The Psychic
and the Swamp Man

The Psychic and the Swamp Man

Kathleen Martell Gordon

The Viking Press New York

Copyright © 1981 by Kathleen Martell Gordon

All rights reserved
First published in 1981 by The Viking Press
625 Madison Avenue, New York, N.Y. 10022
Published simultaneously in Canada by
Penguin Books Canada Limited

Library of Congress Cataloging in Publication Data
Gordon, Kathleen Martell.
The psychic and the swamp man.   I. Title.
PS3557.O6684P7   813'.54   80–52855
ISBN 0–670–58188–7

Grateful acknowledgment is made to Macmillan Publishing Co., Inc.,
and A. P. Watt for permission to reprint an excerpt from "Brown Penny"
from *Collected Poems* by William Butler Yeats. Copyright 1912
by Macmillan Publishing Co., Inc., renewed 1940 by
Bertha Georgie Yeats.

Printed in the United States of America
Set in Fototronic Baskerville

This book is for my husband, Reed,
who believed in me.

I would like also to thank Lester Goran,
who encouraged me to sing;
Whittington Johnson, who reminded me to be patient
when I was in a careless hurry;
Sari Blackman Henkin, who lent me her outer-space visions;
and my mother, Doris Martell, who taught me faith.

O love is the crooked thing,
There is nobody wise enough
To find out all that is in it,
For he would be thinking of love
Till the stars had run away
And the shadows eaten the moon.

William Butler Yeats

The Psychic
and the Swamp Man

1

The vision sprang at me suddenly, like a startled frog, in a hard, clear dream that made the alien dead seem again ferociously alive and the lost remarkably accessible. I sat upright in the dark, moaning. When I reached to take my husband's hand, I found the left side of the bed cool and empty.

Standing at the window with the flowered sheet clutched around me, I stared out over the gloomy, predawn Everglades. As the autumn rain beat steadily against the panes and the vine-covered porch roof below, I considered my dream, in which my mother had appeared as a ghastly specter. I thought of my mother's promiscuity and of my father's running. I was trying to comfort myself by remembering the young man who for weeks had been silently wandering the aisles of my tourist shop, when I saw running across the lawn through the fruit trees the same strange bent figure I had seen in my sleep. The shadowy form, obscured by darkness and rain, stopped to look up at the house for a moment, and I thought I saw his large mouth open.

When the creature groaned, I groaned along with him.

"Swamp man?" I called. I was alarmed when he did not answer. If that was indeed the fanciful creature my mother had promised me, a being who on earth roamed the swamp and away from earth wandered the universe, I could not imagine that he would now appear for any reason but to rebuke me.

By the time I had unlatched and lifted the window, the creature had disappeared into the wilderness that crept to the pole fence at the perimeter of my property. On that darkly silver morning just weeks before the thirteenth anniversary of my mother's death, I thought that my psychic gifts had returned after many years' absence, and that out there, across my lawn and through my woods, might run the alien swamp man for whom my mother had always waited.

Suppose, I thought, such a creature does exist. What if the swamp man knocks at my door this morning, asks for Ruby Holloway, and demands to know if I have been living virtuously the thirty-three years of my life? I fretted over my wardrobe for a long while, ashamed of its frankness, and at last found in the back of my closet an ugly navy smock I had been keeping for funerals. I brushed my light brown hair, which fell just below my hips and sometimes let me feel young and lovely, into two earnest pigtails at either side of my head. I imagined myself in solemn conversation with a creature I had always denied existed, explaining to him that when I was alone and lonely, which was often, I felt old and ugly in a way that only falling in love could fix.

As soon as I heard the howling and groaning again, I rushed to the window and spoke to the fleeing shadow. "I haven't hurt anyone. I don't know what a woman is supposed to be these days. I have an affectionate heart, swamp man."

Downstairs in my mother's kitchen where each window slanted and the floor tiles formed inscrutable ciphers and undecipherable codes, my husband was already hard at work. Over the same table across which my mother had slid the marker of her Ouija board, Artie had spread our bankbooks, deeds to various real estate holdings, and insurance policies on life and property. He appeared to be adding up on a calculator his net worth. His white, curly hair sprang out in familiar and lovely disarray, and his tie was already loosened and drooping down the front of his splendid blue suit. He sang a poignant love song, his pretty pale face bobbing as his fingers flew with important arithmetic.

"Something happened just now, Artie," I said.

He had not heard me. One finger turning aloft, his eyes fixed, I thought, not on the ceiling but on a face he might imagine hovered beyond the plaster, Artie said, "Five months till March twentieth, and I think I've got the world beat."

March twentieth was the day my husband was to turn fifty, the day by which he believed he must be a millionaire or else be doomed to a life of meager accomplishments, decaying health, and a disintegrating marriage. My husband, who was a fine lawyer, who prided himself upon being a careful and rational man, honestly believed all this.

"I saw something in the woods," I said.

"A bobcat, probably. I heard the howling," my husband replied, rubbing his temples and studying his papers.

I looked anxiously toward the rain-spotted windows, beyond which the alien swamp man might be watching me with stern eyes, and sat on my husband's slender lap, carefully holding most of my weight in my knees so that he would think me light and graceful. The scent of the very strong liniment with which he rubbed his back made my nostrils flare and my eyes fill with tears. I wanted to undress him, imagined us making young, tender morning love on the floor, but when I kissed his small ears, his shoulders jerked impatiently.

I thought his lack of interest was the fault of my pigtails, which I unbound, and then of my lipstick, which I rubbed off with the back of my hand. "I didn't see a bobcat," I said.

"Honey bear, my diaphanous daisy, I'm trying to concentrate on these numbers. Look here," Artie said, pointing at one column of figures and then another, his pen dipping and waving as if he were conducting a symphony. That column, he said, indicated how much island property in Curaçao could be bought at a steal of a price; this column indicated projected returns on the investments.

I stared at the figures. "I had this dream, Artie."

My husband said that he too had a dream. With a shining-eyed solemnity due a quote out of Bartlett's, he recited, " 'Let all the learned say what they can, 'Tis ready money makes the man.' William Somerville, 1675–1742. That was one of my father's favorite quotations."

I thought and thought and then held up a proud finger of my own. " 'Put not your trust in money, but your money in trust.' Oliver Wendell Holmes."

Artie grinned and replied that he was putting his money into trust. "Fifteen years ago my father looked at this very land. I want to be able to give you everything, Ruby."

I stalked toward the windows, peered out at the porch, over the wet lawn, and into the rainy Everglades. "Still," I said. "That was no bobcat outside."

Behind me I could hear Artie's fingers tapping on the calculator, and his cheery voice as he resumed his song. When he casually remarked that he might require my half of the tourist and magic shop I owned with my sister Lillian, as collateral, I rushed to him and snatched away his pens. "You're not taking my store," I shouted.

"I was only thinking aloud," Artie said, and looking rather perplexed, pulled me toward him. He touched my nose and said if I loved him—and he did not understand why I should love an old and white-haired man—I would be patient with him. He reminded me that he was the last surviving male of a family whose men were doomed to freakish and untimely ends, "which is why I'd love a son," he said. He recalled that his great grandfather Geoffrey Arthur Holloway, a dignified London barrister, had slipped on a wet marble floor in Old Bailey and, in his fall, had mortally wounded himself with his own gun. His star-crossed uncle Peter had been struck down by lightning on a perfectly clear June day as he had walked along Wall Street. His cousin John, who had been the first to score on the Italians' peculiar mania for lighted yo-yos, had been fatally kicked in the head by a very old, very gentle mare. His father, Albert Holloway, had choked to death on a bit of sandwich at the age of forty-nine as he shouted at a group of quarreling Mexican pickers, "Pack your own parachute!"

"Pack your own parachute," Artie said, his tongue lingering over the syllables, his sweet, caramel-colored eyes glowing at the memory of his quick-witted father. "He was a tough old bird, my dad. That's how I am. He took chances I've been afraid to take, but no more. It's time to make use of his lessons." If a man didn't realize his dreams, he said, he grew old before his time, and if he knew how to stay young and happy, why shouldn't he sacrifice a little now to gain the greater profit? "If you love me, you'll trust me," he said, putting his finger over my mouth.

As I watched him gather his papers into his briefcase, unhappy visions lingering from my dreams took shape and then vanished. But still I smiled and said nothing and fumbled with his collar and tie. "My clumsy little girl," Artie said. "If I didn't want to spend all my time with you later, I wouldn't work so hard now." In Curaçao, he said, he would rent a honeymoon suite, and while he was meeting with his investment group he would imagine me waiting in bed for him. "I really believe this is my year, and that Curaçao is my place. I'll make it just as my father made it. Maybe you'll even become pregnant soon." Artie stooped to kiss my stomach, while I stared toward the windows. No sublimely good alien stood with his face against the panes, watching me.

"You know, Artie, it won't be all roses when we have children. I'll become fat," I warned, a fear not as great as the one Artie had instilled with his family stories. "I'll become short-tempered and shrewish, and then you won't love me."

"I'd love you even more. Then I'd have two babies to take care of." My husband glanced at his watch, adjusted his tie a tenth time, fretted over whether his socks and shoes would look well in the courtroom, and told me not to expect him for supper. After reciting his long list of appointments and the usual precautions I must take to avoid inflaming the passions of the creeps downtown, he walked toward the door with his briefcase and umbrella. There he paused. "Did you want to tell me something before?" he asked. "When you came into the kitchen you said that something had happened."

In a sweet, mouse voice I told Artie that I had bumped my knee.

"Don't ever think I don't hear every word you say. And what was your darling little dream?"

I smiled and tried to invent a gentle dream so that he would still love me. "We were kissing behind the sea grape trees at the beach, just like we did the night I met you."

"You were crying that evening, and I knew then that you needed me." Artie kissed me twice, on the mouth and neck, and hurried down the porch steps.

As soon as his car had moved down the dirt lane, which wound through five miles of woods to the highway, I thought I heard a husky feminine voice whisper my name.

"I'm leaving in a minute," I said. I stamped my foot, as if I were defying her, because I was still uncertain about this swamp man and my dreams. Just as my mother had once done, I gathered together a box of chocolate cookies, two jars of spiced apples, and several oranges, and left the food by the back door so that the swamp man, if that had been he who had groaned so, would not be angry with me. When I heard the voice that furiously called my name, I lost my temper and shouted, "I'm going! Jesus! Why'd you have to come back now, anyway?"

The thunderstorm heightened during my drive into downtown Miami, and by the time I parked my jeep and walked toward the magicians' supply house, hail had begun to bounce against the warm, sand-colored sidewalks. I stood beneath the shop's canvas overhang and waited for my father to fall upon my shoulder, weeping with joy and crying, "Ruby, my darling child."

I stared often and, at last, angrily at my watch, which showed nine-thirty in the morning. Several times I stepped to the dripping edge of the canopy, which bounced in and out like a trampoline in the autumn gale, but no one ran my way with outstretched arms. Just when I decided that my mother had tricked me from going to work so that I would miss the sweet young man who watched me from the corners of my shop, a stroke of lightning split a large palm tree just yards away and forced me into the shop, where magic and miracles were for sale.

Against the counter leaned a pear-shaped, drearily dressed thirty-year-old man named Ellis Shimmel, who was lazily counting a stack of innocent-looking boxes with which a magician might perform the most dazzling feats of wizardry. "Ruby Holloway!" Ellis said, his voice high and melodic. Through his lips shone just a glimmer of angel wire and steel, and for a moment I remembered my fondness for him.

I blushed and stammered and strung together a sentence indicating I needed to order a few articles for my shop.

"Well, excuse me, Ruby, if I don't show you around." Ellis jerked up his chin, so soft, white, and vulnerably folded I had once been convinced that his was one of the prettiest profiles in the world; if my imagination was powerful enough to conjure up ghosts, it had been a simple trick to transform the frog into a prince whose lithe and lovely soul whispered to me. "Why did you come here today after all this time? Did you finally leave your husband?" Ellis asked in a shrill voice.

"I love my husband," I said. "You know I love my husband."

Ellis kicked at something I could not see and then leaned over the counter so that his huge belly rested atop it. "Why did you disappear so suddenly?" His heavy-lidded brown eyes glistened and turned very red. He swept what appeared to be an ordinary feather duster against mammaries that I remembered were as white and softly swelling as my own at thirteen, and with each jerk of his good but not brilliant wrist turned a motley chicken feather into a bright red geranium. "Remember how you used to go crazy watching me do this?"

"No." As I looked at the bouquet I recalled a part of my premonitory predawn dream. I remembered having seen brown chicken feathers being spun into big red blossoms. Just as in my dream, the wind rushed rain against the window, and just as in my dream, I watched the streets for my father.

"Is one of your husband's detectives out there?" Ellis cried. He had dropped the bouquet and was backing away from the entrance, his lower lip bubbling with a delicate foam which had once driven me to the perimeters of human experience, to truth, love, music, and poetry.

"I don't know," I said. Although the sidewalks appeared empty, my father seemed to be churning up the air. He might have been just around the corner, perhaps, on a street lined with Cuban clothes stores and coffee shops, or next door in the lobby of the huge bank building, or across the street beneath the ragged, wind-whipped canopy of the news dealer. "I don't see anything, Ellis," I said, "but that doesn't mean nobody is out there."

When I turned to make my way down the aisle, Ellis whispered that once I had said I loved him.

"I don't remember that," I said. I was certain that my mother was tormenting me, and I rolled my eyes toward the ceiling.

"You used me," Ellis charged as I stalked away, knocking things from the shelves and whispering to my mother that this was all her fault: what a grand place she had arranged for me to meet my father. I felt queasy over the genetic implications of my having fooled with this frog, over the implications of my ever having wished for anyone but my husband and the quiet young man who haunted my shop and stirred me into such sweet, sad daydreams.

At the back of the shop was a rack of scanty, sequinned costumes of the sort in which I myself at eighteen had pranced and performed amazing feats with my magic partners on the stages of Miami Beach hotels. I had fallen in love with each of my three partners and was engaged first to Mitchell, then to Jake, and last to Lee. But Mitchell had suddenly run away to New York, breaking my heart; Jake had confessed he was in love with the hotel lifeguard with whom we used to drink by the oceanside pool after our last show; and Lee had disappeared one evening into a great cloud of pink-and-orange stage smoke from which he never emerged.

A rush of wind and the bang of the shop door made me cry out with fear and hide myself behind the costume rack. When I peeked beyond the clothes and saw the old man's face, I remembered all of my dream.

"I don't like this gift," I whispered. "I'm afraid."

The old man's face was partially obscured by his gray plastic rainhat. Slung over his shoulders was a tattered raincoat, and his undershorts hung an inch below his damp plaid Bermudas. Once my father had strutted through our house in the most splendid white suit, battling my mother's shouting with amused calm and great boxes of chocolates, enchanting me and terrifying Lillian with the Flying Vase and the Headless Corpse, tricks I immediately committed to memory in the hope that he would let me travel with him. But now he looked defeated: as he walked he dragged his bent umbrella along the floor, his back was crooked, and his unshaven chin sank toward his chest. Just as in my dream I shrank farther back, behind a magnetic screen upon which one might make spirit writing appear, and wept a little at how poorly my father, Sam, had aged these twenty-five years. I took his appearance as a moral test and vowed to change his life with my love.

"Mr. Bittner!" Ellis gasped, apparently in great awe of my father. He brought out three red cups and the pea-sized cotton ball for the classic sleight of hand. "I didn't expect to see you in this weather."

"I'm old, and I'm alone, so what else do I have to do?" My father tugged his cap lower on his head. From my hiding place I watched Sam move the cups with hands more dexterous than ever—and as a young man he had been brilliant, astonishing dukes and duchesses all over Europe with his frankly seductive, wildly imaginative brand of magic.

Ellis's brow was wrinkled and wet with concentration. Three times he frowned and chose the empty cup. But Sam seemed to take no pleasure in his success, as a magician ought to when his illusion fools even another magician.

"You don't watch," my father said, his voice petulant. Perhaps the misery of living alone, without his daughters, had made a once sweet-tempered man bitter. "You're not practicing."

"You're extraordinary," I said, my voice trembling, as I walked toward the counter.

When my father stared at me with large hazel eyes twin to mine, my heart jumped. But Sam turned his back to me and, leaning against the counter, fell into conversation with Ellis about old times, about his performances at the Paladium and the Moulin Rouge, about the old greats of magic and the Hindu fakirs.

"You're up there with the best of them," Ellis said, his voice hushed, his jaw hanging. For one moment, when I glanced from my father to Ellis, I imagined that my mother's gay and ruinous blood had tainted mine and had made me unparticular and lecherous. "There's nobody better than you, Mr. Bittner."

"Now," said my father, tears springing into his tired eyes, although perhaps that was only an illusion cast by the rain-filtered light. "Two weeks ago I couldn't do anything with these." Sam waved his gnarled fingers as if he wished to spit at them with contempt. "Even you used to catch me." In a low voice he recalled that a violinist friend of his had finally been able to play the excruciatingly difficult music of Paganini just two weeks before his death. "Paganini's fingers were twice as long as any normal man's—like a devil's—and nobody, except a few monsters, had that kind of string reach. But my friend, two weeks before he died, at the age of seventy-six, found the music like child's play. I'm old, and suddenly I'm better than I ever was before. My only wish is that I could get to Puerto Rico before I die."

My father coughed into his yellowed, mended shirt sleeve, and as any aging magician might, wondered if after his death he would be able to contact the living. He told Ellis, who appeared reluctant to participate in such an experiment, that he should keep a close watch for any unusual stirrings after his funeral. "If my wife can do it, and she was no Houdini, believe me, then I can do it, too. That's the only bad thing about an after-life—having to meet up with the people you thought you'd gotten rid of. What do you think of these swamp man sightings in the papers, eh? I believe this is the work of some clever prankster or illusionist."

"I don't," I called as I backed into a corner crowded with top hats and canes. My father ignored my remark.

"I think," said Ellis, "that this is just some poor gentle fellow who has given up on the world, who decided to run away from everything. I feel like doing the same myself. Still, they say it could be some unknown species of animal."

"A man would become that, running through those swamps." From his raincoat pocket my father took a soggy sandwich, offered half to Ellis, and began to nibble at the crust with lips as delicately fluttering as those of a goat. "Perhaps he's mad or has murdered someone.

Perhaps someone wants to murder him. Maybe he's haunted. But people will believe what they want to believe. I lived out in those swamps many years ago. I knew a woman—a ridiculous woman—who thought a creature from outer space howled outside her house." My father snorted. "There must've been hundreds of these so-called swamp men—men running from something—in the Everglades over the years. People like to confuse illusion and reality. We're all, I suppose, searching for the fantastic."

My father sighed so deeply and sadly that I forgot my fears, stepped forward, and rapped the counter three times. "Now watch, Ellis," I said, smiling brightly, although my heart swelled as if it might pop from my throat like a rabbit pulled from a hat. I began moving the cups and ball. Ellis pointed with confidence. I picked up the cup and laughed. "Wrong!" I said, and smiled at my father.

Just as in my dream, Sam quickly turned his head. He looked like a startled old woman.

Ellis was rather grim. "I admit it. You're better than I am. You always were too good for me, Ruby," he added, so that I winced.

At the mention of my name, my father began creeping toward the door. "I have to catch a bus," he said, taking a cracked watch from his pocket and waving it. At once he bolted.

I ran after him. The sidewalk was slippery in the rain, and already he was far ahead of me. He looked about wildly, one hand clutching his umbrella and the other his hat. For several minutes my father craftily eluded me; he vanished among the rain-blurred storefronts as suddenly as he had vanished from his family many years before.

At last I found him at the luncheonette counter inside the Rexall Drug Store, sipping hot tea behind a newspaper. Shivering and soaked, I sat on the stool beside his and took his hand. He immediately disengaged it.

"Why are you running from me?"

"Because I don't know you," Sam said, without looking at me. Water still dripped from his ruffled hat onto his very pink neck. "If you were an old man and a stranger chased you, wouldn't you run?"

"God strike me dead if I should alarm an old man. But you heard Ellis call me by name. It's me, Ruby, your daughter," I said, smiling at Sam as charmingly as I could.

"You're someone else's daughter—not mine." The color had drained from my father's face, as if I were as unwelcome a visitation as his wife might be, hovering above his pillow. "I'll call the police--annoying an old man this way! You've mistaken me for someone else."

"Mother was right about one thing—she did complain you were stubborn. I'm going to have breakfast. Would you like to join me?" I was trying to play craft for craft, although I knew, by dream, how this meeting would end.

"I wouldn't mind, if you paid," Sam said. Over eggs, grits, and sausage he was quite willing to discuss the old house, which he remembered his wife had spent twelve years building and in which he agreed he had lived. "My wife was an impossible woman," he said, recalling how her visions of ghosts and of aliens curiously compelled her to take naked carpenters into his bed. Sam cheerfully admitted that Sally Bittner had given birth to two daughters, Lillian and Ruby. "Ruby used to be an especially clever child—I used to teach her magic tricks."

"I'm Ruby," I said. "And I've been living in the house for ten years." I explained that Mother had willed Lillian her money and me the old house, but only if I lived there. Of course, I said, this condition was a traditional challenge. "Sometimes," I said, staring thoughtfully across the counter at the steamy wall mirrors, "I think—or imagine—that she's still running around the house, maybe up on the third floor with the rest of her ghosts."

"So, she comes to you, too," Sam said, nodding. He formed bunnies and dogs with his napkin as he ate, his eyes rotating to see if anyone was watching, then nonchalantly flipped smooth the cloth to dab at his mouth. "Another round of everything, Miss," he said, winking at the waitress. In my ear he whispered, "Sally comes to me. In the middle of the night she turns on the radio so I can't get any sleep."

"She must have something particular to tell you."

"You'd like to blame me for your mother's death, wouldn't you?" my father cried, although he still seemed to be playing a crafty game with me, for his appetite remained undiminished. He chuckled as he swept the coins of a tip someone had left our waitress into his pocket.

"I wouldn't blame you," I said softly, "if you'd only look at me now and know I'm your daughter. We agree on everything else."

"You're probably the daughter of some roof worker, or plumber, or carpenter. Your mother had hot pants."

"I don't blame you for being angry with her, but Mother didn't always have other men. There was a time she didn't. Maybe she told you I wasn't your daughter after you left us, to hurt you. Look at me. I look like you."

"You have grown up beautifully, but I wouldn't say that you look like me. Are you married now?" my father asked. I nodded. "And do you fool around on your husband?" Although I said nothing, my father smiled proudly. "I can see you're her daughter," he said, holding up his coffee cup for a refill, "but it's impossible that you're mine."

"Maybe if you talked to Lillian," I said.

"I refuse. I never cared much for the child. I suspect I'd like her even less as a forty-year-old woman. I don't keep much company these days. My life has become routine: Sally haunts me at night, and every other day or so I go to the magicians' supply house and talk to that young imbecile. You must be the woman he's been blabbering about. I didn't plan to go there today, you know," he said, looking at me out of the corner of his eye, "but last night I had a dream, and *she* told me to go there. So you see what kind of dreadful tricks she plays. I suppose you're going to haunt me now, too." He stood and quickly emptied a dish of lump sugar into his pockets. "I've got to go now. The welfare lines are long these days."

"Do you need money, Daddy?"

"Don't call me that. I do need a plane ticket to Puerto Rico. A woman loves me there." When I said that I would be happy to send my father to Puerto Rico, Sam said he would submit to no bribes. "A man has pride, you know. But we'll discuss this another time. She'll send you around again to torment me, I'm sure."

"I'm not trying to torment you," I said, but my father was already walking rapidly toward the door. As he passed the candy display he whisked several chocolate bars into his raincoat and, still a show-off, turned to smile at me.

He shouted suddenly, in a mock-angry voice, "You'll not blame me for her death—oh, no, you won't! I feel sorry for you, but you are not my daughter." Obscured by the rain outside he looked like a gray shadow or a ghost, and then he vanished into the storm.

I left a large tip for the waitress, to compensate for the money my father had stolen. I would have liked to call my husband for advice, but I was afraid to let him know that a man might find me unlovable.

I drove along Biscayne Boulevard in my jeep, meaning to go to work at once to tell Lillian that I had seen our father, but instead continued north on U.S. 1, past the glass-and-ceramic high rises, the beautiful old conch houses, homely concrete fruit stands, and the strip of adult motels. I drove into a neighborhood of rundown trailer villages and faded, pastel-painted tourist courts and motels, and after wrestling for a moment with the steering wheel, I succumbed and turned into the rutted muddy drive of the Orange Blossom Tourist Courts.

Nothing had changed since my mother had gaily, without thought, abandoned my sister and me on Lillian's sixteenth birthday in the cockroach-infested efficiency in which the three of us had lived for eight or so terrible months. When the rain stopped the steamy air became rich and pungent with the spicy smell of rotting fruit, and the fickle sun swelled and scorched. Several small, ragged children were splashing and shrieking in a puddle at the base of a mango tree in the center of the cracked stone. In the shrieking I could hear my mother's voice, muttering madly about the Everglades house she had been forced to flee because its ghosts, no longer pacified by the third-floor addition she had built to contain them, had taken from her all her psychic gifts and any hope that her outer-space alien, that creature who ran through the swamps, would save her with his love.

Behind the ugly backs of the tiny squat cubicles I ran, through the clotheslines of gray wash and over damp, buzzing weeds, until I approached the last cabin. Weeds grew up around the back step, which had been painted so that the cement mocked a grave site. The stories must have lingered. The screen door hung off its rusted hinges and creaked at my timid touch.

Beside the door, on the peeling paint that had been baked nearly to white, was scrawled a misspelled warning. All the windows were smashed, and the sunlight bouncing off the broken glass seemed to bend and refract time: I kept turning my head, my heart beating thunderously, as if I expected to see an angry, lonely child staring toward the railroad tracks, waiting for someone to save her.

Through a side window that resembled a window in my dream, I got into the apartment. At first I saw only the dust, and I choked with its denseness; lost time seemed to have gathered itself together again in gray inches on the rattan sofa and two rattan chairs, and nearly obscured the waist-high partition beyond which was a collapsed double bed. As I walked through the kitchen toward the bathroom, a field mouse ran over my foot. I screamed, and then I imagined that she had come to relive her last years with me.

I could see her sitting on the cracked toilet seat in an old slip with gray stains beneath the underarms, waiting for the foul-smelling dye on her hair to take, reveling in how pretty she would look when one of her real or imaginary boyfriends—or her husband, Sam—knocked on her door the following morning. Her forehead was shiny and shielded by cotton strips to catch the dye. Fanning herself with a movie magazine, she said that she would always love her Sam.

"He must be dead," she sometimes said, weeping, and wept now, I thought. "Otherwise he'd come. I dream of him as if he were dead. If he hadn't run off from me I wouldn't have had to leave my house, and my swamp man would've come for me. Men kill the dreams of women. I shouldn't have to live in a place like this. I'll die here, unless my swamp man or my Sam comes for me. I'm afraid I'll die here."

I saw myself as a child, insisting that no swamp creature existed and that Sam was forever gone.

"I hate this gift," I whispered, shutting my eyes, but she would not stay away.

"I'm getting married soon," my mother had said as she handed over a checkbook the day she left Lillian and me alone. When I saw with my vision that she was not and sadly said so, my mother called me a little girl witch, accused me of turning her husband and swamp man against her, and vowed to get even with me some day. That night my vision went gray and then darkened completely, and that same night Lillian insisted that the gift had flown over to her, and said she saw that our father was dead.

Each time Mother came to visit my sister and me she seemed to have grown more mad and more pathetic; she always dressed in rags, although she imagined she looked like a princess, her hair was matted and filthy, and the scent of rotted sex breathed from beneath her torn, stained skirts.

"I'm going to get even with you, Ruby," she often said, wagging a finger at me. "You'll live where I've lived."

Even now I tried to banish her and to fight her. "All right, I've come here, just like you wanted, but I swear I'm not going to pity you."

On a Christmas Eve nearly thirteen years ago my mother had returned to the Orange Blossom Tourist Courts dressed in ragged red satin and had gone into the bathroom with her rope. I dared to look into the shower now, and she took up the challenge. From the fixture I saw her hanging, a dreadful grimace on her face. Sticking from her pocket was the note a police officer had handed me just before she had been carted off before my perfectly dry, perfectly calm eyes. Even in high dread my mother had been maliciously gay.

"You haven't won yet, Ruby!" she had written. "He'll come to you—I promise!"

"I can't cry now," I said, my eyes roaming over the

broken tiles, the rusted faucets, the mildewed walls. "I've tried—but I can't cry for you now."

As I climbed through the window into the blinding sun, I began to tell myself a pretty story. Once upon a time, I said as I walked toward the jeep, lived a very good and beautiful princess, who wandered in disguise among her subjects till she forgot who she was.

2

Sisters' Tourist and Magic Emporium stood at the end
of a pitted narrow street of old, salt-weathered conch
houses in downtown Miami. The street abutted the
marina, the huge city library among whose amber
shadows I had spent much time researching accounts of
ghostly appearances and other supernatural phe-
nomena, and a large bayfront park where withered,
sore-eyed men slept and sunned, and starving, mange-
mottled dogs and cats roamed the spotted shade of the
sea grape trees. Although my sister Lillian had been
twice mugged and three times bitten on the walk beside
the bay, she still insisted upon going to the park each
morning to perform the good deeds she dreamed would
show her the way to the Everglades swamp man, who
would speak to her of strange, uncharted planets and
engage her help in making a world without misery or
evil.

"I will not be daunted," Lillian always said. For
these outings into the park she wore one of several white
caftans she hoped would suggest her sublime goodness
and preserve, by concealing her large breasts and legs,
the chaste life she claimed to have been keeping since

her third marriage had failed. "There's no one around worth having, anyway," she remarked on the day she took back, as part of her reclaimed virtue, her maiden name of Bittner. "Men kill the dreams of women."

That Thursday morning as I loitered on the sidewalk before the shop, I saw my sister inside standing before a dusty display of faded plaster fruits, doling out packets of pet food and wrapped baloney sandwiches. Lillian was a tall, stout, red-haired woman with thick bristling brows, a bumped and hooked nose, and a large-lipped and crooked-toothed mouth. But her voice was deep and resonant, her blue eyes were clear and strikingly beautiful, and her pale complexion was as smooth and as unlined as if she had not known a moment's trouble in her life. Lillian's psychic followers, all women over sixty-five—my sister would abide no men in her group, since sex obscured sight—clamored to fill their shopping bags and to be out on their charitable mission. This good-hearted group included the meticulously coiffed and synonymously dressed Grace and Clara Thurnwood, identical twins who had been married to identical twins who had died by impressive coincidence on the same day, October 14, 1971, although of different ailments; the deep-voiced, eighty-seven-year-old former Berlin cabaret singer Lyla Zimmerman, whose father had been a cabinet minister in the Weimar Republic and now directed by occult means his daughter's financial affairs; and an earnest writer of very bad nature poems, Posy Adams, who claimed to commune with Charles Darwin and who encouraged Lillian in her own literary pursuits—a collection of verse dealing exclusively with suicide, unrequited love, and life on other planets.

The members of the group had made many forays into the Everglades near my home to search for the swamp man, filling me with anxiety that one of the old

women would step on a snake or break a limb. These
eerie excursions, conducted with the sincerest pomp,
had been unproductive. The problem was not that the
extraordinary did not reveal itself in the jungle, but
that each of the women perceived the extraordinary
differently: Grace and Clara Thurnwood, for instance,
persisted in seeing the vision of a young woman with a
hairy hand, similar to the May Moulach whom Wilkie
recorded as having haunted Tullock Gorms, giving
warnings of imminent deaths in the Grant family; Lyla
Zimmerman gazed into the brackish, algae-clogged
ponds and saw gigantic fish that sang opera in the voice
of Caruso, but in an incomprehensible tongue; along
the river bank Posy Adams sensed the poetically shimmering footprints of glad angels; and Lillian perceived
the presence of a creature who, like most elves, loved
music and dance and had the ability to change his appearance to confuse the mortals who sought him.

Although these inconsistencies at last had prompted
my sister to postpone her active search, she remained
optimistic that she would greet her alien swamp man
before the new year; she determined by various signs
that the creature wished to be left alone to observe, test,
and steel her group into a state of worthiness that
would render them capable of working alongside the
rest of the aliens when they descended into the Everglades with a celestial burst of music not unlike Bach's
Brandenburg Concertos.

What I imagined was a stealthy entrance into the
shop caused a great commotion. Lillian's psychic followers glimpsed me sliding around an obscure aisle and
rushed to caress my hair and admire my "aura." These
old women, who previously had noticed me only for my
youth, asked me many questions about their dead relatives, lost wills, and the creature who, according to the
newspapers, roamed the swamps once again.

"Have you seen him, darling?" Grace Thurnwood asked.

"I know she must have, even if she doesn't realize," said her twin sister, Clara, whose wide blue eyes brimmed with tears. I was unnerved and flushed, and insisted I had seen nothing extraordinary in the swamps. "I don't see a thing anymore, and so I couldn't be of any help," I said.

"You're going to see again soon," Lillian predicted, with a tremulous smile.

"Oh, the information we got about you in our séance last night," said Lyla Zimmerman. She had a ferocious grasp on my arm, and her crossed eyes twirled like a little wind toy. "You're going to take us to this charming swamp creature. You're going to be our leader."

"No, thank you," I whispered. My sister was still smiling at me, her hands clasped against her white saint's garb, her eyes and mouth tender. Behind her Victor Riley, the sixty-year-old retired cruise director who helped run the magic section of the shop, scowled and preened his magnificent silver hair.

"Into the park now, girls, like soldiers," Lillian said, tossing back her hair and raising a ghost-sleeved arm. "I'll join you soon."

Lyla Zimmerman whispered an important, wet message in my ear: "My dead father rapped a message last night that you're a very special woman."

"Well, you thank him for me," I said. I guided the old woman through the perilous aisles of orange T-shirts, postcard racks, citrus perfumes, alligator ashtrays, and Florida fudge. At the front door we shook hands.

As soon as the store emptied, Victor Riley tapped his silver temples and let loose a melancholy laugh. While my sister dreamily smiled and sighed, he busied himself shuffling and unshuffling, with the most flamboyant, peacock manner, a deck of cards. For an amateur he was an excellent magician. The card he flipped across the store grazed Lillian's cheek and broke her reverie. She frowned, blushed, and stamped her feet. "You're always taunting me." Victor smiled and said in a soothing voice that although he adored Lillian, he feared she had fallen prey to paranoia. "I am not paranoid," Lillian said, taking me aside. Lillian whispered that she suspected Victor worked in the shop only to annoy her and to meet seducible women. "When I first met him he was different—he was a gentleman. Are you in love with him?"

"Are you?" I asked.

"He means nothing to me except another test of my patience," Lillian said, although her eyes slid with sad yearning toward the chair where Victor sat, obviously eavesdropping. "Where were you this morning, Ruby?"

I took her arm and, begging her to remain calm, revealed that I had seen our father, by accident, at the magicians' supply house. "He's alive," I told my sister, who had grown much paler. "I talked to him. But he's looking poorly, Lillian." As I planned how together we might talk to him and coax him back to us, Lillian, oddly serene, turned away and said that she was quite certain I was mistaken.

"Our father is dead. He died in a car crash in Puerto Rico, where he was cheating on Mother—I had proof of that long ago," Lillian said, meaning of course her psychic proof. "What you saw is a spirit!"

Confronted by such adamance I became confused and doubted my own senses. But after reminding myself that ghosts did not eat and that I had seen my father consume an enormous breakfast, I said, "I'm sure, Lillian, that I saw a live man." I had touched him, I said, and had seen tears in his eyes.

Lillian said that my "apparition" made absolute

sense to her. "Your life is going to change dramatically," she told me, in a voice deep and rough with emotion.

"Listen to your sister, Ruby," Victor called. "Angels dance on her tongue." Lillian smoothed her caftan over her thick trunk and said that last night she learned in séance that my psychic gifts had been returned after a long and perhaps willful lapse. "This is just the beginning," she said. I was unable to meet her eyes, which seemed to burn with a prophetic light, and crouching before the nearest shelves, I began rearranging a display of guava jelly Lillian had stacked carefully the day before. As I fumbled with the jars my sister continued to instruct me. "This can only mean one thing: Mother wants you to join me in the search for the swamp man. When he makes you believe in him, Ruby, you who always denied he existed, he'll remember who he is, and why he came to earth."

My hands jerked, and I dropped and broke eight jars of guava jelly. Lillian stared through the splattered lenses of her glasses toward the magic table, which wobbled with Victor's laughter. Gelatinous globs, like bugs of another world, quivered on my hair and skin. Lillian patted my shoulder, told me not to cry, that I was as graceful as a ballet dancer when I concentrated on what I was doing, and attempted to clean off my face with her sleeve.

"You can't continue to deny your gift," she said, now licking her glasses and rubbing her own face. She glanced toward Victor Riley, who leaned with his elbow propped on the table, where he still played with his deck of cards, fanning them out, snapping them together, letting them drop like dominoes along his luxuriously tanned and slender forearm. Lillian warned me to watch my behavior in the next weeks; the fact that my psychic gifts had returned at the same time the swamp man had been sighted again in the Everglades was clearly a sign of some sort. "To deny your gift is to deny Mother and what she gave to us both. Think of the promise our swamp man—the outer-space alien—offers!"

"I've told you before," I said, in a voice as timid and as alien as if the sound had just seeped from a crack in the plaster walls, "it's all gone."

"The gift was always there, but you've been afraid to look." Sometimes even Lillian saw the truth and interpreted it correctly. She put her arms around me. "You're afraid of the truth when you can see it all. I bow to your abilities, Ruby, they're far greater than mine. You'll join us soon." Her voice, as gay as our mother's had been, made me shudder: my research into the supernatural indicated that by tradition—and creatures of the supernatural seemed bound by tradition—when one was asked to join, one did so or else suffered dreadfully. "Soon you won't have any choice." Lillian helped me clean up the broken jelly jars, singing as she swept and mopped, and then picked up her heavy shopping bag with the melancholy air of one who carried a great burden indeed. "The search for truth is so difficult," she said but smiled as she departed, for if the world must be magically interpreted, then the world was a delightfully magical place.

Victor Riley held his small pink hand above his head, displayed a coin in his palm, fisted it, and snapped a crisp one-dollar bill before my eyes. "Your sister is crazy," he said. When I did not take this bait, he slid his fingers through his silver hair, displayed the dollar, and with a rubbing of his slender fingers transformed the bill into a twenty, which immediately caught flame and vanished. "I know debilitating madness when I see it—I've had thirty-six years' experience with my poor mad wife. Your sister is going to destroy herself." Victor chuckled and winked as if he had said something very charming indeed.

I picked up a well-trod-upon gum wrapper from the floor, displayed it, and snapped a fifty-dollar bill before Victor's aristocratic nose. His white-and-silver eyebrows, shaped so they appeared to have been plucked, arched with surprise. "My sister does a lot of good," I said. Through the shop windows I could see Lillian dawdling on the sidewalk, her glasses shining with an almost supernatural brilliance, offering a sandwich to someone who must have been sprawled on the hot cement. "She feeds hungry people, and she's made those old women feel useful. At least she has hope."

"The hope of the hopeless." Victor's round gray eyes grew small with mirth. Fingering the medallion that hung over his opened pink-and-purple shirt he insisted, citing many mad examples as proof, that my sister meant to be my ruin. "She hates you. She hasn't said so precisely, but I'm a man who can see beyond the obvious. Your sister hates you because she knows you love me—please, Ruby, don't interrupt me now. Every morning she tells me she's in love with me. I'm afraid your sister is a vulgar whore. This morning she asked me if I wanted her to come down on me behind the counter. When I explained that would be unseemly, she accused me of having an affair with you." Victor sighed and shrugged, as if to ask how went this strange and coarse world.

I started angrily toward the front door, meaning to confront my sister, but Lillian had disappeared; only a very old man in a brown suit and red suspenders sat on the sidewalk, chewing on a baloney sandwich.

Victor stood at the full-length mirror preening his subtly winged silver mustache. "I'm not surprised at your sister's question. You've been sending me obvious signals all morning," he said, nodding at me in the mirror and at last tearing himself away. "Don't get me wrong, I like it. But your sister suspects that we've consummated here, and that burns her. Why do you suppose she hired me? She was infatuated with the Silver Fox."

"I don't think so," I said, but when I imagined Victor's eyes softened with despair, I threw up my hands and said, "Maybe she is—who knows?"

"She wouldn't be the first to fall head over heels for me," Victor said. He launched into a long and whining account of his trials with ten or more women he had met while hanging around the cruise ships at the Port of Miami, each one big-breasted, beautiful, well-groomed, and ladylike, and all so gratefully cured of their frigidity they wished to marry him. "My endurance at sixty astonishes me, but I come from manly stock. Tell me you love me, Ruby."

"But I don't."

Victor was so incredulous and argued so vehemently that I allowed finally as how I might not know my own mind. I stared at his face, at his rapidly blinking eyes, and agreed it was possible, though minutely, that I might be in love with him without realizing it. "You see, I'm confused," I said.

Victor said that I was confused because I had been suppressing my sexual urges. "A lovely, original, modern woman like you shouldn't worry about middle-class morality. If I had a sister, I'd tell her the same thing."

"I haven't been suppressing my sexual urges," I said softly. I understood at once that I had made a mistake.

"You've cheated on me," Victor cried.

"Not on you, Victor," I said. "Not on you."

He paced before me and predicted that I would destroy myself by fooling around with other men, while he would be discreet and would take care not to ruin my life with unnecessary dramatics. With my vulgar behavior I would lose not only my husband but my chance for a delightful affair with him, and be very, very sorry. "You're a callous woman." "I'm not callous—I thought I was in love," I said. "Dissembler," Victor shouted, so that an elderly woman who had just entered the shop immediately turned and staggered out again. "You only want to be flattered. It's sad how you women prance and preen. Even your ugly sister does it. I think maybe you've reached the stage where you'll take anyone for an adventure and pretend it's love. Shakespeare was right about women."

I was very much alarmed and begged to know, so that I might be improved, what Shakespeare had said about women.

"I suppose you want to argue now with Shakespeare?" Victor said in ringing, triumphant tones. I stared toward the windows, but no outer-space alien stood outside my shop ready to battle for my honor. "You led me on. You made me think you cared for me. Could I have been so wrong?" When he slumped so, he seemed handsome. He remarked that if he ever found a woman who was truly tenderhearted—"someone who would love me the way I'd like"—he would be the happiest man alive. "Don't I deserve love?"

"Oh, Victor, I'm very fond of you," I said. Having given myself over I waited for him to tell me the same, waited for him to kiss me and so perhaps save me.

Victor gazed toward the street, his fingers clasped behind him. He lifted his pinky in listless greeting, and over his shoulders and through the plate-glass windows I could see a stunning young woman standing on the sidewalk. "She's a trapeze artist," Victor said, rolling his eyes meaningfully. "Even so, she was a mistake. She wants to marry me—I thought she understood this wasn't to be serious—and if she keeps calling my house, my wife will surely poison my coffee."

"When did your wife go mad?" I asked.

Victor seemed surprised. "Why, she was mad when I married her. I imagined I could change her, and now I'm being punished for the thought." Victor smiled through the windows at the young woman who waited for him, and then strutted out the door, smoothing his hair, which shone like tinsel in the afternoon sun.

"You don't know me," I said. I watched Victor shake off the hand of the trapeze artist and walk rapidly, followed at several paces by the girl, across the street and into the parking lot.

"I know you!" I thundered.

I sat on the stool behind the cash register with the lost-and-found section of the newspaper opened before me, eating chocolate-covered coconut patties and trying to determine if indeed my psychic gifts had suddenly returned. The swamp man might have been a homely apparition, and meeting my father just the coincidence that teases the already limber imagination. I would try a test: a Mrs. Gretta Reborado advertised that her Dalmation dog, answering to the name of Knecht, had been lost the previous Tuesday in the vicinity of the airport. I let my sticky fingers trace the newsprint, shut my eyes, and seemed about to arrange and give substance to the shimmering, colored globes that danced behind my lids when the buzzer above the shop door sounded.

The young man who haunted my shop and my thoughts as persistently as any ghost walked over the threshold and ducked behind a postcard stand. I rattled my newspaper pages, picked up a pen and circled several advertisements, and several times summoned the courage to open my mouth. But speech seemed to have fled me. Behind fluttering eyelashes I watched the kid move down a side aisle. I was disarmed by his beauty, by his shiny, rumpled dark hair and his huge dark eyes, so energetic they seemed to snap. He wore, as always, a faded T-shirt and tight faded jeans, the softness of which I had memorized in imagination, and he carried a white motorcycle helmet in his thin, fetching arms. He looked around the shop, making certain that we were alone, and then he spoke to me for the first time.

His voice was soft and husky and had a lover's lilt to it. "Ruby Holloway?" he asked. When I peered beyond the newspaper pages he smiled, showing me the most beautifully white and wickedly even teeth. This smile had me trembling, just as my mother had trembled when she had glimpsed a young carpenter who made her catch fire. The young man humbled me.

"I'm Ruby Holloway," I said. As I rounded the counter, brushing hair from my face, the young man caught my arm.

"I've come to announce my feelings. For weeks I've been watching you, your face, your beautiful long hair," the young man said in a melancholy voice that hurt my skin. When he touched my hair, I moaned and stepped back. "I've spoken to your sister about you. I've seen your husband come into the shop and listened to him talk about you. You've been watching me, too. I saw you, Ruby. Oh, I know a lot about you." He knew, for instance, that my husband was a lawyer who traveled a great deal, that I lived in the Everglades, that I was a magician, and that I was haunted.

"Haunted?" I felt a sudden shock and had an instant vision of a complex, convoluted danger but pushed those sensations aside. "I'm not haunted. If my sister said so, you've got to discount her. She has delusions."

"My name's Rolando Ramirez," said the young

man, sticking out his hand. When I shook it, he lifted my fingers to his lips and kissed each knuckle. "I've been waiting for you for weeks. I think you're my angel. Don't talk yet," he warned, and seeing me stare toward the street, twisted his head to look through the windows also. "We're alone. I know you're going to remind me that you're married, but I want to think you're not happy. Don't talk to me about happiness that way! I've had a terrible time with women."

"And I thought you were shy," I said, shaking my head and feeling a little bolder. "All these weeks, standing in the corner."

"I am shy, but I know you. I work part-time for my uncle," the young man recited in an unhappy voice, "but I have better prospects. I'm studying to be a silversmith." The boy removed from his pocket a tiny and intricately carved silver fish, showed me how he had scrolled my name on its underbelly, and gave me the charm for remembrance. He would admit that he was very poor, he said, but he was still young enough so that his poverty could not be taken as a measure of his abilities. "I'm twenty-six years old," he continued, frowning now and speaking very rapidly. "I know you're thirty-three, but when a man and a woman are born to be with each other, age doesn't matter. Nothing matters except that I've been in love with you a long time." The boy took a deep breath, smiled, and touched my cheek. "Will you come away with me now, Ruby?"

I laughed and said as gently as I could that of course I could not go away with him. The kid held my eyes as if he were a hypnotist, and in the depths of his pupils, where my face shone in miniature, I imagined I could see a heart and soul very much like my own. "Forgive me," I said.

"Tomorrow then?" When I shook my head, the boy held up his hand. "I know you. You're lonely like me.

You look hurt—don't talk, Ruby! If you won't go away with me now, I'll come back tomorrow. I'm going to love you better than you've ever been loved, and make you feel more beautiful than you've ever felt. Once I have you I'll never let you go."

"My husband," I said, softly, gladly, "will kill us." I had begun watching the street again for my sister, indeed had begun to hope that she would return, but the sidewalk, shimmering violet rainbows in the heat, was empty.

"This is where you can reach me," Rolando said, scribbling on a piece of paper. When I seemed loath to take it, he thrust the paper into my pocket. "I think you're going to come to me. I think you're going to be my angel, and I can be your angel, too."

"My sister's coming back," I said, although I could see not a soul beyond the streaked windows. I pushed the kid toward the door. As he let himself onto the street my sister appeared, waving and shouting, and spoke to him for several minutes. When she came into the shop she was smiling and sighing, and for a long while she stood with her face pressed against the windows. Her hair was matted and full of leaves and stickers, and in her hands she held a little yellow flower.

"That's one beautiful-looking boy, isn't it?" Lillian said. "If I hadn't decided to give up men, if, say, I decided to have a relationship with anyone, I think it would be him." She was not interested in him, not in the least, she told me, pushing her flower to her nostrils and staring dreamily over the petals. "But sometimes I think he's in love with me."

"He's very pretty," I said.

In the small courtyard at the back of the shop I pulled the spider monkey from its cage, fed him, cuddled and kissed him, watched the baby alligator swimming round its tank to pursue the dried fish I tossed, returned the monkey to its cage, sat on the stockroom floor, took from my pocket the silver fish Rolando had given me, and began to cry.

"Not that I care, but where's Victor?" Lillian asked later that afternoon. She had been sitting in his chair at the magic table, her head propped in her hands, staring toward the street. When I said that I thought he had gone off with some girl, Lillian muttered that Victor Riley was a devil. "He has no heart at all. He ridicules me just like my husbands did. I'm only trying to do something for others with my life. It was like being reborn, when Mother left me her money to finish her work. If a woman doesn't have her work, she only has men. And I'm not pretty, and I'm forty, and I've never had any luck with men anyway."

All afternoon my sister talked about her failed marriages, not, she said, that she cared about all that any longer. Near closing time, as she was ringing up a sale, she began to weep, for she suddenly realized that no man, not even her husbands, had ever told her he loved her. "I dream of my husbands all the time. They laugh at me. They haunt."

3

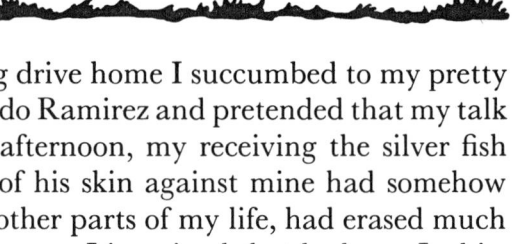

During the long drive home I succumbed to my pretty stories of Rolando Ramirez and pretended that my talk with him that afternoon, my receiving the silver fish and the touch of his skin against mine had somehow diminished all other parts of my life, had erased much of my adult memory. I imagined that he knew I whispered to him, and that he whispered back and was waiting for me. In imagination I found him sweeter and more playful than any lover I had ever known.

Thirty miles west on the Tamiami Trail, over an old wooden bridge and five miles down a dirt road that crooked through pine woods and palmetto, was the house my mother had designed and begun to build some years before my birth. For years my mother had sat on the front lawn, dressed in the heavy velvets and satins she called her princess clothing, plotting on blue-print paper yet another addition or crafty architectural joke. The slanting windows that she hoped would somehow sharpen her vision had been just the beginning. At the back of the house was a narrow, winding staircase that stopped at a blind landing some feet short of the second floor, and somewhere in the maze of wings was a low-ceilinged hallway along which were no rooms at all. Several doors and two sitting rooms had been boarded up. On high ground surrounded by citrus, gumbo-limbo, crab apple, and pine trees the house stood, a white wood, twin-towered spook that had come to resemble a gigantic starfish with broken, veering limbs.

My husband and I used only a third of the house, and sometimes, when I was alone, I was certain that along dark, dusty halls or in rooms unentered for over twenty years my mother roamed in shadow with the other ghosts of whom she had often spoken: the boyfriends and lovers she imagined had committed suicide over her, the angry victims of the rifles her father had manufactured, several footloose murderers, and a pitifully weeping young bride whose husband had died on her wedding night. All these haunts the swamp man was to have banished eventually for my mother, when he recognized that she was a woman of tender, charitable heart.

"Although you couldn't be charitable to your children, or to your husband, who loved you very much," I said, daring to conjure her up.

As the dusk deepened the house filled with a poignant and weighty blue shade, and the wind blowing through the opened windows smelled as sweet as cake. Insects thumped against the screens, frogs croaked, crickets hummed, and alligators bellowed. Outside the kitchen, purple bougainvillea wound up the white porch pillars, and down by the teetering, vine-covered pole fence were the rich green jungle, the river, and far beyond that, miles and miles of saw grass.

From the pile of food I had placed on the porch that morning the cookies and two jars of spiced apples were missing. The oranges, however, had been ignored. I trembled at a cry from the swamps beyond, which must certainly have come from an earth animal, and stepped to the porch railing; over the sweep of lawn in the deepening evening scrambled the silhouette of a man or beast—it was impossible to tell which, although it stood nearly upright. The thing howled pitifully.

I rushed down the porch steps and hollered, "Swamp man?" but the thing only howled again, slipped through the fence poles, and ran, limping, into the woods. A great feeling of pity engulfed me. I imagined I could feel the very rhythm of the creature's heart and blood and had to restrain myself from rushing into the swamps after him.

I was ashudder when I reentered the kitchen and was unable to prevent myself from again gathering up those foods I thought would delectably tempt an outer-space alien's palate—potato chips, cookies, and sugary cereals—and I pushed them, with my foot, beyond the door. "Mother?" I whispered. "Why did you send Daddy around, and now him? Don't tell me. I don't want to know." I rushed about the house turning on lights and locking doors, and then sat in the living room, trying to ignore what seemed to be my mother's powerful presence.

The telephone rang, and I picked up the receiver, expecting to hear my husband's voice. "Ruby?" a man said. "I love you. If you don't love me back, I'll die."

I hung up the phone immediately. I was entranced. I took a long bath and then tried on several pretty dresses, wondering what Rolando would think of me in each. In imagination I stand outside his apartment door, wearing green, a rose tucked behind my ear; he answers my single knock and then leads me, in eloquent silence, into the bedroom, where we make exquisitely choreographed, swollen love. But then my story became hopelessly fouled. He answers the door disheveled and smelling of another woman, of her perfume and her sex, and only after I have knocked and pounded for several minutes. He reddens over the obviousness of the rose in my hair and stammers that he did not expect me. Over his shoulder I can see into his bedroom, where his eighteen-year-old steady girl friend lies naked except for her knee socks. She is not jealous.

At eight o'clock I heard Artie's anguished voice in the hall. I ran downstairs and poked his curls, kissed his smooth fair cheek, his jaw, and the back of his neck. He stared at me as if I had suddenly sprouted whiskers. "Where are you going all dressed up?" he asked.

"I got dressed up for you," I said.

Artie held me at arm's length, a mortified expression on his face. He was evasive about telling me the reason for his mortification. "I've got pride, you know, Ruby," he began, as he looked through the mail. He did not want to judge me before the facts were in, but a man needed his peace. "I'm forty-nine years old," he cried at last.

I rubbed his neck, and slipping my fingers beneath his blue silk jacket, kneaded the sharp little bones along his spine. "Tell me," I kept saying. "Tell your honey dear."

"It must be a mistake," Artie said, his yellow eyes narrowing, "or someone's idea of a joke. It isn't your fault, Ruby, I know, but this new situation is intolerable." Artie told me that some man had been calling his law offices all day long, "every hour precisely on the hour," and had spoken with his secretaries and law partners, all of whom must be having a good laugh for themselves. "What are people going to think of me?" he asked, shaking my wrists. "The lunatic told everyone he was in love with you."

I pressed my face against Artie's chest. In the dim hall, hiding beyond the concern in our eyes, must have been an instigating little demon. "I'm afraid this is the same crazy fellow who bothered me the other times you were away," I said. I reminded Artie of the peculiar calls we had received after he had returned home from his three-week trip in May to California, where he had been looking at a Mexican food franchise; and of the strange love letters I had received at the shop in June, when he had been in Philadelphia looking over his new office building, and during all of August and September, when he had rushed off to Switzerland to persuade an Italian corporation to invest in his now-scrapped cruise ship company.

"They were Germans, and I was in Amsterdam," Artie said. He paced before the front door, jingling coins in the pockets of his still properly buttoned blue jacket, and occasionally stooping to the floor to pluck up debris tracked in from the yard. "You attract lunatics. You always did. Did you tell this fellow what your husband would do to him if he catches him around you again?"

"I did," I said solemnly. "He called me his angel, but I think he'll stay away now. He's afraid of you."

Artie seemed very pleased, and forming fists, rolling and shrugging his shoulders, swiped twice at his shadow. "You see," he told me, placing a tender finger on my chin, "men only respect power. When a beautiful young woman is married to an older, white-haired man, all sorts of punks take the liberty of making inappropriate advances. To a young punk a fifty-year-old man is little more than a ridiculous heap of bones in an unstylish suit."

"They respect you—it's me they're after."

"This is just another reason why I want my million dollars." Artie smiled fondly at me and said that he wished to put me in a pretty little bird cage where no one could ever hurt me. "But the gilded cage is expensive. You know, this morning I really wasn't certain about sinking my savings into this Curaçao deal. My father's friend—the Judge—can be more heavy-handed than I like. But this reminds me how vulnerable we both are, and when I think of that, I think I've got to go ahead with this deal."

He got an erection, he told me, blushing at his brazenness, just thinking of what lay in store for him in the islands. "I'm expecting the Judge with the papers any minute. The world will soon know what kind of man Arthur Holloway is. And nobody will be able to hurt me."

"Deal not," I said, "with the gold currency of any nation, but in the currency of the heart—death refuses bribes."

"Who said that?" Artie asked.

"I did," I told him.

At nine-thirty I heard the door chimes ring the plaintive melody of which my mother had been very fond. I crept, hidden by shadow, halfway down the stairs. A stooped old man wearing an ancient black suit moved slowly into the hall, and I saw him embrace my husband.

The old man spoke in a rough, cracked voice, as if he had been asleep for days or years. "I still have many people to see tonight," he said. He cast a nasty, squat shadow against the walls. "I've got the papers here—don't sign unless you're certain. My scheme is no sure thing. Already our little group has made enemies in Curaçao—I've always been blunt." The old man laughed merrily and said he enjoyed the drama of business more than any profit he might gain. "If you sign, you're mine. When I tell you to jump, you'll have to jump."

Artie said that he would jump as often as Judge Howard wished, until he made his money. "I trust your judgment. More to the point, I trust my father's judgment. Remember the time I went with you and Dad to Buenos Aires? You were both brilliant."

The old man laughed and shuffled his lustrous shoes;

he remarked that Albert Holloway had been a greedy man.

"Not greedy. Ambitious," Artie said.

As if by rote, or as if I were miming to a well-known record, I could, sitting on the stairs peering between the finely carved banisters, repeat words before they were spoken and see what was far beyond the normal range of vision: I could see the old man's black pirate eyes glittering and his pale hands making a sweeping circle to indicate how much island property in Curaçao could be bought at a bargain price. "The owners, I happen to know, are desperate to sell. They've had a couple of recent financial disasters, which I helped along—all legally, of course, but I get what I want." He might, the old man said, begin building condominiums in the next couple of months, or he might sell the land very quickly. "The chance for profit either way staggers even my imagination. But you might—and I bring this into the discussion only because I've known you since you were a boy—lose all your money. Consider that you already make a very good living. You have a fine law practice, Arthur."

"It isn't enough anymore," Artie said. "I want what my father had."

A howling started up outside, but neither of the two men seemed to notice.

"If you want what your father had, it certainly isn't up to me to dissuade you." The old man's hands, distorted by shadow, flew up. It was now time to begin jumping: Artie was to meet him at the airport the next morning at nine. "All the investors are going to Curaçao to look over the land, have some meetings, plan the project, do a little wheeling and dealing. Bring a check," the old man said. "You know the amount."

"I've already got it set," Artie replied. "Remember when I was five, the time I went along with you and Dad to Mexico City?"

"The only thing I remember about Mexico City," the old man cried in a booming voice, "was that I destroyed my opposition. What's that howling outside?" "A bobcat, probably," Artie said.

I ran upstairs and waited beside the window, but no outer-space alien attacked the old man as he stood beside his car, talking to Artie. I put on a ridiculous negligee Artie had bought me, of peach-colored silk, with lacy crotchless panties, and slipped on the matching feathered slippers. I was sitting at the edge of the bed, worrying, when my husband strolled into the bedroom. He seemed not to see me but paced a circle, grinning and rubbing his hands.

"It all looks so good!" he said, addressing the ceiling.

"Artie?" My husband seemed startled by my voice, and I felt very shy. "Are you ever lonesome?"

He blushed and replied he had no time to be lonesome. Then he seized my breasts. "You're such a darling in that outfit." He stooped to bite my nipples, but then straightened and struck his forehead with his fist. "The lunatic," he said. "I'd forgotten about the lunatic."

"What about him? You promised I could go to Curaçao with you."

"I can't take you with me. The other wives aren't going along." While I rummaged through my purse and slyly licked a birth control pill from my fingers, Artie fretted over what his father would have done if he had been torn between making vast amounts of money or leaving his wife in a dangerous situation. "Fish or cut bait! My father would have gone ahead to Curaçao, I know, but then, he didn't have you for a wife." Artie's eyes grew melancholy as he pondered what steps his father would have taken to protect his home and family, and his pale cheeks puffed with thoughtful breath. "The times I've taken you with me and given you a bodyguard, you still managed to get yourself in trouble or lost. And Curaçao is full of gigolos and creeps. It's worse than Miami, and far worse than Paris. I remember Rome, and I remember Paris," Artie said, recalling the April afternoon his innocent had been cajoled into a derelict artist's studio while he was off trying to put together what had then seemed a very promising deal in New Guinea. "If it hadn't been for that crooked Carlyle, I'd be rich now and wouldn't have this problem." My husband was working himself into an erotic fit; his fingers inched up my legs and kneaded the flesh of my thighs. "Promise me, Ruby, you won't talk to another man while I'm gone. Promise me you won't encourage any lunatics."

I laughed and slipped away. "Trust me," I said. "To love is to trust and to trust is to love."

"But men," Artie said, in a voice not unhappy, "have their clever ways." He rushed into the bathroom and sang loudly while he shaved. He emerged showered and well-scented, wearing his black silk pajamas and red velvet slippers. He kissed me and placed a finger between my legs.

Just then the telephone rang. Artie cursed and rushed to answer it. He listened quietly for a few moments, frowned, and then shouted, "If you call here again I'll kill you! It was that lunatic," Artie told me, throwing me on the bed and pouncing. "He told me to tell you—put your legs around my waist—that he can't live without you."

"Consider the devotion," I said. "It's so nice." Artie cried out angrily and bobbed for a breast, but I pushed him away and sat up in the darkness. "Do you hear anything?" I asked.

"Nothing but the crickets and the wind. Don't tease me, Ruby." Artie pushed his head between my breasts and noisily sucked a nipple.

"How long will you be in Curaçao?" I looked about

the room for any unusual stirrings, for the shadow of a woman's hand, for instance, or the rustling of her shadowy skirts.

"We're going to hold meetings through next week." Artie tried to lick my stomach, which was bared by the tart's sleepwear he had bought his innocent child, but I rolled to the side of the bed.

"A week," I said. I stared at my round breasts, my flat stomach, and my slender hips, searching for the first signs of decay. When I saw what I had been looking for, I imagined that my handsome and successful husband would soon launch into a series of affairs with young, beautiful women, that he would come home from work one early afternoon to inform me that he had fallen in love with a virgin. "Are you going to have a woman in Curaçao?"

"Don't be silly, my love," Artie cried, plunging my little toe into his hot mouth. "Why should I go hunting when I have the best at home? You're so sweet." Artie rolled me off the bed and onto the floor, begging me to behave myself while he was in Curaçao, to keep all the doors and windows locked, and to avoid speaking with strangers. Then he began whispering in my ear every obscene word he knew. "Say something dirty," he pleaded.

"I can't think of anything," I said. "Would you like to pretend to attack me?"

Artie roared like a lion and fought me into the rocking chair. We positioned ourselves with difficulty and rocked, groaning, until the chair toppled. Then my husband came at me from the rear.

"I love you," I whispered. "Your sweet eyes." But the eyes whose sweetness I praised belonged to the young, dark-haired man who saw in my face an angel's smile, and when I came, I imagined that Rolando had somehow felt my heat.

Artie lay beside me on the floor, stroking my hair, my cheeks, and crooning little love songs. "You're all mine," he said. He recalled the days when I had been neither his nor any man's. He remembered the night he had discovered me weeping in the bar of the hotel at which I had worked as a magician, and how, despite his persistence, I had refused to let him bed me for weeks. "My little virgin," he said now.

I remembered that the night Artie had asked me to marry him I had wept with wonder. I remembered that when my sister had hinted that I was not the innocent Artie imagined, that I had been "liberal and several times engaged to magicians," Artie had shouted that he would not listen to another word of such talk. "Not from you either," he had said when I started to tell him the truth and rid him of any misconceptions. "You're perfect. Perfect."

"You're perfect, you know," Artie told me now, taking my hand and leading me back to bed.

"You're perfect," I said. At that moment the telephone rang again, and I cried, "Don't answer that!"

"I told you not to call here anymore," Artie shouted into the receiver. Then he paced, his back stooped, his head lowered, and said that the lunatic who was making these phone calls would soon be sorry. "A man shouldn't be disturbed in his own house this way. Are you sure, Ruby, you haven't encouraged this fellow?"

"There isn't anyone but you, Artie," I said softly. As I gazed over his shoulder onto the moonlit lawn I seemed to see, or rather perceive, an awful shade, a maliciously gay presence. She was out there. I cried out and broke away from my husband. "All these suspicions—it's humiliating. If you can't believe I'm faithful to you, then you don't love me."

"I love you more than anything in the world," Artie whispered. His hair was in the sweetest disarray, and calling me his honey dear, his little feathered quail, he tucked me into bed. He lay with his cheek next to mine and talked of the great fortune he would soon make and how grand and lazy a life we would lead with our beautiful children. Within a few minutes he was snoring. I lay awake, thinking of the telephone calls, of the dark-eyed young man who spooked my heart, and of my dead mother, who spooked my bedroom. I fell asleep with her pressing against me, it seemed, and in a dream I watched her grow old very rapidly until her skin shriveled to bone and only a dry white skeleton with gray hair and a pointing finger hung before my eyes.

In the morning, when Artie prepared to leave for Curaçao, fussing over what he should wear and what he should pack, I cried, which should have pleased him very much. Instead, he looked at me askance.

"These young punks burn me up," he said, refolding a shirt I had just folded and handed him. "But your admirer is going to pay for his little joke. I made some arrangements while you were still asleep."

"That again," I shouted. I thought perhaps it was not worth living with men at all, for they either become inattentive or keep a woman in chains. I'd sooner live with my sister than with a man. "What have you got planned? If you put a detective on me again I'll never forgive you. I can take care of myself."

"I hope so," Artie said grimly, and even as he called his detective agency, he insisted that he had not been wrong to want to protect me, that as always, he had in mind only my best interests. "It isn't that I don't trust you. I just don't trust the lunatic. You can come with me to Curaçao if you still want to," he said.

"Go yourself," I shouted and flung his red slipper across the room at him.

4

A lonely, anxious mood fell upon me when my husband left for Curaçao. I walked around the outside of the house, kicking at coral rocks and ancient shells, and tried to convince myself that I was not afraid of spending seven nights alone in a place where ghosts might hover and some howling thing or creature might show himself at odd and startling intervals. In seven nights I could paint the kitchen, the hall, and the living room; could by the light of a kerosene lantern dig several flower beds to replace those that had dried up in the scorching August heat; or see seven movies with Lillian. After gathering together and placing outside the kitchen door my most ambitious bribe yet, a tin of imported pâté, a large slice of roast beef, a box of butter cookies, and an uncorked bottle of French wine, I drove downtown, figuring up how many years of beauty— four or five at the most, I thought—were left to me.

By the time I reached the shop the world seemed a black and desolate place. Lillian and her psychic followers were again preparing to go into the park with food and a message of hope, but when I asked if I might accompany them on their excursion, my sister tried to coerce me into a declaration of faith. "Does this mean you've seen our alien?" she asked.

"He has no reason to come to me," I said. I brooded all morning and told myself that my always preoccupied husband might just as well have tumbled me into the beds of other men. Each time the buzzer above the front door sounded I jerked in alarm and anticipation and rushed into the storage room to rearrange my hair and powder my face, so that at least I would have the pleasure of looking pretty when I told Rolando Ramirez that I could not have him. Each time I returned to the shopping area I saw no adoring and adorable boy, but only an elderly couple wishing to buy a stuffed toy monkey for their grandson, a group of Canadian tourists who rifled over the shelves and left without buying anything, and a well-dressed Colombian woman for whom Victor Riley was putting on quite a magic show.

"What's wrong with you today?" Victor asked me once, just before Lillian returned from her errand of mercy.

"All men are jerks," I said, wiping my eyes.

Victor assumed that I had been gravely hurt by our conversation of the day before, when he had threatened me with Shakespeare's opinions and the loss of my husband. "I only talked that way because I care," he said. "I think you care, too, Ruby. Don't you love me?" I looked toward the empty street and then at Victor. Some sadness in his face while he waited for my answer, some inexplicable guilt and a longing for tenderness made me think that I must say I loved him.

"I might love you, Victor," I said. As soon as I had uttered the words he seemed transformed, beyond my closed eyes, into the worthiest and grandest of men. Victor cupped my face in his hands, and I breathlessly waited for the kiss of the century.

When I finally opened my eyes, Victor was seated at

his magic table, gazing into the plastic crystal ball he used to tease gullible women with predictions of gay romances with sensitive and intelligent silver-haired strangers.

My sister flew back from the park in such high spirits my own seemed to shrink in response. She placed on the counter three white duck feathers, which she claimed to have discovered lying on the ground in the form of the letter A, and removed from her purse several muddy leaves, which she held to the light, exclaiming over their shapes, colors, and fragile veins; all these qualities together, she called to Victor, formed letters and words to guide her in her search.

"You should be as happy as I am," she chided, and pinched my cheek to make me smile. "Everything in the world instructs."

I was anxious to examine the leaves and feathers and distract myself and learn how everything in the world instructed, but when Victor spread his arms and said, "My charming, unpredictable Lillian," my sister rushed to his side. She spent most of the late morning and afternoon giggling with him. I was jealous and imagined that my sister had a far better way with men than I did. Several times I saw Victor rub her buttocks, and minutes after he left the shop for the day, Lillian prepared to depart also.

"Have a wonderful weekend," she said brightly. Her eyes blazed with energy behind her thick glasses.

"Artie's gone. Do you want to go to the movies with me tonight?"

"I can't." Although I attempted to hide my suspicions, Lillian scowled, and a blush crept over her cheeks and nose. "I'm going to work all weekend. Somebody has to keep Mother's dream alive."

"If Mother's swamp man saw me, would he be angry?" I asked.

"About what?"

"I don't know. I guess I've forgotten," I said.

"You forget because you're afraid to remember," my sister told me in a voice that was horrible in its sweetness. Then, crying out that she was certain all the pieces of her puzzle would fall together this weekend, she stepped out into the street shadows and was gone with all of her remarkable hope.

The young man approached me in the twilight just as I was locking the shop door. "Ruby," he whispered, clutching his motorcycle helmet to his broad chest and looking at me with beautiful eyes that, like dark evening water, seemed to catch and intensify the first light of the moon and stars. When he touched my shoulder and then my hair, my legs bent beneath me. "Ruby, please have dinner with me. I know your husband's away, and that means it's time for us to start."

A horror crept and then ebbed as I looked into his face. "You're crazy. How do you know my husband's away?"

Rolando smiled and said in a soft, halting voice, "I called his office."

"You've been calling my house, too—it's got to stop."

But Rolando shook his head and insisted he had never called my house. "I'd never do anything to hurt you. I want you, Ruby, and I know you want me. I've never seen a woman as beautiful as you. Look how your hair blows in the wind." He caught and kissed a strand, and I felt eighteen again. "Will you come with me now?"

"I can't," I said, looking about us. The street was deserted now, and its end seemed to melt into the soft, diffused lights of the park.

"Don't be afraid," Rolando said. "Come later, if you like. Please." He twisted his fingers as if he were suddenly anxious. "Do you still have my address?"

I nodded.

"I'll be waiting for you."

"I won't come," I said and then rushed past him to my jeep. If I kept him in my imagination, he would remain safe and sweet forever.

An hour later as I parked before my mother's house, I saw the small, half-bent creature standing by one of the gumbo-limbo trees. The creature was oddly illuminated by the lowering red sun that always lingered over the swamps. As I climbed from the car the creature took a step forward and, throwing back its head, began to howl. I was terrified.

"Swamp man," I called. "I'm a friend, not an enemy. When are you going to speak to me?"

The creature stopped howling for only a second, as if to catch its anguished breath. Animals in the woods now bellowed and called. I took a step toward the shadowy form, to see if it would run, but it stood its ground and waved its thin limbs at me. When the creature opened its mouth to shriek, I shrieked also.

"Who sent you?" I screamed at last, but I was afraid of its answer and ran up the porch steps and locked myself in the house. When the wailing stopped, I peered outside and saw the creature climb over the vine-covered pole fence and dart into the thick green woods. The roast beef and butter cookies I had left by the kitchen door that morning were gone.

I paced for a time in the dining room, before the never-completed mural my mother had begun to paint years and years ago—a brilliant, tortured composition of angels and devils battling against a surrealistic sky. "What do you mean by sending him around tonight, when I'm all alone? Are you sending him to torment me?" I whispered, and in my rage it seemed that all the grins of the devils were directed at me. "Sending these people to test me—I'm not like you."

I paced and paced and grew warmer and warmer, as if some thing or some one were pressing up against my arms, my chest, my heart. I picked up a vase and threw it at the wall. The force of the blow left a great nick in one of the angels' delicately formed ear. "What do you want from me now?" I shouted. "I don't want to remember you. Why won't you just leave me?"

I waited for a moment, perfectly still, as if she might answer me, but all was now quiet in the sweet-scented early evening, except for the frogs and crickets outside and the cries, perhaps, of a swamp man, an outer-space alien speaking in a strange new tongue as he wandered from the silver ship my mother had been sure would nestle in the underbrush on the very land upon which she had built her house.

I went to the living room and stood before one of the tilted windows. Fireflies darted like tiny fairies or like tiny space men, whose dignity must be so great and whose power so immense that physical size had dwindled until only the light of the soul remained. The outline of the treetops burned with the last light of the sun.

I put a call through to Artie's hotel in Curaçao, but no one answered the phone in his room.

"You leave me here," I whispered, feeling as if I were battling her and the message she had written to me just before she had ended her life: "You haven't won yet, Ruby!" That was true.

I found one of Artie's sweaters and was a little warmed and comforted when I wrapped myself in the soft blue wool that smelled of him. I looked out my bedroom window at the moon and stars and heard once again the cry of some creature perhaps part animal and part alien, or perhaps otherworldly altogether, as incongruent to this planet as I felt now.

"Ruby," I heard my mother gasp, and I picked up

the phone in the sort of trance that had once angered and frightened her.

"Oh, it's you again," my father said in an easy, amiable voice. "How did you get my number? Never mind," Sam said, groaning. "I know she gave it to you. What do you want now?"

"I want to come see you tonight."

"Are you bringing me a ticket to Puerto Rico?"

"Yes," I said. "I will." When my father suggested I save myself a long trip by dropping the ticket in the mail the next morning, I shouted, "I'm your daughter."

"You are not my daughter," Sam said. "But you sound upset. Have you seen her?"

"I think I saw the creature she talked about. I think he runs through the woods here."

"Your mother must have sent him around to bother you. There are ways and ways of haunting, you know, and I wouldn't put anything past Sally. If she sends him around here, I'll kill him. I don't want to see anything of hers."

"Listen," I said, trying very hard not to sob, "I'm alone here. I'm frightened. I need to see you."

"I'm afraid that's impossible. Why should you women be so terrified of being alone? Your mother had the same affliction." My father lowered his voice. "I have feminine company now. Perhaps we can meet next week. Call me next week. And don't forget to put my ticket in the mail."

"If I do that, you'll take off before I have the chance to see you."

"I have honor," my father said. "I am an honorable man."

"If you had any honor you'd admit I'm your daughter."

"But you're not," Sam said. "Good evening to you, Ruby."

"You leave me," I said, and then I dialed Rolando Ramirez's apartment. "I thought you might want some company," I told the boy.

I parked my jeep on Calle Ocho, Southwest Eighth Street, near a vacant lot where old men sat at folding tables playing dominoes beneath blue clouds of cigar smoke and strings of yellow electric lights. The main street of Little Havana was crowded, and rumba music swept through the open doors of the cafés and restaurants. I felt wonderful, as a woman should, walking along. Finally I stood before a Cuban bakery, staring up at the lighted apartment just above its red canopy. When I saw Rolando lean out of the window and smile down at me, all my lower muscles contracted and quivered with pleasure. Now that, on this evening, was love.

"Ruby, you look so beautiful," Rolando said when he opened the door. I was overwhelmed by the beauty of his large dark eyes, his perfectly shaped head, his long neck. "I prayed you would come." He was wearing a black silk kimono, a gift, he told me ruefully, from a girl friend who had recently left him for a plastic surgeon. "Women only like rich men."

"I don't. Rich men only care about becoming richer," I said. Rolando smiled, and his eyes caught a marvelous, merry light. He kissed my cheek and apologized for the disorder of his apartment. Books, puzzles, magazines, and clothing were strewn all over; inside a glass tank was coiled a boa constrictor, which, Rolando said when he noticed my eyes widening, was an intelligent, clean, and affectionate pet; and resting on newspapers spread on the faded carpeting were several dismantled typewriters and adding machines.

"I'm supposed to be fixing those for my uncle's shop, but I haven't had the concentration lately," Rolando said, leading me to the couch. From the pillows he brushed books, bits of food, and a great many bills. He stepped back, his eyes very melancholy, and looked so sweet and sensual I thought I could be happy every day of my life if only I could gaze into that face. "Before you called I was thinking of either killing myself or going to a mental hospital." Rolando turned and went into the kitchen.

"I don't understand. You seemed happy when I saw you before." Rolando did not answer, and when I leaned forward, I saw several very large cockroaches, apparently disturbed by his movements as he uncorked a bottle of wine, run up the kitchen walls just inches from the face of a man who, I liked to think, must have led so complete an inner life that the external, by and large, went unnoticed.

Rolando sat on the couch a respectable distance from me and sipped his wine, his lower lip trembling. "I hate living here," he said, a remark that sent me rushing back to my life at the Orange Blossom Tourist Courts. He pouted so fetchingly I kissed his fine jaw and put my arm over his shoulders. Rolando immediately turned his face into my neck and began to sob. "I have nothing to live for, nothing," he kept saying.

"Of course you do—don't ever think that," I said, hugging Rolando as any alarmed, affectionate mother might. Perhaps some spirit had sent me here to save this young man's life however I could. On the bookshelves that flanked the beaded entry into Rolando's bedroom were a collection of animal skulls, a stuffed, black-painted frog, and several books whose grim titles and brittle bindings suggested an old and terrible depression. "You have everything to live for. We have to believe that."

"I don't." Rolando's full lips were pressed against my bosom, and his tears trickled down the front of my summer blouse and wet my breasts.

"You're extremely handsome," I said, rubbing his head, "and you're young. You should have all the hope in the world."

"I'm not handsome, and I'm poor. There's hope for the rich, maybe, and the beautiful—for people like you—but not for me. My last girl friend left me in such a financial mess," he said, staring at me with his eyes still full of tears. "You'd think she'd at least pay her own way, or help me out by cooking once in a while, but no: she had to have the best and I had to pay for it. I'm behind in my rent, my bills, I have nightmares all the time, and nobody in the world cares."

"Don't you have any family to help you?" I asked, thinking how alike were the circumstances of our lives.

"My family's poor. We lost everything in Cuba. They'd have me move back with them, but I need my independence. I'm a grown man." Rolando ceased his crying then, pulled away from me, and stood before the small window overlooking the street. "I'm sorry. I don't know what you must think of me now."

"I think you're wonderful," I said softly, looking at the way his hair curled over the nape of his neck, at the way the silk of his kimono clung to his broad shoulders and slender hips. I took out my checkbook. "Listen. How much money do you need? I'll write you a check. Any amount at all."

"If I took any money from you, you'd never respect me." The poor young man seemed to shudder; he whispered that when he was half-awake, half-asleep at night, he saw the face of a woman in his window, a woman he was certain was dead, so pale was her skin and fixed her gaze. "You'd be doing me a favor, and yourself, too, if you just took me to the mental hospital and left me there for good."

"That's ridiculous," I said, wondering at his nightmare vision. "I've been depressed, too. I've seen things, and I've wanted to kill myself. I have the money to spare, and if I didn't lend it, I couldn't respect myself now."

The kid turned, and I was inflamed by the way his wet lashes glittered against his high cheekbones. "My rent's two hundred," he whispered. "I owe Master Charge another two hundred. Are you sure your husband won't miss the money?"

"He's practically a millionaire. He gives me whatever I want."

"You're an angel," Rolando said, placing the check I had written him, for an amount well above what he had asked, beneath the skull of what once must have been a rather large bird. "What made you so good, beautiful angel?"

I said I was not very good at all.

"Why did you change your mind and come here tonight?"

"To save your life," I said, laughing nervously.

"Tell the truth now," Rolando said, "like my angel."

"I heard strange noises in the swamps. And," I said, unable to look at Rolando for more than a moment at a time because his beauty hurt me so much, "I think maybe I'm in love with you. I don't want to be, but I think I am."

Rolando sat beside me and hugged me for a long time. "You know," he said, "I don't believe it was an accident that I went into your shop so long ago and saw you. You looked so lovely—why do you suddenly seem afraid of me, Ruby?"

"I've seen how things like this can end," I said. "My mother—she had man after man, and none of them ever loved her. The only one who did, my father, left her. She ended up killing herself." Rolando wished to know all the details of my mother's death, which I related with as much bitter sorrow as if I had known him all my life. "She was always running after the impossible. I used to warn her about that even when I was a kid. She blamed me for trying to ruin her life."

"I'm sorry for you," Rolando said at last. "But you shouldn't let guilt over your mother destroy your chance for happiness. You aren't her."

"I want to be a strong woman—a brave and good woman. But I don't know how." I shut my eyes, and the gaunt, strong face of a vaguely familiar woman popped into my mind. I got up from the couch and said, "I'll be leaving now."

"You only came here to tease me then. That was cruel," Rolando said, in a voice as quiet as blown silk. His hand fumbled for mine, and I let him pull me toward him.

The kiss was so soft and so delicate I felt as if I were a very young girl again—very young and very innocent— and I began to cry over having grown up when inside I still felt like a child.

"It's okay," Rolando said, touching my tears and looking at his wet fingertips as if his skin sparkled with diamonds. I thought there could not be a man as gentle as he was. "I think maybe you've been hiding your feelings for a long time, and it's made you lonely and afraid. But Ruby," he said, taking me by the arm and leading me into the bedroom, "your heart is safe with me."

"Do you promise?" I asked, as if humans could indeed keep such vows, such flowers were their hearts.

We made love all night long, the kind of marvelously slow, detailed love that I must have forgotten about, when every curve is a source of great delight, each moan a grand inspiration, and every orgasm seems sanctified and holy and connected to life and death and God. Rolando had me crying out, he was so good and delicate. I thought he had made me wondrous, too, for even to touch his finger, or kiss the small of his back, or tip his tongue with mine made him moan.

We lay across the water bed and watched the sky pinken into dawn. I stroked Rolando's slim tanned stomach.

"I wish I'd met you long ago, before you were married," he said. "I think God made a little mistake. We belong together."

We fell asleep for a few hours, and then I awoke to the most awful shrieking: Rolando was standing by the window, and when I rose and touched his shoulder, he shuddered. "I saw that woman again. She was wearing a red satin dress, and she was laughing at me."

"My mother," I said. "That's my mother."

"Was it?" Rolando asked, smiling weakly. "I've been dreaming about her for weeks."

"I'm afraid of you."

"I'm afraid of you, too. Let's not talk about it," Rolando said.

My eyes roamed the room, which was full of sunlight, and fixed upon the clock on the shelves above Rolando's bed. "Oh, God, it's nearly one," I cried, searching frantically for my jeans. "I'll get killed, surely. Artie's probably been calling all morning. And you don't know Lillian. If she notices anything odd at all she'll tell my husband."

"So what?" Rolando said. His voice and face were dreadfully sullen as he watched me dress.

"I'm a married woman," I said. "I do care about my husband, you know."

"I don't believe you. You told me you love me. I love you."

I said nothing.

At the door Rolando kissed me so sweetly and looked so sad that I agreed to meet him after work Monday. He spoke with such fear about what he imagined would be an endless succession of empty, lonely nights during

which he would see my dead mother at his windows
that I said I would meet him for lunch and dinner on
Tuesday, too.

"I love you," I said, "but this can't become a regular
thing. I'm thinking of you now. My husband's a very
jealous man. He'd kill us both if he ever found out."
Rolando laughed. "If he was that jealous he
would've taken you to Curaçao with him. No, he left
you alone, and now you're mine."

"I've only been here once," I said. I was terrified:
Rolando's face evoked the memory of a hundred men
to whose whispers my mother had succumbed.

"It doesn't matter. You're mine. I'm going to marry
you—I love you more than you've ever been loved. Will
you marry me, Ruby? If you won't, then I can't see you
anymore. Just say it," he whispered, slowly kissing my
neck from top to bottom.

Lost to my imagination, I said, "Maybe I'll marry
you. This is a great love, isn't it?"

5

I drove the bumpy dirt lane toward the house at great speed. As I rounded a curve, I saw a tall, stout, red-haired woman I would have sworn was my sister running through the woods. I braked and drove on very slowly, catching every now and then a glimpse of the white-clothed figure. A half-mile from the house I saw a face peering out at me from behind a tangle of palmetto, and binoculars pointed in my direction.

My sister's rusting Datsun was parked in my driveway beside the pink Cadillac that belonged to the woman who had been cleaning my house ten years. Janet Monsterville was an exceedingly handsome fat woman with a very dark complexion, which she tried to lighten with skin bleach and lemon juice, and huge almond eyes, which she painted a nightclub-green even for work. She was standing on the front porch wielding her switchblade when I ran up the steps.

"Oh, I ain't pointing that at you," Janet said sweetly. She turned her wide cheek to me for a kiss, and my lips slid against her wet, warm flesh. "Your bad sister's out here running through those woods. She came here about twelve, wanting to know where you were and talking about some swamp spook." Of course, Janet said, she normally would not believe anything my sister said, "but when I got here this morning the kitchen was broken into, and, girl, what a mess! But we don't need to worry, women out here all alone. I can cut up people and animals. I'd cut up your stupid crazy sister if you told me to—getting you in trouble with the boss."

"What happened?" I was trying to keep my legs close together to clench the smell of sex.

"Damn sister went and told him you never came to work this morning. She's a sly one. She grabbed the phone right from my hand and told the poor old boss you were gone all last night and this morning, too—getting him all upset. You're in trouble now," Janet Monsterville said.

I walked inside the hall, screeched at a frog that jumped out from behind an antique Chinese cabinet Janet thought compared poorly to her own new furniture, and dialed Artie in Curaçao. I let his phone ring several times while Janet attacked the frog with a broom, crying out that she meant to have frog legs for lunch. Finally I threw down the receiver and stalked up the stairs to the bathroom.

Janet came into the bathroom just as I got into the tub. "All the eggs and milk were stolen," she informed me, sliding over the shower curtain a couple of inches so that she could peek at me. I saw her nostrils flare when she bent, grunting, to pick up my reeking jeans and panties. "And whoever broke in this place tracked in mud and grease and blood all over the kitchen floor. I mopped, but you'll have to call the wax man. Slavery's abolished, and I ain't going to kill myself over any floor. I'm fifty-seven long years old," Janet said, "and I'm sick."

When I stepped from the tub Janet praised my

breasts, waist, and hips, and recalled how she herself used to be the talk of the little Georgia town in which her poor old mother still lived. Oh, she said, she used to sway along the road with her long hair and her twenty-six-inch waist. "Even those white crackers called to me. Shit, I had some men in those days! Georgia's my heaven, and soon I'm going back home. Last night I walked up and down the street two hours before I could find a boyfriend. If I could shove off some of this weight maybe I wouldn't die young," Janet said, lifting her big belly and then her breasts.

"You've been talking about dying ever since I've known you," I said. "You aren't going to die young."

"Am too. You got another boyfriend?" Janet demanded. "I fasted last night—dry yourself before you get sick, too—and I heard the Lord. I know the truth when I hear it."

"What," I asked, reaching for a towel, "does the Lord think about you running around with all these different men? Wouldn't he mind?"

"You can fuck and pray, too," Janet said. "God don't expect a woman to be perfect. Long as you apologize before you die. Who'd you spend the night with?"

When I told her about the boy and my guilt, Janet growled that a woman ought to keep extras around so that she would never be alone. She herself had been going with a mechanic named Alonzo for eight years, and she was good to him, but she always kept her postman, her gardener, and her truck driver on the side.

"I ain't putting all my heart into one man. I just feel sorry for my boss—he's old-fashioned, and he's so proud of you. Poor thing. You say this Cuban got no money?" Janet asked, incredulous that a woman would give a man money instead of getting all she could for herself.

"I don't need his money," I said.

"Us poor folks got to watch out for ourselves. Even

Alonzo, if he didn't give me money he'd get none of my pie. I can't afford no beans and rice. I like young ones, but they'll take all your money and leave you flat." Her first husband, she said, had taken all her money and left her flat, and God had smote him dead with his huge fist for doing so. Janet reminded me that my magician fiancés had taken my last dollars and had left me flat.

"Rolando isn't going to leave me until I tell him to," I said, lighting a cigarette from the pack that had fallen from my jeans. "He loves me. He told me that."

"Love don't come easy as you say—not even when you're pretty. I guess you're lonely, your husband being away so much, working nights, flying off all the time. We could go to the movies. I get lonesome nights, too."

"I'm never lonesome," I began, but Janet interrupted.

"Bad people running all over my neighborhood from the projects down the block. The bad boys'd rape me. And what if I get sick when I'm alone? Go into a coma?" At this my face fell, and I promised, as I had so many other times, that we would have a night out together very soon. But Janet shouted, "I got my boyfriends. And I got my money."

I stood wrapped in a towel before the opened bathroom window. In the waist-high grasses beyond the back fence I could see my sister standing with binoculars held to her eyes. "What the hell is she doing?" I said.

"Spying on you! She says you're in for some trouble—says some outer-space spook tells her. She says she knows your future. Shit, that crazy sister of yours is about as psychic as my foot. She says you hate her and your poor crazy mama."

"I don't hate Lillian."

"She thinks so," Janet said. "You're going to have to

commit her. I had a cousin like your sister. Lela-Mae was the jealous and the back-stabbing kind, too. She's dead now. God took her and put her in hell because she was so bad. That bitch tried to take my first husband from me and then my second one, too. Telling those stories. Wouldn't stop that crap till I cut her arm up. Don't you trust any bitches," Janet cried.

"Maybe Lillian was only worried when I didn't show up for work."

Janet uttered something that sounded like a prayer and rolled her eyes toward heaven. "Don't be stupid," she said. "You act like you ain't a part of this world."

I dressed and went downstairs for coffee. Janet set up the ironing board beside my chair, spit several times on the iron, and insisted on pressing the underwear. She spoke of her three husbands, all dead now, and her three stillborn daughters. "I'm better off without them, I guess. Otherwise God would've made them live."

"Are you ever haunted?" I asked.

"Every day," Janet moaned. "Every day."

I tried to escape from her into the living room, but Janet picked up the ironing board under one fat arm and the clothes basket beneath the other. The iron cord in her teeth, steam hissing dangerously close to her breasts, she followed me. While she ironed she said something about her diabetes, and later something about cancer, or cancer smears, or an aunt who had died of cancer. When she quietly accused me of not listening to her, I noticed that she was gray in the face and that her wide, deep eyes were bloodshot.

"I'm going to meet my Maker soon, when I get back to my Georgia," she crowed, as if she were singing. On and on Janet talked about how beautiful Georgia was and how much her mother loved her.

I carried a glass of wine upstairs and lay across the bed with my chin on the window sill. The sheets still smelled of my husband, and I suddenly missed him dreadfully. When I stared down at his red velvet slippers, I could not imagine what had compelled me to tell a sobbing boy I might marry him.

Janet Monsterville burst into the room on the pretext of dusting and launched into an account of her sexual activities with her bus driver and her postman, each of whom had given her fifty dollars without her having to ask. "I can pay off my china cabinet now," she said, and then, pulling at her plaited hair, "and go to the beauty parlor. Alonzo—he don't know who he's dealing with here. I'm roller skates!" cried the woman who, like my husband, claimed she was destined for an early death.

When I opened my mouth to ask Janet why she thought Rolando had wept so and why he might have seen a dead woman in his window, Janet cried, "You want me to pray for you tonight?" Before I could ask her why she thought I needed prayers, she was deep into the history of a grievance she held against one of her other employers, "my second Tuesday. That crazy old lady," Janet muttered. "I said to her last time, 'I ain't taking any crap from you, crazy old bitch.' She still likes sex, though, always telling me about rubbing up against her pillow." Janet sighed. "Well, I guess she's just ignorant. I may be getting old but I ain't never going to rub up against no pillow. I got to earn my money."

I went downstairs to sit on the front porch with another glass of wine. Janet Monsterville followed me with the broom and swept along the lovely weathered planks.

"You're my only true friend," Janet said, "just like family. I'm sure going to pray for you tonight."

"Why?" I was staring off into the countryside; in the woods my sister stalked with a dangerous idea, and in those woods crept either an alien or a man deranged by fear.

"So you don't lose your husband. Beans and rice'll

leave you flat, and when your husband finds out about him, he'll leave you flat, too. I wish I had a husband. Alonzo won't even take me out to clubs and he falls asleep right after dinner. I got hot blood. Stupid old man, I'll get rid of him yet!" Janet grasped the handle of the broom as if it were her sixty-five-year-old boyfriend and she meant to strangle him lifeless.

"But last week you said you were going to marry Alonzo."

"Did not," Janet said. "Wouldn't have him." She went into the house and returned to the porch with a gin and tonic. She squeezed herself beside me on the big wooden porch swing, noisily chewing on her ice. "I ain't letting no man make a fool of me."

"Rolando thinks I'm all his now," I said. "Maybe that means trouble and I shouldn't see him anymore."

"Long as you don't go getting carried away. You get carried away, you'll be dead." Janet rocked us back and forth on the swing, her feet thumping, her plump knees cracking.

"Sometimes," I said, "when I think there's no romance left in life, and no surprises, I feel old. I become very frightened. Do you?"

"That's why I keep so busy with my men. You couldn't come see me at night, anyhow. Tonight I'm going to put on my red slacks and my green-and-red-striped top from Saks and, girl, I'm going to jump." Her eyes widened as Lillian appeared in the distance. My sister climbed clumsily over the fence and fell into the grass. Her binoculars bounced between her breasts as she walked toward the house.

"Your sister's trying to break up you and the boss," Janet said.

I insisted that Lillian could not manage that even if she tried, because I loved Artie more than anything in the world. "And he loves me just as much."

"Maybe so. But a man's going to put up with just so much. You love him like you're telling me, you better not get carried away. I'm your friend. I'm your real sister. I tell the truth." When Lillian approached the porch steps and smiled at Janet Monsterville, Janet said, "Somebody round here ain't no good. Somebody round here aims to cause trouble."

"Well, it isn't me," Lillian said, with great dignity. "I want to speak with Ruby—alone."

"I'm finished here, anyway." Janet stuck out her hand, and I gave her thirty-five dollars, which she snatched and stuffed into her bra. "I ain't staying in a house full of ghosts and traitors," she said.

"You won't get a rise out of me, Janet. Grief has taught me patience," Lillian said.

Janet Monsterville bullied her way into the front hall as if the very molecules of the air were ghosts and traitors. Through the kitchen window, beneath which my sister and I sat silently, came Janet's grumbling as she squeezed into her long-line bra and girdle. Moments later she rushed through the front door, pausing just long enough to kiss me and spit at Lillian's feet.

"I hope you die tonight," she shouted at my sister. Janet drove away in her Cadillac, singing at the top of her husky lungs to an Otis Redding tape.

Lillian asked in a troubled voice where I had been all last night and this morning. "I happened to be here when Artie called—he's very worried about you. What are you hiding, Ruby?"

"You find out, since you're such a great psychic. I don't like you spying on me, Lillian."

My sister's eyes were shiny with tears. "I wasn't spying on you. I was looking for the swamp man."

I smiled. "Do you want to find what Mother looked for? I'll take you there tonight. Maybe we'll even see your future. Go get the flashlight from the kitchen." I

thought then that I was bluffing, that I had no intention of using my gift to take Lillian to see the swamp
man that evening or any other.

My sister's face was rosy and triumphant when she
returned to the porch. "I knew it," she said. "I knew
that your gift had returned." She let her fingers quiver
to the vibrations of spirits she insisted I, too, must sense,
and together we stepped out across the lawn, which was
caught between the last of day and the beginning of a
full-moon night. The moon over the Everglades was
huge, orange, and looked as if it were made to be
streaked by ghosts and the black shadows of witches.
My sister's glasses shone as brightly as the windows of a
church, and her mouth was determined as we walked
toward the path that wound through the woods to the
river.

"Does Mother ever come to you?" Lillian asked.
"Tell the truth now, Ruby."

"No," I said. "I keep her off."

"You shouldn't. She wants to forgive you. Once you
loved her, Ruby, I saw it. Why don't you remember
that you loved her?"

I pushed my way through thigh-high grasses and
brush. "Maybe I'm too sad."

"Your gift will save you. Mine saves me every day,
even when I think it won't. We're going to see something marvelous tonight." Lillian hugged me, her
cheeks wet with glad tears that broke my heart over my
meanness. Hope as fragile and sweet as hers was difficult for a hopeless woman to bear, but her disappointment would have crushed me.

"Let's go back to the house now. You're trembling
so," I said.

Lillian insisted she would not be daunted. She leaned
against me as we walked deeper into the pine and
cypress; lizards rustled from our path and spiderwebs

wound into our hair. My sister was not frightened of spiders or snakes; she wanted to be a wonderful woman. "God gives us all gifts," she said, pushing aside the razor-sharp fronds of palmetto that grew along the path. "Now your gift has returned, and you're taking me to the swamp man. It's a crucial time for women all over the world. I could kill myself," she cried suddenly, "for sleeping with Victor."

"It doesn't matter," I said, hugging her with both an unexpected surge of great love for her dreams and a fear of the woods and the swamps at night, when I could not see what crawled, or hung, or crouched in painful breathing. But the shine in my sister's eyes made me think what I had never before thought about another woman—that in her face was reflected a heart and soul much like my own, but stronger, more resilient. "We've been through a lot together, haven't we?"

"I used to think sometimes we'd never make it," Lillian replied as we made our way toward the river, from which, she now recalled, our mother used to sail us to a make-believe land of fairies and kind, funny ghosts. I could not remember this. Lillian said that if our mother and father had not left us alone to make our way as best we could, we might not have been strong enough for the grand events that would occur this very year. One alien was already running through the swamps, she said, and she was certain the rest would follow once this swamp man had accepted us as worthy brethren.

The dock from which we used to launch our rowboat now sloped toward the water like a lame old man. Its rotted planks shone nearly white beneath the moon. "I'm going to faint. My God," Lillian said.

She shouted something incomprehensible—she often spoke in tongues—and pointed at the sky, where the moon drifted between clouds as easily as a coin tumbled through the nimble fingers of a handsome magician father. "He's coming to us," Lillian whispered, as if she had been enchanted by a fragment of some miraculous outer-space sight, or by the music she imagined would swell the skies when alien ships, as bright as angel eyes, hurtled toward earth. "Soon, soon."

I shivered with fear of ghosts and of swamp men, who might expect too much from this weak, bad Ruby Holloway, and huddled beside my sister on the crumbling cement boat ramp. The river reflected a thousand moons and glowing animal eyes, and it lapped and licked at my shoes. My sister mumbled to herself as if she were in a trance. She knelt before the water, and her muddy high-heeled boots sank into the sand as she dipped her fingers and touched them in pious gesture to her forehead. The hem of her dress was soaked. A cry of some thing, some animal, perhaps, sounded in the distance. Lillian said, "That's her, or them. I'm trying for you, Mother, can't you see that I'm trying?"

I was frightened for my sister and cried, "They're coming, Lillian, I promise you." In my arms she moaned and twisted her head, as if she had suddenly caught a dangerously high fever. I had begun to work up a healing incantation when Lillian alerted and stood erect.

"I'm all right now," she said, but her lower lip wobbled with disappointment because her alien had not shown himself to her by the river.

"I shouldn't have brought you here," I said.

"We'll see him yet," my sister replied.

When we were just a mile or so from the house my sister tripped, fell over a bush, and landed in a small clearing. She sat, dazed, her fingers touching a bruise on her cheek. Looking down, she discovered a woman's stiff and filthy velvet hat. Beside her, she noticed a fire pit and a length of rope lying next to the charred wood. Lillian began to screech at the top of her lungs.

As I helped her up, we heard the wailing behind us. About five yards away crouched a human, or what appeared to be a human but was so caked with mud, so bizarrely dressed in a woman's flowered blouse and old suspendered trousers, and so bent, as if with pain, it was possible to imagine that a form of life not belonging to this world had been revealed to us. When the creature groaned, it seemed to groan for the universe, and my own mouth opened again unwittingly at the sound, and again I groaned along with it.

Lillian gagged as a skunklike stench thickened the air. My sister stepped forward, coughing, and took a small notebook and a flashlight pen from her pocket. "What do you want? Who are you?" she asked, articulating each syllable slowly and distinctly, as if she were speaking with one unfamiliar with the English language.

The painfully moving cramp of limbs was as thin and as knotted as a mass of mangrove roots struck suddenly and miraculously with life. Its filthy, matted head twisted to one side, and its quite human mouth opened as if to implore; its eyes burned, and splinters of human heart and aspiring human bone seemed to burrow into my heart. I gave myself up for a moment, and for a moment I knew the creature and was astonished at my mother and Lillian and myself, and at all the frightened world waiting to be saved.

For a moment I thought the creature knew me and was not at all angry. I shouted without thinking, "Run!" In the blink of an eye—and in this the swamp creature adhered to supernatural tradition—the being I imagined loved me had vanished.

"Why did you tell him to run?" Lillian cried, grabbing the flashlight and running through the still-quivering brush. By quivering leaf and shaky intuition my sister stalked the swamp creature. I was forced to run after her to remain near the elucidating beam of her flashlight. We ran deeper and deeper into the jungle, until finally Lillian stopped, breathing very hard, and slapped a spiderweb from her sweating brow.

"We're lost now," I cried.

"Hush! Don't ruin this for me, Ruby! I hear something. Do you?"

"A voice, and the branches rubbing together," I said. My eyes teared at a confused and complicated emotion, and at some vision I was unable to piece together. My sister and I moved sideways through the brush, holding hands and tripping often. "Let him alone tonight," I whispered, but my sister refused and grasped my hair to lead me on, so that I wanted to fight her on the damp ground among the leeches and snakes.

A flung branch, let loose by my sister, struck my face and knocked me to the jungle floor. Above me Lillian screamed, "The witch of the woods. Ruby, get up and run!" She was weeping and tugging at me, and the folds of her white caftan tangled in snakelike branches. "I don't want to know my future from her," she shouted, stamping her foot and glowering at someone behind me.

When I stood up, I came face to face with the other woman in these woods who also had the gift of vision: my aunt Catherine Doris Lillian O'Connell. "You," I said, taking a step backward. "I'd forgotten all about you." I rubbed my eyes and looked again, and there she still stood, smiling sadly at me.

"You didn't forget about me," said my aunt in a low, hoarse voice. "It's impossible that you would forget me. You just didn't want to think of me, Ruby, although I used to hold you in my lap."

I rubbed my eyes again and gawked at her in the light from her kerosene lamp. My aunt was a peculiar, marvelous woman who, although she leaned upon a bumpy stick for support, loomed above me by four inches. She had a beautiful long throat and a nobly shaped head, upon which was coiled a neat red bun, well-streaked with gray. She wore heavy boots, an ankle-length cotton dress, and an apron stuck with all sorts of small cutting and measuring devices. I recalled once watching her draw maps for the Parks Department, remembered that making maps, acting as a guide, and saving those lost in the Everglades had been her work. My mother always claimed my aunt had come to live in the Everglades because she had suffered a broken heart. I had not seen her since the day my father left us and my mother led Lillian and me to Aunt Catherine's small, steeply pitched cabin and demanded to know the future, which Catherine could never be persuaded to reveal.

That day my aunt looked gravely at my mother and said, "You know your future, Sally." My mother collapsed with fear. Later she said that Catherine meant to kill us with her visions, and weeping as wildly as if my aunt had actually shown her the dreadful end that would be hers, shouted out, "Forget her—she lies! That will not be my future." A couple of days later we left the Everglades, and by the time I returned to the old house, two years after the funeral (to which Catherine had not gone), all memory of my aunt had fled me.

"I remember you very well now," I said finally. I pulled my arm from my sister, who was still tugging at me.

"Don't speak to her!" Lillian gave me a vicious shove backward and then hid behind me, peeping over my shoulder at Catherine. "She'll kill us, too—she'll tell us things. She'll tell you things about me." My sister, overcome by what my aunt might have to say about her, sobbed that she would never murder our mother's dream.

"Shut up," I said, gently rapping my sister's head.

"This isn't a chance meeting, is it, Aunt?" Catherine shook her head, and I averted my eyes. Somewhere in the dark shapes of the trees croaked a blackbird, and from nearby came the gentle sounds of roosting quails.

"You girls are in trouble," Catherine said, still looking directly at me. She had the strongest face of any woman I had ever known, a face of majestic bones, sudden angles, strong chin, and large, clear blue eyes very much like those of my sister and mother. But these eyes saw everything, and at once I remembered that this was the face that had flashed before me at Rolando's apartment, a vision that for one moment had convinced me that I ought to leave.

"We're lost," I said, staring at the cane with which my aunt now walked. Her legs must have grown stiff, but she looked prepared to help and to save. Hanging from her wide belt were a canteen, a knife, some rope, and the same worn leather purse filled with medicines and suction cups she had carried when I was a child. "You came for us because you knew we were lost. Isn't that right?"

"It's easy to get lost out here," my aunt said. "I'll help you get back."

"I won't walk with her," Lillian said. "Mother told us never to talk to her."

"You're so afraid—you aren't your mother," my aunt said, looking not at me but at my sister. Catherine pointed the way toward the river, which Lillian and I could follow back to my dock. "Who were you looking for, Ruby?" Catherine asked.

"It's none of your business," Lillian shouted. Once again she tugged at me and pleaded with me to run.

"We thought we saw something strange by the river," I said.

"But you know what that was, Ruby. You hide your knowledge as if it were a hump on your back." My aunt

smiled at me. "You should come see me. But you'll be
coming soon enough—I'll be seeing you soon." My aunt
made her way through the brush, and I could hear her
humming, a low, soft, gospellike tune, as if every step
she took were through a church.

As soon as we could neither see nor hear Catherine,
Lillian stepped forward and shouted, "We're never
coming to your house, for your information." Lillian
seemed both shaken and relieved that Catherine
O'Connell had not revealed anything about her life
and its end. "I never said I felt like Mother."

Lillian walked rapidly in the direction my aunt had
just indicated, snapping twigs and sharp-edged leaves
into my eyes, her boots crunching snails and land crabs.
She complained that she would not be surprised if
Catherine had sent us deeper into the jungle to starve
and then rot. "Why'd you have to talk to her? You'll
ruin everything."

"But Catherine knows what we're supposed to do," I
said. "She's the one who could really help—if only I
could be her."

"Judas," Lillian whispered. Whether she was refer-
ring to me or my aunt I did not know. "Why'd you tell
the swamp man to run when I've been waiting so long
for him? He could've been the first of the aliens. He
might've spoken with me, asked me for help. It
might've all happened tonight, except for you."

Then Lillian began to cry. I told my sister that I had
shouted inadvertently at the creature; it was as if some
spirit had taken over my tongue. And this was so. "I'm
sure this means we weren't supposed to speak with the
swamp man just yet. Can't you see that?"

"Maybe," my sister said, in low, cold, frightened
tones that sounded all of teeth and twisted tongue.

"Why are you trying to keep Mother alive?"

"I don't have to answer that. It's the dream that's

going to live." As we walked toward the house Lillian scribbled in her notebook. All around her in the Everglades she heard the sound of alien voices, but that night the crickets bloomed in chorus, and I thought no otherworldly sounds filtered our way. Lillian pointed at the stars, around which, she said, circled planets possessing highly advanced civilizations, and she felt a coded rhythm and beat in the night. She claimed to hear the sounds of long-dead Miccosukee Indians making a mockery of time and space. She sensed the thick sweet air was quivering with the sonic beams of a craft hovering thousands and thousands of miles above us, and about her head she intuited myriad spirits, ready to help all those ready to embrace a noble dream.

I thought of Christmas, which was still many weeks away, and saw myself attempting to save a young boy from death.

6

In the years since my mother's death I had read and carefully compared nearly two hundred stories of ghosts, sprites, fairies, elves, bogarts, or what we might now call outer-space aliens, what we who live in the Everglades might say are swamp men. The elements of supernatural folklore are remarkably similar, whether the ghostly visitations occur in Great Britain or in the Polynesian Islands, but one detail in particular struck me as perhaps the most expressive of the human will to be haunted, and that was the utter inability of women and men to flee what clattered in their houses, overturned the milk churns, ruined the butter, or pinched them while they slept.

As I hoisted myself over my fence, I recalled the story of Hinzelmann, a nineteenth-century German sprite who so exasperated the free-living nobleman in whose rooms he dwelled that the gentleman fled his castle. This Hinzelmann then floated in the form of a white feather beside his master's coach and, as the feather, summoned a voice to warn the nobleman to return home before the worst luck befell him. To emphasize his point the sprite toppled wagon and horses into a stream; the nobleman, finally convinced of the futility of his escape, returned to his castle, where felicity and a quiet life awaited him.

"We saw him, Ruby, didn't we?" Lillian said. "And Aunt was just behind him, as if we had to go through her to get to him." As she flung her legs over the fence, Lillian cried that she had just seen a strange shadow passing through the illuminated rooms of the house. "Catherine says we're in trouble." When Lillian spat her syllables so, her mouth was awash and saliva sprang. "If I were to go out now with my group, looking for him, she'd stop me somehow and ruin everything." Lillian stomped the earth as she walked along beside me, her eyes fixed on the ground so that she would not have to look up at the house and the shadows the house contained. "I might've talked to him tonight, except for you and her. He has amnesia, you know. Entering the earth atmosphere has caused him to forget who he is. Now she's out there keeping him from me. She knows I'm afraid of her."

Lillian had always entertained a great many comic-book superstitions, not the least of which dealt with our aunt's part in our mother's death. Now she was worried that a hair had perhaps dropped from her head as she wandered through the slash pine. She wondered if Catherine O'Connell might burn the red strand before a full midnight moon, chanting strange rhymes to do her harm. With her superior psychic knowledge, Catherine O'Connell might turn Mother against her. "I think our aunt is a witch," Lillian said. "She prophesized trouble."

"I think she was just speaking in a general way, to warn us to be careful. We don't want to rush things. Catherine meant that we might be in trouble if we behave foolishly."

"I'm afraid," Lillian said. She moved slowly, heavily, without joy.

"I won't be," I said, trotting along in front of her, full of the energy that comes from noble resolve. I thought that my life was to be fixed and that suddenly, miraculously, without any effort of my own, I had grown into the woman I had always wished to become. Rolando Ramirez would not tempt me. "Fear has led me wrong in the past. Who cares about growing old? Look to the future!" As I unlocked the front door the rusty chimes played their tinkling melody, and Lillian gasped and seized my arm.

"I'm not going inside. I've been sinful," she said.

Although I had a firm grasp upon her muddy dress sleeve, Lillian stood frozen on the plank boards of the porch. I said, "I won't have you driving back to the city now. If we see ghosts, we see ghosts. We can't run from them, anyway."

"I think you're right about that," Lillian said. She entered the hall on mouse feet, whining. Her face and lips were swollen with mosquito bites, and I attended to our swellings and scrapes in the kitchen. Lillian's eyes rolled as I swabbed her arms and face with ammonia, as if every slanted cupboard and window, each scrolled faucet and bizarre light fixture, signaled some dreadful message about her future.

When a field mouse ran across the kitchen floor, Lillian screamed. "I think I'm haunted. She haunts me."

I smoothed her hair from her face. "I'm haunted, too."

"But not like me. Oh," she said, "Mother was so desperate and so ugly."

"Not so ugly," I said. "She knew about the swamp man."

But Lillian was still uncertain. "But that didn't save her, did it? I'm afraid. I'm afraid I'll do what she did."

Lillian stood for several moments at the window above

the kitchen sink, stooped and defeated. She told me, her eyes as still and fixed as if they had been shellacked, that ever since our mother's suicide on Christmas Eve nearly thirteen years ago there had been a terrible darkness inside of her. Nearly always, she said, she doubted Mother's dream, but even in her doubt there seemed no choice but to try to realize that dream. "If she hadn't hated me, she wouldn't have killed herself. We failed her in some awful way."

My sister and I had never been able to speak seriously about our mother's suicide. In Lillian's face I saw the shadow of my mother's face, and perhaps she saw the same in mine. When I spoke now, my voice trembled with fear and shame. "Maybe we didn't fail her. Maybe her death can't be explained. She was so delicate, and such a child. A woman has to grow up some day. She wanted love so badly. We would have loved her, wouldn't we?"

"But Daddy wouldn't, not the way she wanted him to. Don't tell me he's alive, Ruby, I couldn't bear it. Maybe it's his fault she died."

"Maybe it's nobody's fault."

"But he left her alone. All her dreams were lonely. I'm alone. I have her dreams now. I wish some man would love me." My sister continued to stare through the tilted window, her head cocked to the right and her eyelashes blinking rapidly. "If I had that—a good man who told me he loved me and treated me like a princess—I'm sure I'd have everything that matters in the world. Fooling around with Victor!" She turned toward me with the most dismayed expression. "How could I have done that?"

"He's clever," I said, swallowing hard. "He knows how to work on us. I won't let him do it anymore. You don't love him, do you?"

"No," Lillian said. "I love a man who's sweet and sensitive and full of life, and maybe he'll save me."

Lillian insisted upon sleeping in our old bedroom, and she cried out in delight and clapped her hands when I switched on the overhead light. The huge bed still remained, although I had repainted the pink walls, first blue and then ivory, and had added plush ivory carpeting, an antique desk with a telephone and type-writer, and shelves full of books dealing with the supernatural. Lillian, her eyes filled with tears, softly read the titles aloud. My sister had not entered the room since we had left the house as children, and only once since our mother's death, shortly after Lillian's second divorce, had she peered through the doorway. Thin and smiling, she had stood in the hall and suddenly wept at the sight of her old doll lying on the bed.

My sister wrenched my head against her shoulder. She threw off her muddy dress and shoes and sat naked, her breasts hanging below her thick puckered waist, thumbing through a beautifully illustrated book on fairies and elves. From time to time she picked up her dress from the floor and wiped her eyes and nose with the soiled cotton. "I want this to be true," she said.

"Maybe it is true. We saw him in the swamps tonight, didn't we?" I asked.

Later, when we were in bed, I touched my sister's shoulder and whispered, "Lillian?" My sister turned her head toward me, and in the gentle moonlight I could see her smiling. "We can't let anyone make us forget we're sisters, we're family."

"We're sisters forever, no matter what," Lillian said. We lay close together in the dark and plotted swamp man strategy. It was enough for the time being, Lillian agreed, that we knew such a creature existed. Lillian decided to occupy herself with the harmless task of attempting, with Mother's guidance in séance, to trace more exactly the swamp man's outer-space origins. "I don't know what else to do to make her not angry with me," Lillian said. In the dark she shuddered, and in the dark she squeezed my hand.

At that moment the telephone on the desk rang. When Lillian reached for the receiver, I said, "Don't answer that."

My sister had a very throaty, beautiful way of answering the phone. She listened quietly for a few minutes, her breathing becoming more and more rapid, and at last put her hand over the receiver. "It's Rolando Ramirez," she whispered. She settled with the phone among the bed pillows, her ankles crossed, her red hair spread over her white, plump arms and shoulders.

The two spoke very intimately for nearly a half hour. Lillian told Rolando that she had seen the swamp man, for whom, he knew, she had been searching many years; discussed and minutely analyzed his nightmares according to the theories of Freud and astrology; and related, in tiny, tender detail, the story of how she had met her first husband, the Italian cornet player, and with what pain she had reached the conclusion that he would never love her. When she hung up the phone, she sucked her pinky and said she thought that she and Rolando were psychically linked.

"He knew I was here, for one thing. And he's described seeing Mother in his bedroom window—she wears the same red satin dressing gown she died in. Minds like ours would meet." She sighed and hugged her pillow as if it were he. "I shouldn't be astonished that he knew where to reach me. I know where he is, every second. We speak together nearly every night." Even in the dark I could see Lillian's tongue slipping around her knuckles.

It was difficult to find my voice. I felt suddenly very ugly and as stupid as if I had been tricked by a small child with a magic cane. "Do you?" I said. "Have you been to his apartment?"

"You're asking me if we've made love—we haven't yet." My sister laughed softly, huskily. She said she was still waiting for her first kiss. "There's a man who cares about being friends with a woman."

Lillian fell asleep, first raving and then murmuring about Rolando's hair, his eyes, his slim stomach, and his dainty, well-shod feet. As soon as she was unconscious I crept down the hall into my own bedroom and called Rolando.

"Why are you doing this?" I demanded.

"Doing what?" Rolando's voice was sullen and cold, and when I imagined that I had already lost him to my sister, I cared not at all that an hour ago I had pledged to give him up.

"Lillian thinks you love her. She's in love with you," I said.

Rolando said this was all a part of his plan to keep our affair a secret. "I've dreamed of you every night since the day I saw you. I love to go to sleep, Ruby, so that I can be with you in my dreams."

Frowning, I said that I loved Rolando in my dreams, too. "I just don't want Lillian to be hurt."

"You care more about your sister than you do me," Rolando charged. Then he began to cry. He was so terribly lonely without me, he said. He was unable to sleep or eat, and one of his few joys was listening to my sister talk about me. No woman he had ever known had given him so much glorious pain. If he ever lost me, he would be unable to live.

"And I," I cried, so overwhelmed by these declarations that I called him my honey bear, my sweet cake, my diaphanous daisy, "would be unable to live without you."

I returned to bed in mad conflict, not thinking at all

of my swamp man. I tried to imagine telling Artie that I wanted to leave him, but could only visualize falling to the ground at his feet in bone-breaking, heart-breaking, and spirit-breaking pain. Nor could I imagine telling Rolando I wanted to be a faithful wife, for as soon as he fell to the ground at my feet—in my vision he wore a cream-colored silk suit and a rose-colored shirt—I lost all my will and collapsed on the ground beside him.

In dreams I saw my mother at one side of the room; her lips were frozen in an awful grimace while she swung from her rope. Her brilliant red satin dressing gown split light and years and heart, and she howled terrifyingly, pointing her finger and telling me that I had not won, never would win. Across the room my vision swept, and I saw Catherine O'Connell and beside her a swamp man. Both were talking to me, imploring me, but my mother's howls grew louder. When I jerked awake, I saw that the bed beside was empty: Lillian was gone.

"Lillian," I whispered. I reached for the light, then swung my legs over the side of the bed to the soft white carpeting. "Lillian!"

No sound answered my small voice. I leaned against the door frame and peered out into the hall. "Lillian," I screamed. Already tears were running down my cheeks, and I trembled with the autumn chill and with a fear of inescapable ghosts in great, empty old houses. I searched each room on the second floor, and then, turning on lights ahead of me, went downstairs. But my sister was not in the living room, nor in Artie's den, not in the kitchen, nor swinging on the front porch. I was afraid that she was dead, and I collapsed into the porch swing and wept hard.

Some thing, some creature, paused for a moment on the front lawn as if it had heard my crying and pitied me, and then disappeared behind the house. I ran out onto the lawn, and then, realizing I was alone, looked up toward the third floor. There, where I had been warned as a child never to go, I saw the shadow of a heavyset woman pass a suddenly lit window. The third floor was where my mother had housed her haunts, and now I had to save my sister from them.

It took me a long time to climb the stairs. I stumbled as I passed the second floor, the staircase narrowed, and the dusty old banisters leaned out with my slightest touch. When I looked up and down the third-floor hall, lighted for the first time in years, I saw something small and quick dart down the long passage. At first I shrank and then shouted and ran after it. Huge balls of dust clung to my bare feet, and I coughed and shouted my sister's name as I passed first one closed door and then several others. A dust-shrouded rocking chair leaned against a mildewed wall, and I thought that on its cushion sat the old dead woman my mother had often mentioned. She seemed to rock and wail, rock and wail. Standing by her side, one beautifully shaped fair hand on the old woman's shoulder, was the young bride who wept over the death of her husband. The wailing became mixed with the sounds of the Everglades animals outside, and when I saw a door ajar, I bolted inside the room and tripped, falling flat, over an empty milk bottle.

Yards beyond me, across red-and-beige carpeting and beneath the voluminous folds of floor-length curtains, I saw the most execrable, cracked muddy shoes. Someone or something moved behind the curtains.

"Where are you from?" I cried. "Who are you?"

A voice, eerily high-pitched, shrieked, "Ruby Holloway." At once the room was in darkness, and I heard the sound of a door slamming and knew I was again alone. When I crept into the hall, I saw my sister standing by the stairs, one hand clutching her throat. Lillian turned and grinned when I rushed to her, and then sank to the floor, her eyes wide and swollen with fear.

"I saw her," she whispered. Her head swung from side to side as if she were mimicking our mother hanging from her rope. "I saw her. We spoke for a long time. She warned me—Mother warned me."

"Oh, God, don't listen!" I said. I helped my sister up and dragged her down the stairs and back to our old bedroom. She sat on the bed, dazed, and seemed unable to answer my questions. Her eyes remained fixed on something not visible, until finally she sighed and smiled and lay on the bed.

"I'm thirsty," she said.

When I went downstairs to the refrigerator for some juice, I found in place of the carton a note written in a tiny, pleasant fairy hand: "I'm sorry I have to take this. Don't be afraid. And please don't hurt me. Best wishes, Eugene."

"Are *you* who my mother was waiting for?" I asked.

My sister drank the glass of water I brought her and then fell into a restless sleep. All night I dreamed of fairies and of elf-shot: my sister had all the dazed symptoms of elf-shot. Perhaps Eugene did not like her and had stunned her for a time.

In the morning I consulted my library of the supernatural to see what must be done about Lillian. She awoke just as I was making a sign of the cross over her head, crying out, "Be gone," to rid her of the elf-shot. My sister blushed, frowned, and crossed over, naked, to the armchair just opposite the bed. From her purse she took her notebook and filled first one page and then another with her scribbling.

"What are you doing there?" I asked.

"Nothing," Lillian said, continuing to write with inspired speed.

"What happened to you last night? Why did you leave this room?"

"I don't know," Lillian said, sucking on her pen. "I can only tell you that I was warned by Mother. Did you see anything up on the third floor?"

For some reason I insisted that I had not seen anything at all.

"Nothing?" When Lillian saw me approaching her—I had meant to snatch her notebook from her hands—she lifted her great white buttocks and slipped the pages beneath her. "I'm going to get dressed," she said. "I have plans to make, a lot to do."

"Let me come into town with you," I said.

"No," Lillian said. "You stay here. You've never liked séances, anyway, and I'm planning a big one. I'm in love," she said, "and maybe that's a good sign."

7

I wandered through the woods and underbrush until afternoon. Beneath the chilly, overcast sky, perhaps watching me through mist-shrouded palmetto thickets, might also wander the swamp man who had chosen the earthling name Eugene and perhaps this Ruby Holloway as his primary earth contact. Several times I approached Aunt Catherine's cabin, where, I could now easily recall, I had sat as a child with my mother and my sister, watching glowing embers snap up into the chimney and listening to stories of the strange creatures that lived in the Everglades. But always, as I rounded a curve in the river and approached the first of Catherine's vegetable patches, I fell back and ran into the slash pine again. At last I crouched on the banks of the river, on the old boat ramp where my sister and I had sat the evening before in moonlight as compelling as sexual attraction, and there I thought how sad it was that a woman could not love when and whom she pleased without risk.

But in these woods despair now seemed inappropriate, for here roamed a swamp man who might rid me of my haunts. By the banks of the river, on the boat ramp beside my sloping dock, I waited for him to approach me.

"Swamp man," I cried, holding out my arms to embrace what spell of his had lingered into this day. But I noted nothing out of the ordinary, except for one small, strange animal that might have ridden an intergalactic space ship to these swamps. The animal, which was just four or five inches long and seemed to be part lizard, part insect, crawled slowly over the wet leather toe of my boot and then onto the cement ramp upon which I sat. The creature had a hundred spindly legs, a head the shape of an alligator's, the most delicate row of sharp teeth, and what struck me as very human, terribly intelligent black eyes.

"Can you understand me?" I asked. When I touched the long scaly tail and the scaly body, I shrieked and drew back my hand. I watched the strange creature hang suspended on a sharp green frond, then fly off into a tangle of brush that bowed over the dull river surface. I called once again, "Swamp man," and stood, shivering in my flannel shirt. Soon enough, I thought, Christmas would arrive, and perhaps with Christmas a glad miracle would occur, and we would all—even I—be elevated to the ranks of angels.

"I think I want to be good, swamp man," I said.

As I approached the house and rounded the fruit trees, I was startled to see my husband's Mercedes in the driveway, and behind it, a black El Dorado. At the southeast side of the house Artie, a cigar clenched between his teeth, stood over a jasmine hedge as a younger man parted branches with a gun.

I was as crafty as my magician father as I crept toward the two. I hid for some minutes behind a large pink hibiscus bush, apologizing to my swamp man for my cursing—but surely I had been found out. Artie was crying out that if I did not return soon he would call the sheriff. The strange man kept telling him in a rough voice to calm down; he continued to push aside branches with his gun and stooped from time to time, as if he had discovered some proof of my infidelities in the bushes. Perhaps Artie had hoped to find me in the act at the side of the house and had hired a detective to bear witness.

When I thought that my husband planned to leave me, I ran into the house and called Rolando Ramirez. "I love you," I said.

"And I love you more than my life," he said.

Seconds after I had hung up the phone, Artie walked into the hall. His damp white curls glittered with moisture, his cigar wiggled between his teeth, and his yellow eyes looked about merrily. Pointing a charming, angry finger, he accused me of having had a lover in his absence.

"I didn't," I cried.

My husband kissed me gently, and then, seizing my shoulders, said, "Where are you hiding him?"

"Who?" I asked, trying to catch him as he broke away.

"The man from your shop." Artie stalked up the stairs, shrugging off my hands and crying out that he had spoken twice to Lillian. In their first conversation she had hinted that I had expressed an interest in, as he said, "the same fellow who followed you in London, no doubt. When she talked to me this morning, she wanted to change her story. You've got your sister protecting you now, but nothing escapes my eyes. I'm going to search our bedroom."

"I don't like this game," I said, as Artie tore the sheets from the bed, looked beneath the mattress, scrutinized the bathroom, and flung open the closet doors.

"Escaped," he said. "The fellow won't dare show his face around here again."

"I don't like this game."

Artie jerked me toward him and, bending, kissed me so long and violently I felt dizzy and confused. "I've missed you," he said.

"What's going on here?" I asked. "You're home early."

Artie grinned and marched about the room securing each window. The searching and securing procedure he repeated in every room on the first and second floor of the house. When he returned to the bedroom, he shoved me to the mattress and told me in a proud voice that there had been trouble in Curaçao.

"You mean like in Rome?" I said, recalling the time when Artie and his associates had determined from a series of trivial annoyances, beginning with a missing tire on my husband's rented Fiat, that a radical Italian group wanted to prevent the construction of a bridge from the mainland to Sicily. My husband had been wrong about this but had had a wonderful time considering the possibilities of kidnappings and assassinations. "You mean like in Paris and London?"

"I mean for real this time," Artie said. "There's a chance we could be in danger, but that won't defeat Arthur Holloway." Artie's chest seemed to expand as he strutted back and forth across the room. He told me that someone close to the investment group—not actually a member of the group but close to it—had been put in the hospital the night before with two broken arms and a broken left leg. No doubt, Artie said smiling, someone was trying to ruin the group's prospects.

"Did you see the man, or just hear about him?" I asked.

Artie refused to tell me. "The less you know, the less you'll be in danger yourself. If anybody but my father's old friend were running this deal, I'd certainly have gotten out of it by now. I never expected to see anything like this. I've always led a calm life, a careful life, practicing law and taking care of you. But now!" He had aroused himself considerably. Squeezing my thigh, he told me that the land in Curaçao looked wonderful, and that the deal seemed extraordinarily promising. "I'll be a wealthy man soon, and all for my sweet wet wonder."

"Why do you always have to run around with men who want to be crooks?" I said. "Get out of the deal, Artie."

Artie looked at me sternly, although his eyes still glowed with boyish delight. "My father's friends are not crooks. The old man, the Judge, was at my christening—I love him. Important men always have enemies, I think. Your husband is an important man now. Don't cry, Ruby." Artie was so moved to clumsy haste by my tears that he was scarcely able to unbutton my flannel shirt and unzip my jeans. "As soon as the hitman is caught, I'll be going back to Curaçao. I'll have to insist that you stay away from the shop for a while."

I was as much aroused as he. "I won't," I said.

"Don't fight me on this, please, Ruby," Artie said, suddenly serious. He undressed, and wearing only his dark socks and his shoes, rummaged through the suitcases he had placed by the door. From one of these he plucked a transparent scarlet nightgown and wiggled his fingers through the breast cut-outs.

Artie blushed and stammered sweetly, "It's just that I have this picture of you in New Orleans, leaning over a balcony." I let him dress me like a French Quarter floozy. Then I admired myself in the full-length wall mirror and was touched by his present. "I'm going to fuck you all afternoon and night," Artie said. He picked me up, grunting with the strain—he outweighed me by just twenty pounds—and threw me on the bed. When I spread my legs he cried out how wonderful I was, and how beautiful and young and exciting. "No man is going to kidnap my wife," he said, his feet, still modestly attired in socks and shoes, kicking out with anger. During the third hour of our play and our third attempt at resurrection, Artie fell away from me and said in a melancholy voice, "I'm forty-nine. I can't cut it the way I used to."

"Artie, you're as wonderful a lover as you've ever been. I'm satisfied. I am deeply satisfied."

"Then why do you hurt me?" he asked, staring with sick eyes through the locked window and across the dusk-rolled lawn.

"What are you talking about?"

"I don't know," Artie said. "I'm sorry. You're my life. I was nothing until I met you."

"It's the other way around," I whispered. "You made me important."

"Then let's forget everything else but that. I don't want to think—life is so short, Ruby." Artie put his arms around me and fell to sleep, whimpering in what must have been anxiety-ridden dreams. He awoke an hour later, gasping that he was having a heart attack. He lay on his side, his eyes stricken, his fingers in his mouth, his arms and legs twitching. When I screamed, he screamed also.

"This may be it. I thought that if it came in Curaçao, at least I'd be alive and really fighting." His voice was only the shell of a normal voice, and the light in his eyes seemed to be growing dimmer. He said he had written me instructions for just such a time. "Get in touch with my law partners. They'll know what to do. You're a young woman—if you want to get married again, I'll understand."

When I dialed the county rescue squad and cried out that my husband was dying, Artie wrenched my arm. "Hang up that phone and listen to me! If you're kid-

napped by the mob—listen to me closely now, Ruby—
and you're forced to submit, don't worry about me. I
can handle it."

"Thank you," I said. I struck his chest to revitalize his
heart, and when I pressed my ear to his breast, the
rhythm sounded strong and vital. "You're fine, Artie." I
was crying with relief. "You were dreaming, that's all.
Dreaming."

"I never dream. Ah, but look at you, you're an angel," Artie said. His eyes rolled and seemed unable to
focus. "A vision of feminine perfection. I'd like to make
love to you again, but I can't."

"It doesn't matter."

"It does to me. Bring me a drink. One last triple
scotch."

I put on a robe and went downstairs to the bar. As I
crossed the living room with Artie's drink, I looked up
and gasped in surprise: on the stairs above me stood a
slight, crooked-backed, and bizarrely dressed creature,
who turned and ran as soon as my eyes fell upon him.

"Swamp man," I said, hurrying after him. "Swamp
man, oh, Eugene." I stood at the end of the hall, looking
up the winding stairs to the third floor. For several minutes I stood fixed to the same spot, trembling with both
fear and a curious, pleasant anticipation. Outer-space
aliens would be elusive and prankish, but in the end,
however childish, willful, and spiteful they might be,
supernatural house sprites would be guiding. "Sweet
dreams, Eugene," I called.

Artie, pale and dour, quickly drained the tumbler of
scotch. Then he lay against the pillows, and while I
smoothed back his curls, he wondered what he could do
for the family of the man who had been beaten up in
Curaçao.

"His wife, if he has one, must be beside herself." He
seemed lost in sad thought, and when I suggested that I

might visit the poor woman, he said, "No. I expect he has no one, poor fellow. You look so beautiful in that nightgown, Ruby. You'd never really look at another man, would you?" I shook my head. "What would you do if you were kidnapped, and some man wanted to press his advantage?"

"I would tell him I had syphilis," I said.

"Good, good," Artie said.

While Artie's eyes slowly closed I sang him a soft lullaby, and while I sang I saw a lovely, blue-gray shadow creep toward my bedroom door to listen.

In the morning when I awoke I saw that the small round table which usually stood in a corner of the bedroom topped with a vase of supermarket carnations had been set at the side of the bed. On the table was a tray with cereal, milk, and some warm, expertly baked cinnamon rolls. Artie was still sleeping soundly, and I smiled at my good fortune to have found such a husband and vowed that beginning at this moment I would be forever faithful.

"That's so lovely," I said, sliding my cheek from his sweetly haired belly up to his chin.

"What?" Artie asked, sitting bolt upright.

I poured two cups of coffee and chided Artie for trying to disown his gentle deed. "You're still like a kid on his honeymoon. You make me feel like I'm on a honeymoon when you do things like this."

Artie rubbed his eyes and looked very pleased as he reached for a cinnamon roll. "My darling is up early baking for her husband to thank him for the good time last night."

"Stop this," I said. "When did you get up?"

"Getting up early, creeping downstairs like a little fairy."

I crawled forward on the bed and looked out into the hall. "It wasn't me," I said. "I saw a creature while you were away—I saw a swamp man. He lives here now, I think. My swamp man—he calls himself Eugene—has brought up breakfast for us."

Artie licked each of my sticky fingers and, calling me his pink periwinkle, his jelly doughnut, and his wet custard pie, climbed atop my hips. There was our first kid, he cried, and now twins. I was so lovely. I loved him.

After we had dressed and walked downstairs for vitamins, we discovered that a small miracle had been worked in the kitchen. Artie examined the gleaming, spotless stove and counters, and would have made love to me again, he said, had he not been pressed for time. "You certainly were busy this morning—what a good lady you are! I must be crazy ever to leave you."

Clean hearth, happy home—my swamp man had done all this, I told Artie. Artie winked at me, and when I insisted that I had been blessed, he blushed and said, "That's sweet of you. I feel blessed, too."

8

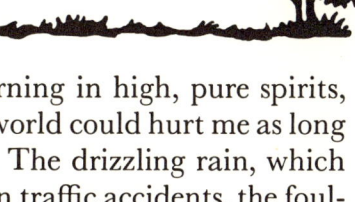

I drove into town that morning in high, pure spirits, certain that nothing in the world could hurt me as long as Eugene was on my side. The drizzling rain, which usually fixed my thoughts on traffic accidents, the foulness of aging, the stain of sin, and lonely, unmourned deaths, instead buoyed my mood. Now was the time, I told myself, to seize my destiny, look to the future, jump on that wild horse, and wrestle that steer to the ground.

As I pulled into my parking space I saw that beneath the leaking canopy of the shuttered drugstore beside my shop stood a man pretending to read a newspaper. Rain dripped from his detective's hat—I supposed that my husband had hired another fellow infatuated with Humphrey Bogart—and when I gunned my jeep motor, he flicked his cigarette to the ground and rapidly walked away. I followed him for several blocks, slowly, obviously, until he dashed into the First National Bank building, where my husband practiced law.

I called Artie from a phone booth across the street. "Take your man off," I said, as pleasantly as I could. "A game's a game, but now you've gone too far."

"I will not take him off," Artie said. "You need him for protection. Even the Judge thinks he's a good idea. I've told you before, there are some who want to ruin all of us involved in this deal. Someone might try to get to me through you."

"That's a romance," I said, trying very hard to be patient. "Nobody was trying to get to you in Rome or Paris, not really, and you put a guard on me then, too. If I could see that this fellow is a detective, don't you think a professional hitman would?"

"He's supposed to be one of the best investigators in town. Don't fight him, Ruby, please, like you did the others. I'm asking you to cooperate with me on this. I can't watch out for you now." He said he would be forced to work until midnight every evening until he returned to Curaçao and would be frantic if he thought I was without protection.

"I'll come to your office and help you," I said. But when Artie hesitated, I said, "Never mind. I promised an old friend I'd go to dinner."

For some minutes I leaned against the glass side of the telephone booth, sweating in my yellow rain slicker and watching the rain bead on the folding doors. Finally I smiled and dialed my house. I had to let the phone ring for several minutes before it was picked up. "Eugene," I said, "this is Ruby. Artie has a detective after me. Swamp man?"

My swamp man whimpered into the phone.

"What I'm trying to figure out is, should I dodge the detective fellow or what? My sins are more Artie's idea than mine. Swamp man? Eugene?"

Again my swamp man whimpered.

"Don't tell me then," I said. "I'll figure things out for myself. I thought you came to help me. What's a woman supposed to be these days?"

When I walked inside the shop, Lillian's psychic

group gathered around me. The ancient, cross-eyed Lyla Zimmerman wore a Baggie over her head and dry cleaner's plastic over her navy crepe dress; Grace and Clara Thurnwood wore bright pink trench coats and matching pink hats; and Posy Adams had flung a gigantic rubber army cape over her thin shoulders.

Posy took my arm. "Lillian learned all about our swamp man last night—we all learned about him."

"Good, good," I said and pushed through the crowd toward the counter, stopping to thank Grace and Clara for the marigolds they thrust into my hands. Behind the cash register Lillian and Victor were arguing fiercely about the swamp man and the possibilities of outer-space aliens landing in the Everglades near my house.

"I'm telling you I worked on it all last night," Lillian said. "I spoke with Mother, among others, and I know his name and where he's from. Tell Victor you saw him, Ruby," my sister pleaded, and then launched into a lengthy description of the swamp man we had seen in the woods, adding the fantastic detail of a silver aura about his head. "He is the victim of temporary amnesia, which we must cure." Victor Riley laughed aloud and tapped his temples. "Ruby," Lillian said, taking my arm, "I've learned his name. Relga! When you see him, call him by that name, he'll remember who he is and where he's from. Relga has arrived. When I heard that name, I felt an enormous power surge through me."

"You're horny," Victor said. "That was the power you felt."

"You're an old fool, and you'll be sorry soon," Lillian said. She must have slept in the same white caftan in which she had trudged with me through the woods, for the dress was muddy about the hem and torn in several places. "I haven't rested two hours since I saw you last," Lillian told me.

As the elderly women blinked back tears, Lillian revealed that the evening before, as Grace, Clara, Lyla,
and Posy had watched, her hand had been taken over
by an outer-space alien, a friend of Relga, who wrote,
through her, the alphabet of a universal space language
and its earth equivalents. "He's going to be all ours,"
Lillian said, "as soon as we prove our goodness."
    "It's astounding how specific these delusions can be."
Victor's voice rose above the cries of the old women.
"My wife, for instance, Ruby, is certain that I intend to
murder her one day with a slicing gadget, a Vegomatic,
she ordered by mail. Each night she hides it in a different place."
    "You would like to murder her—you've told me so
many times," Lillian said. Casting many inflamed
looks at Victor, Lillian explained that this Relga who
ran through the swamps was the leader of an enormous
and complex hierarchy of outer-space beings who had
in ancient times visited earth for the purpose of coup-
ling with humans preselected for their virtue. The off-
spring, Lillian said, still retained the powers of flying
and mental telepathy, and the gift of vision special to
their spiritual origins. She said that we both revealed
our kinship with the aliens because of our intelligence,
the fullness and length of our eyebrows, the shape of
our eyes, and the vision that allowed us to see into the
future and more accurately interpret our pasts. She
imagined her own disproportionately thin arms were
vestiges of winglike appendages. Relga, who on his
planet was spirit without flesh, had appeared in human
form on earth so he would not startle us.
    "If you hadn't taken me into the swamps the other
night, I might have never seen him," Lillian said.
"When he first speaks as Relga, he's going to speak to
you. You're in the highest spirit category of all—double
Vivas Nimas. Your beauty and goodness prove that."
    Victor Riley scowled and muttered that I was not so

beautiful and certainly not very good. I scowled back at him and said in a loud voice that this was the best news I had heard in a long time. "Maybe, Lillian, you'll be a world-famous psychic some day."

"We'll both be world-famous and loved, too," Lillian said wistfully. "And nobody—not a thing in this world—will be able to hurt us."

"Do you think so?" I asked, suddenly as wistful as she.

I listened as Lillian meted out the assignments for angelic deeds. Lyla Zimmerman and Posy Adams were to go into the park as usual to feed stray cats, dogs, and humans—who knew but that aliens might be testing their faith by taking the form of degenerates and drifters sipping whiskey beneath the sea grape trees? Grace and Clara Thurnwood were to drive into the Everglades and take up those stations indicated on the maps Lillian had drawn the evening before.

Grace and Clara crossed themselves as they left the shop, their plump pink chins lowered in obeisance. Posy Adams helped Lyla Zimmerman along the sidewalk in the direction of the park. I saw the old German woman slip in the rain and fall heavily against Posy.

"Lillian, I don't think these women are able," I said. I was suddenly frightened that events had gotten out of control.

"You shouldn't feel sorry for them," Victor said. He had thought and thought about the matter, he said sweetly, and had decided that the reason these women engaged themselves in such an undignified pursuit was that they knew no Silver Fox, no Victor Riley, would ever want them again. He had noticed that the women became inflamed when he entered the shop, as if he were a painful reminder that sex was slipping away. "In short, they only do this because they know that no one will ever fuck them again."

"Imbecile!" Lillian shouted. "Pompous jackass. You

don't know a damn thing about anything. You haven't any love at all." Saying that she was unable to bear the sight of his face a moment longer, she rushed into the stockroom and kicked the door shut.

"I wonder what that was all about." Victor appeared genuinely hurt and confused, but after having analyzed the situation, he smiled and relaxed and said he knew more about love than any man he had ever met. "Yesterday I slept with three different women and my wife, too, and still I had the energy to take my nephew out for ice cream—there's a boy for you. Don't worry, Ruby." Victor winked at me. "Your time will come soon. You're special to me. Am I special to you?"

"You're special to me," I muttered.

That afternoon Shakespeare seized control of Lillian's hands while she was making entries into the books and scrawled lines of psychoanalytical and erotic poetry across the columns of numbers. When she read the poems aloud, Victor asked, "Do I have to listen to this garbage?"

Lillian said that anyone who called Shakespeare garbage was out of his mind.

"You're out of your mind. You wrote that," Victor said.

"You never really loved me. Do you know that he bit my nipples?" Lillian shoved at her breasts, as if to show me. "He left disgusting marks all over my body." Lillian flung a basket full of five-for-a-dollar shells at Victor and, grabbing her purse, rushed from the shop.

"You see how much she cares about me," Victor said in a bleak voice. "She's not enough of a lady for me. She's too old."

"She's forty. You're sixty."

"I'm not sixty here," Victor said, tapping his heart. "Maybe I ought to quit—I know that she loves me. I came here to work in good faith. I wanted only a pleasant part-time job, and now I'm badgered by your sister's fantasies. What you saw in the swamps was just a man, and he can't help you any more than anybody else can. Faith is only a product of the wishful imagination insisting we're not alone. I expect no miracles." Victor might have continued, but two teenage girls entered the shop and walked, their sandal heels clicking smartly and vibrantly, to the magic section. Never had Victor performed so brilliantly and seductively. He spoke in whispers to his audience for a long while, pointing at his crystal ball, and when they left the shop, he stared at their gorgeous teenage thighs and round teenage buttocks.

"I think I'll leave now," he said. "I think I'll have them both at the same time. Why not? What else is there for a man?"

As I watched Victor walk down the street, I saw the man Artie had hired to watch me leave the bay-front park and stroll toward the shop. From his sports jacket he took a folded paper and then sat behind the pages on a nearby bench.

I called Rolando and painted for him grim possibilities of violence maiming his pretty face; I said that if he lost an eye or an ear, I could never forgive myself. "You'd better not meet me this evening. I won't have your broken bones on my conscience."

Rolando immediately accused me of no longer caring for him. "I don't blame you. Why should you love me?" he asked in the most morose, lifeless voice.

"I love you," I snapped, "but I'm telling you there's a detective sitting in front of my shop."

Rolando said he might as well just kill himself right now.

"No!" I shouted.

"I see your mother in my window," he said softly. "Did you send her around to haunt me?"

"I wouldn't. You can come see me, Rolando," I whispered.

"I'll see you in a half hour. Oh, Ruby, you've got such a hold on me."

"And you," I said, feeling forlorn and frightened, "have got a hold on me."

I ran outside and informed my husband's startled detective that I had just received an odd telephone call, the exact words of which I was unable to repeat, from a man who claimed to be waiting for me at the Greyhound Bus station in North Miami.

"I'm off," said the detective.

Now it was true that ever since I had seen my swamp man I had been having grave misgivings about my affair with Rolando Ramirez. It was also true, I thought now, that the boy and I had little in common after all, except a strong will to imagine that after a single night of love-making—and certainly we had made love—we ought to marry. Perhaps, I said, twisting up my finger, I had been a little hasty, but that decision, as certain and as sound as the floor beneath my feet, faded and distorted into a hundred confused questions as soon as I saw Rolando pull up to the shop on his motorcycle.

Now here, I thought, is masculinity poetically expressed. I stood at the window, smiling with joy at seeing him, at the delight of watching the late sun shine in his hair and on his black leather jeans, which must have been very hot and soft against his skin.

"I'd rather have him than a swamp man," I said, running for my purse.

In sullen, argumentative stance Rolando told me where he wanted to go and what he wanted to do, as if he had somehow caught all of my worst fantasies. When I said that his was an impossible idea, he remarked that I did not care at all for his feelings. "It doesn't matter," he said, widening his eyes and leaving a horrible threat expressively unspoken.

"It does matter," I cried.

"Then you shouldn't worry so much about your husband. If he cared as much about you as I do, he'd be with you now."

"You look like the devil, all dressed in black," I said. I could see no evidence that I was being followed as I drove west along the Tamiami Trail. I parked my jeep in the woods, got on the back of Rolando's motorcycle, and wrapped my arms around his waist. When we reached the lane that led to my house, I thought I could hear the sound of a car behind us, although no headlights were visible. "Get off the road," I said. Rolando swerved his motorcycle into the pines. Somewhere in the deep woods, close enough to my river so that I could see its mist, Rolando stopped the motorcycle, pulled the helmet from my head, and pointed up at a tree. In the dark a fluorescent arrow gleamed on its trunk.

"I did that today," Rolando told me, nuzzling my neck. "Look around, Ruby!"

All around me were trees painted with those orange fluorescent arrows. "Why did you do this here?"

"I've buried you a treasure," Rolando said.

Rolando insisted upon the extravagance of his love for me as I made my way toward the river by the direction of his clumsily painted arrows. "You're crazy," I said, but then I hoped that he could make my world enchanted, because he loved me so hugely, and that in an enchanted world no thing and no one could ever hurt me. "Oh, you're so crazy."

"Dig here," Rolando said, turning me by the shoulders.

I scooped up sand with my hands, and when the pit was two feet deep I struck something smooth and hard.

I brushed wet sand away from a decorative corked jar like those I sold in my shop. I was annoyed at the thought that Rolando might have purchased it from Lillian. "You're not going to hurt my sister," I said. "Tell me again you're not going to hurt her."

"Read this," Rolando said. He tapped the label,

upon which I could just make out the message, "Moon-beams for Ruby."

Now this was passion poetically expressed, I thought. My husband had not once ever captured moonbeams in a jar for me. I could have rolled as easily with the jar as with Rolando, indeed might have cared more for the jar than for him, but at that moment my vision was confused. I knew nothing but the pride of ownership—I imagined that I owned this lovely boy, his eyes, tongue, heart, soul, and hot leather jeans. "This is the best present I've ever gotten," I kept saying.

Rolando nibbled my shoulders and neck. His love was proved by his delicacy, about which, he assured me, he never had been complimented by other women because he was moved to such artistry only by my face. "When are we getting married?" he asked several times. "When will you tell your husband?"

"Soon." I was certain that I heard Rolando's infinitely rich, tender, and intelligent soul whispering to me.

We rolled solemnly on the sand, under trees so thick the stars and moon seemed to have broken apart to fit into the silver crevices between the branches. Rolando said my eyes were as quiet and mysteriously lit as moonlight—and I believed him. I think I must have even widened my eyes, to make them larger and brighter, as if the moon were another woman whose beauty I envied. I said I wished we could stay in the woods forever. I felt brave and careless, as if I could throw away all of my past and never regret the lost moments.

Rolando promised that he would make my life a dream, when I let him. "Is it true, baby, about the swamp creature?" He lifted his head from my stomach and peered around us. "Lillian told me about some swamp creature."

"He's gone now," I said. "He was just someone passing through, an escaped convict, probably." When I said that the woods seemed a black slate full of large wild eyes.

"Your sister says you agree with her that some guy from outer space runs through these woods."

"I've got to humor her. You know she's crazy, don't you? She's dangerous."

Rolando said that I was dangerous. He led me into the center of a thicket of palmetto, to a soft, hidden bed of sand and spicy pine needles. We spread our clothing over the ground and lay there for a long time in the cool night air. Rolando had the most remarkable tongue and the most inventive hips and legs. There wasn't a single trick he did not know, and there wasn't a single pause which I could not fill with moaning or shouting, or he with poetic homage to me. Rolando declared I was the most beautiful woman, both inside and out, that he had ever seen, and the most glorious lover, too. I believed every word, and I became lost in a world without memory.

"Most women don't like to make love as much as you do," Rolando said later. "If I had my way I'd make love to you every moment of every day."

"If you want to make love to me that much, you'll have to marry me." I picked up my blouse, which lay beside my jar of moonbeams, and slid it over my head. I left my panties in the sand, because Rolando wore no underwear, and pulled on my jeans. Rolando stuffed the scant bit of lace into one of his pockets.

A wailing sound, perhaps of a rare Florida panther or of my swamp man, Eugene, suddenly broke the spell. I asked for my underwear back, but Rolando refused. "Why do you want to keep them?" I asked, suddenly anxious.

"When you're not around, I'll have these. I think you

don't trust me, Ruby. I think you're not serious about marrying me. But you will be. You may've tossed away a hundred men, but I won't leave so easily."

"You just want to marry rich, I think, and anybody will do," I said, joking.

"That isn't true," Rolando said and, ducking through a gap in the brush, walked away.

I ran after him. When I touched his thin shoulders, the muscles quivered, as if he had just brushed a spiderweb.

"Don't!"

"I'm sorry. I was only kidding."

"I can't prove how I feel about you—not yet, I guess. You don't respect me because you had to lend me money, but I'll have money tomorrow, you'll see." I probably believed he was nothing but a leech, he said, but that was not true: he helped his uncle as best he could, and he was figuring out all sorts of ways he might further himself and leave a great mark upon the world. "I'll have as much money as your mother-fucker husband some day," Rolando said, kicking at a stone in his path.

At the side of my jeep he suddenly began weeping. "Why should I keep seeing your mother, Ruby? Your sister wonders, too. You're not really going to leave your husband, are you?"

"Yes—I'll come home with you right now," I said. "I don't care if I am followed. The hell with alimony."

Rolando immediately wiped his eyes and urged me into my jeep. "You don't want to be foolish and give up everything, do you?"

"No," I said. "I don't want to give up everything." I lifted my face for a kiss, but when I opened my eyes I saw that he was already wandering away. When he was gone, it seemed that he had never existed.

•••

The front door was open when I arrived home, and as I walked up the porch steps, I could hear anguished cries, as if someone were being beaten in the living room.

"I'll save you," I shouted, before I could think, and looked about for a big stick or rock.

"Help!" a man's voice screamed. "Police—for God's sake—help!"

Artie's detective rushed past me, screaming and holding his bleeding head. I watched him run down the dirt road into the approaching headlights of what I knew was Artie's car. Suddenly, the headlights went out.

I tripped over a broom in the hall. "Swamp man," I said.

Minutes later Artie walked into the house and lectured me so severely about leaving the door unlocked and about the dangers of roaming alone through the swamps at night that I knew he had not found me out.

"But I wasn't alone—you hired someone to watch me," I said. I was so full of contempt for my husband when I compared the meagerness of his love to Rolando's that I wished he were dead.

"The detective turned out to be a drunk. He couldn't even follow you. He came up with some crazy story about a wild animal attacking him in our living room. It's the most ridiculous thing I've ever heard—he'll not see a cent from me. You gave him the slip, didn't you, Ruby?"

"Not purposely," I said. The swamp man had beaten Artie's detective and in doing so had revealed that he was on the side of romance: he understood my nature perfectly. "But I do not like being followed, Artie."

"It doesn't matter. Today I found out what's going on in Curaçao. Judge Howard had the authorities pick up the guy who attacked our man—nothing to worry about, he said, the incident had nothing to do with us. We might just resell the land soon, Ruby. I'm flying back to the island tomorrow. You'll be all right now." Artie grumbled all the way up the stairs. At the landing he turned and asked if I was coming with him. I called, "In a moment." In the kitchen I poured a big glass of milk and set out some cookies for my swamp man. "You're on my side," I said softly. "Does this mean I'm right after all?"

That evening I dreamed I was being pinched, and I cried out with pain. When I awoke in the morning, I discovered that my arms were bruised. So were Artie's.

"You've been kicking all night in your sleep," Artie said, examining a large welt on his bicep and another on his slender thigh.

"Those are outer-space-fairy pinches," I said. "You're being punished for something."

"And what are you being punished for?" Artie asked, pointing at my arms. I was unable to look at him and glanced nervously about the room. My eyes fell upon the dressing table, where Eugene had set up a tray of food.

"Here's breakfast," I said, getting up and bringing the tray back to bed.

"I'm not hungry. I have an early plane to catch." Artie was in a foul mood as he dressed and packed a small suitcase; he carried on about my walking around in the woods late at night, where I might be raped or murdered, carried on about his drunk detective. "He must have no respect for me," Artie said. "I'm an important man now, and I'll see that his license is revoked." When Artie opened his bureau drawer, he smiled and cried out, "How sweet you are, Ruby." He held up several pairs of neatly folded socks—socks he had been waiting for me to mend for two years. "The stitching is a little rough, Ruby, but I do appreciate the effort."

"I didn't mend your socks," I said. "I told you before to buy new ones. You're so cheap sometimes, Artie." When I sat before my dressing table to put on my makeup, I winced and shifted my weight: my swamp man had pinched my buttocks, as a joke of some sort, for I truly believed he must have been on my side in all matters. I could hear Artie singing downstairs. Moments later he returned, complaining that he was unable to find his car keys. By concentration and second sight I helped him locate the keys, which had been dropped into the washing machine.

"Ruby," Artie said, at first severely and then smiling. "Will you never understand that a man must tend to business?"

"I did not take your car keys," I said.

Artie kissed me and said, "You must love me very much."

"I've told you I do," I said sadly. I helped him carry his luggage to the front door, cried as I kissed him good-bye, and then went upstairs. I put on a black silk shirt, beneath which the subtlest outline of my nipples showed, and a white silk skirt slit to my thigh. As I stood before the mirror, meaning to admire myself, a voice that belonged to either my mother or my swamp man whispered, "Ruby."

"I don't look very well at all," I said.

My husband clumped up the stairs and into the bedroom. "My car won't start," he said. "Did you fool with my car? It's essential that I be in Curaçao this evening. I stand to lose a lot of money if I'm not."

"I don't know anything about cars," I said, swinging my hair over my breasts. "This is a sign, I think. Stay home for a while, Artie."

"I have a plane to catch in one hour." Artie's teeth were grinding. "Take me to the airport on your way to work."

Behind him I thought I saw a downcast little face

and a slight body slip past in the hall.

I was quiet all the way to the airport. "Have you arranged for another detective?" I asked Artie as we stood before the terminal.

"I told you that you don't need one now."

I knew Artie was telling me the truth, but somehow this truth disappointed me. "What if I'm kidnapped by the mob?"

"You won't be. Sometimes I think, Ruby, that the only protection you need is from yourself."

"I do love you," I said.

"Oh, Ruby," Artie said, shaking his head and looking pale and distressed, "I'm afraid you really do."

9

I imagined that a spirit, possibly angelic or possibly demonic, took hold of me when I left the airport and directed me to drive past my shop, over the MacArthur Causeway, which bridged Biscayne Bay, and into the cramped, narrow streets of old Miami Beach. I parked my jeep outside a yellow stucco apartment building and worried as I mounted its steps that the flash of thigh exposed by my slit skirt might make my father think unkindly of me.

An eye shaped and colored like my own peered out at me from behind a barely cracked door, a chain rattled off its hook, and an old man's arm pulled me inside a musty efficiency apartment.

"I don't want to make my lady friends here jealous," my father told me. When my eyes adjusted to the dim light, I saw that Sam was wearing a magician's top hat. My father smiled and said, "You see I haven't lost my style yet." He took precious pains to adjust his tattered bathrobe, his fingers flying over buttons and smoothing wrinkles as if he wore satin instead of badly stained flannel. On his feet were a filthy pair of pink woman's slippers. "It's so kind of you, Ruby, to deliver my plane ticket to Puerto Rico in person. But I told you not to bother—you could have mailed it." He sat me at a wobbly card table between his tiny kitchen and unmade bed, whose faded, patched spread I recognized as having once belonged to my mother. On the walls hung pictures of Sam Bittner in tails, top hat, and stiff collar, standing with the rich and the famous he had once amused. "I hope you left the departure day open. I do have to pack and get my affairs in order."

"You know I didn't bring you a plane ticket." I clutched my purse over my bare thigh; it would not do to have my father think that I was an exhibitionist or a woman on a hunt.

Sam smiled. "Then she must have sent you to murder me. How else could you find me?"

"By need," I said. "I still need you. I'd get you a plane ticket today, I'd do it this moment, if you'd say you're my father."

My father turned and rummaged through the stacks of cans behind curtained shelves. "I don't know why you want me, Ruby. It speaks badly of you, this need. I was a dreadful father even when I believed you were my own. I wouldn't change now."

"But Mother hurt you," I persisted. "She wounded you, so you just don't trust anyone anymore. I could change all that."

"We'll discuss this over a civilized breakfast," Sam said. In the kitchen, Sam poured two cans of spaghetti into a dented saucepan, saying that he certainly hoped that the elderly woman across the way, who was in love with "yours truly," would not think that he had begun courting a very young woman. "I dislike taking her money, but a man must do what he must. Sadie isn't my type—she's eighty years old with a twenty-year-old's libido. It isn't the eighty years that bother me so much—

almost anything has its attractions for a man of the world—but I can't stand the combination. A woman should be one thing or another. Don't act twenty if you're eighty. Act as ugly as you are. If only someone who truly loved me"—and my father let his eyes water as they fixed upon my face—"would send me back to Puerto Rico."

Sam shuffled across the room to the bureau beside his bed and returned with an ancient map of San Juan. He pointed to the street on which he would live, if only he could go back.

"A man like me needs adventure. But my woman there, my Lourdes, has memories of how I looked before." When Sam swooped off his top hat, he revealed an absolutely bald scalp. I assured him that many women found bald men terribly attractive, and he said, "That's true, I know that. But my Lourdes used to love to run her fingers through my hair. It's horrible when your looks go, Ruby. You'll see how horrible it is." My father sighed and said that in San Juan people remembered and respected him, while in Miami he was tormented by his greedy landlord, careless surfers and skaters on the beach, rude bus drivers, sullen grocery clerks, vicious dogs, his dead wife, and now me. "You blame me for not being able to live with Sally. You think I murdered her." From apparently thin air my father grabbed a large spoon. "I haven't lost it at all, Ruby," he said as he stirred the now-bubbling spaghetti.

"I never said you murdered Mother."

"You don't need to say. You imply it by your presence." I shook my head and bit my lips as Sam put a tea kettle on to boil. He removed a folded paper towel from a drawer with such caution one would have thought it held diamonds instead of two tea bags. When he looked once again at me, I imagined his expression had become gentle and worried. "Why, you're crying," he said. He tapped his nose twice, and from his closed fist magically appeared a handkerchief, which he handed to me.

"Why is forgetting so easy for you?" I asked. "How can you be happy trying to forget?"

"So you have come to accuse me! But you know that your mother made my life miserable. She never cared about me. She was a dirty woman—smelled to high heavens." Now there was a gleam to Sam's eyes, and he grimaced as if he was both delighted and shocked at his memories. "Filled up the whole room with the smell. I couldn't stand it. Sometimes I wanted to suggest using a cork until the last minute. I've known several women with the problem. One of them I did cork once, some whore in Haiti. She didn't seem to mind. Despite her odor, she was a beautiful woman."

"When I was little, you used to say you'd take me traveling with you, that we'd have a father-daughter magic act," I said.

"It's your mother's fault I didn't take you—I thought I was making a promise to my own child. Sam Bittner was born honorable. I'm basically a one-woman man, Ruby. That's why I want to get back to Puerto Rico before I die. I can get a job there—people still remember the old Sam Bittner—and pay you back for my plane fare. My sweetheart lives in San Juan." My father's voice softened, and his eyes became dreamy. "I want to find the love I missed. You could help me with that, Ruby." My father looked at me with such pleading I was almost swayed.

"Not until you say I'm your daughter."

"When you prove you're my daughter by giving me the air ticket, I'll acknowledge you. You prove my claim, Ruby, you realize that, don't you? If you really believed you're my daughter, you'd lend me the money without conditions. I'll pay you back every cent. I'll write you every week if you like. Give me the money, and I'll be your father. I promise." My father placed his hand over his heart. Behind him the spaghetti boiled and the tea kettle hissed.

"I know your promises," I said, smiling and wiping away tears.

"I'll tell you what," Sam said, as he dished the spaghetti into two Melmac bowls and poured hot water over the tea bags. "I'll take you with me to Puerto Rico. We can work together now."

"I have a husband," I said. "A husband who's rarely at home, maybe, but still, I have a husband. This is a trick, anyway."

"You're the one who is trying to trick me, by coming here." My father's voice sounded anguished, but his eyes were still gleeful, as if he enjoyed our argument. "I do believe you're conspiring against me with your mother. She told me last night—I just remembered now—that you would come to me today. How else could you have found me if she hadn't directed you?"

"Why would I conspire with her against you? I don't pay any attention to her at all."

"Then you do see her."

"She's in my house," I admitted. "But why hurt me because of what she did?"

"You're hurting yourself, because I am not your father, and you want what you cannot have." My father placed two bowls of spaghetti and two cups of tea on the card table and, politely excusing himself, went into the bathroom. He emerged wearing shiny gray trousers pinned at the waist and a yellowed shirt that sported a variety of buttons, including a woman's rhinestone.

"Perhaps I don't dress as elegantly as I did once," said Sam, sitting down across from me, "but don't turn up your nose at me, Ruby, or my breakfast either. I'm poor, but I'm not ashamed, and I'll do what I must to survive. I figure I have five more years left, if I can get to Puerto Rico. You could," Sam said, his lips curling away from the hot spoon he lifted to his mouth, "lengthen an old man's life, and then I would love you forever. Generosity is the real test of your affection, you know."

"You go to hell," I said, "with your tests and your terms."

My father suddenly sobbed. "Help me, Ruby! You're the only one who can help me. No one else cares enough."

When I looked into his face, wishful thinking transformed true vision: poor, lonely old man, I thought, too proud to let his daughter love him. From my father's pocket I appeared to pluck a twenty-dollar bill. "Buy yourself a new shirt," I said, throwing the money on the table.

"It isn't nice of you to steal from my pockets, Ruby," Sam said.

"I saw Daddy again today," I told my sister when I entered the shop.

Lillian removed her glasses and, rubbing her eyes, quietly said that if I could not accept her theory that an apparition had been appearing to me, I might at least do her a favor by ceasing to dwell upon the subject of our father. "I've trials enough without your bringing him up all the time."

Lillian told me that Victor Riley had called her from a motel and asked her to meet him there, just to talk. As soon as she had written down the address—"I thought he really needed a sympathetic ear, Ruby"—he had greatly alarmed her by remarking that her life as a middle-aged woman would be agonizingly lonely, that she would probably begin drinking and then have to get a hysterectomy. During this tirade she could hear the hilarious noises of at least two, and possibly three, other women. "He wants me to be as hopeless as he is. Do you see what can happen when a woman is careless?"

Lillian said that she had been unable to conjure up a single guiding spirit the evening before, and that the watch kept by her psychic friends in the Everglades had been fruitless. She was, she said, afraid of going into the swamps herself, because Catherine O'Connell might tell her something dreadful. "You're going to have to give up everything and help me now, Ruby."

When I timidly refused Lillian's request to take her into the swamps again, she became enraged. "What could you be doing with your evenings while Artie is away that's more important than this?"

We waited upon customers, avoiding all conversation, until it was nearing noon. Then Rolando strolled into the shop, elegantly transformed by a cream-colored linen suit I suspected he had bought with some of the funds I had lent him to straighten out his financial affairs. He greeted me casually, and when he kissed Lillian's hands, my sister blushed violently.

"I thought maybe you'd have lunch with me, Lillian." Rolando bestowed the most dazzling smile on my sister, whose legs seemed to tremble from the light of his teeth and eyes.

"I'd love to, but I don't think I should leave poor Ruby." Her hands fluttered to her hair, which had become snarled by her constant nervous tugging. She pulled two stools close together by the counter, and when Rolando sat beside her, she gave his cheek a kiss. "Maybe we ought to have lunch here."

"You don't want to be alone with me—you're afraid," Rolando said, but when Lillian covered her face to hide her blushes and smiles, Rolando winked at me. I turned and walked into the stockroom.

For a long while I remained in the back, my ear

pressed against the door, listening as the two talked. Rolando told Lillian that his great loneliness had not abated. He was just a walking target, he supposed, for a beautiful and cruel woman. "We've suffered in the same way," Lillian said. "We've suffered in love, and we suffer now in our dreams." Each night in sleep, she said, she murdered her three ex-husbands, one by one, and tossed their broken-limbed bodies down a dark, dark stairwell.

"It's a pity," Rolando said, "that your husbands never appreciated you. Such a lovely, sensitive, mature woman."

"Well, I have my gifts," Lillian said. "Soon the whole world will know what I've been doing. Then my husbands will love me again, but they won't be able to have me."

"They'll have to fight me," Rolando said.

"If only Ruby would help me. With her gift of vision, she can see into the future whenever she likes."

Rolando said that he had never quite understood what Lillian meant by this. "Or maybe I've been afraid to ask. Do you mean that she could tell me exactly what will happen tomorrow?"

"Exactly. But she won't. I could tell you most things, but my sister, Ruby Holloway, could tell you everything. But she's not as mature or as generous as I am. She's still afraid."

"I love generous, mature women," Rolando replied. My sister answered that this preference spoke well of him, for most men preferred very young women, who were bound to be self-absorbed. When their voices lowered, I rushed from the stockroom and took my place behind the counter, frequently looking up from the ledgers I rattled to glower at Rolando.

"Your sister and I were having quite a talk, Mrs. Holloway," Rolando said.

"I bet you were. Aren't you two going to lunch?"
My face must have visibly crumpled—certainly my mouth twitched and I blinked back tears—for Lillian again insisted that she would not leave me alone. "Her Artie is never at home. What a life for a young woman. Loneliness has made my sister stubborn, but I still love her."

"That's because you're so good," Rolando said.

My sister was magnanimous in what she perceived as a victorious moment and said she would just run down the street and bring back sandwiches. "Rolando, see if you can cheer up my sister." Lillian gaily swung her seashell-studded purse over her shoulder and said she wouldn't be ten minutes.

Rolando laughed in a tone that made me ashamed. When Lillian had left the shop, he came around the corner to kiss me. I pushed him away. "You're going after my sister. At least she thinks you are. This isn't the way, Rolando. She hasn't any gift," I said, as if that were a terribly important matter to clarify.

"Some Cubans believe very much in all that, but I understand your sister fantasizes. She's in love with me." Rolando smiled and shrugged and placed his hands on my rigid shoulders. "Don't you see? I've thrown her wonderfully off track. It's you I love, and you I want."

"But you're hurting her again," I said. "She's been hurt so often, Rolando."

When Rolando demanded to know if I cared more for my sister than for him, I began to weep. He took my hand and led me into the back room. He kissed my breasts, praising the quality of my black silk shirt. He wanted to know how much my skirt cost and was pleased by its slit. "I love your legs," he said, biting my inner right thigh. "Don't be angry with me. You're still coming to my apartment after work, aren't you?"

"I'm tired," I said. "I need to think."

"You think too much," Rolando said, kissing my throat, my breasts, my inner thighs. He was too painful a pleasure.

"What's wrong with me," I asked, "that I can't stay away from you?" Rolando only laughed and pocketed my bikini underwear.

"I'm starting a collection. Be careful when you bend over this afternoon," he said.

"Lillian's coming back," I said, buttoning my shirt.

My gleaming-eyed sister rushed into the shop crying out to Rolando that she had bought him two submarine sandwiches—a meatball and a turkey—and a large chocolate milk shake, into which her tongue now dipped. "I hope you're hungry," she said, her voice husky, her hands caressing her throat. "I know I'm hungry." When she placed her packages on the counter, she frowned at me and remarked that my face looked peculiarly red. "Are you sick?" she asked. Her eyes seemed so full of concern that for a moment I wished Rolando were dead.

"It's this heat, Lillian. The air conditioner in here isn't adequate."

"I'm feeling the heat myself in this dress," Lillian said, flapping her arms like a great awkward pelican. Rolando said that she looked just like a beautiful saint from another world.

"You don't know how accurate you are," Lillian replied. With tender hands she tucked a napkin into Rolando's shirt and said if he had not been about she would certainly pull all the shutters and stand naked for a moment or two in front of the air conditioner. "I hate clothes," she said, tossing back her damp, limp hair.

"Then I think I'll have to break the air conditioner and make this place a furnace," Rolando said.

Lillian said, "You're terrible," and when she swatted Rolando with the sandwich wrappings, she left grease stains on the lapels of his jacket.

Lillian insisted upon reading Rolando's palm after lunch. "I see much love and passion in your life soon," Lillian said. "A marriage, perhaps, by spring. Have you fallen in love with anyone in particular?"

Rolando replied that he was in love with all pretty women. "When I look into your eyes, I'm in love with you."

"Lillian," I called. "Help this woman with the colognes. You know the stock better than I do."

"My sister's so helpless sometimes." As Lillian passed me, she squeezed my arm.

I took her place on the stool near Rolando and leaned toward him. "I'll kill you, lover, if you make things more complicated than they already are."

Rolando smiled, and hidden by the counter, slid his hand beneath my skirt. "Then I'd better leave now." While Lillian was bent to a bottom shelf, Rolando quietly departed.

Lillian was blinking with confusion as she rang up her sale. After she escorted the customer to the door and gazed up and down the street, she turned and pointed her finger at me. "Did you tell Rolando anything bad about me? Why did he leave so suddenly?"

"I don't know. I guess that's just the way men are." My sister looked so forlorn and disappointed as she stared toward the windows that I came around from the counter and hugged her. "You're looking so pretty these days. You shouldn't worry about that kid. You're too good for him."

"Am I?" Lillian asked. She twisted the ends of her hair into her mouth and chewed thoughtfully. At last she said, "Won't you please take me into the woods tonight?"

"I can't."

"Why not?"

"Don't you know, Lillian?" I asked. My sister's mouth opened in astonishment, and my eyes filled with tears when they met hers.

"Poor Ruby. I understand. I'll wait for you," Lillian said. Whatever she had just understood was making her wring her hands and cry quietly into her sleeve.

I took the most extravagantly circuitous route to Rolando's apartment that evening, just in case another detective—or my sister, out of concerned good will—might be following me. I parked far from his Little Havana apartment, and as I walked along the street, I was alert for a plump woman in a caftan who might be crouched behind one of the rubber trees lining Calle Ocho.

Rolando greeted me with wet eyes. "You're so late. I thought you weren't coming," he said, turning away abruptly.

"I have to be careful which way I come here. I've explained how things are." I stood in the doorway of Rolando's kitchen, watching him chop vegetables and raw chicken. His mouth was terribly grim. "What's wrong?" I asked.

"Nothing. Please don't watch me cooking. I don't like it."

I walked into the living room, where the typewriters and adding machines were still dismantled upon sheets of newspapers; clothing, books, and magazines were still strewn over the furniture and floor; and the very bills for which I had lent Rolando money were scattered upon the coffee table, as if he had dashed them down in despair.

"I thought you were going to pay Master Charge," I called. "I lent you a lot of money, Rolando."

I heard the sound of a glass breaking. Rolando stood slumped in the kitchen doorway, sucking on his fingers, his black hair nearly hiding his black eyes. "I didn't know you were placing conditions on the loan. I had to take my boa constrictor to the veterinarian," he told me, waving toward the fish tank in which the lazy snake was coiled. I took it as a sign of great love that at either corner of the tank were hung my two pairs of gaily colored silk bikini underwear.

He scarcely spoke to me over dinner, which we ate sitting on the floor before the coffee table. "Will you tell me what's wrong?" I asked, all patience flying.

"Nothing." From time to time Rolando wiped his eyes; finally he threw down his fork and said his stomach hurt. He roamed his two tiny rooms, pushing in and out of the beaded curtain that hung before the bedroom entry, kicking at books, scowling with distaste at the mildewed walls and carpeting, at the ragged couch and ugly, crushed-velvet chairs. "You don't have the slightest idea, Ruby, of what it's like to live in poverty."

"I lived in poverty for years, after my mother left."

"But not now. Your husband gives you jewels," Rolando said, lifting the gold-and-diamond locket around my neck. "I could never do that. I never even know where my next meal's coming from." Rolando kicked an ancient typewriter. "I'd like to go to college. I'm just twenty-six, and I feel that I have no future. If I had the money, I'd get a degree and fix up this place and make something of myself. Because I know if I don't you'll never marry me. You didn't mean it," he said bitterly, "when you agreed to marry me."

"Money has nothing to do with it." When I imagined that in Rolando's face was once again the implied threat that my mother had made good, I said, "I want to marry you, but I'm afraid."

"You're afraid because you're not sure," Rolando said, rubbing his cheek against my breasts. "Sometimes I become so angry with you, I'd like to do something dreadful. I love you, though. I'll wait for you forever. You own me, Ruby."

I was immensely moved by his last statement—what woman could have resisted owning such a beautiful and devoted young man? "If you need more money," I said, kissing the wet skin around his eyes, "just tell me."

"It's my parents—they're in terrible straits." Rolando's lovely face swayed me into believing everything he said. I had to believe everything he said. "My father's been laid off by the sugar-refining company, and my mother's very sick." He had, he said, given his parents most of the money I had lent him, because after all, they were old and infirm, and what else could a good Cuban son do?

I promptly wrote Rolando a check for a thousand dollars, scarcely worrying about how I would explain the absence of such a large sum to Artie. Rolando smiled when I handed him the check, and sat beside me on the couch, his arms around my neck. "Ruby," he asked, nuzzling my ears, "do you really see the future?"

"I don't talk about that." I was suddenly frightened. Though the night had fallen deeply, Rolando did not turn on the lights. He held me, and rocked me, and said there was no secret I should keep from him.

"You're afraid I wouldn't love you if you told me everything, but I'd love you even more. Oh, what your sister has been telling me is stupid, I know." Rolando stood before the fish tank, and caressed first his coiled snake and then the panties he had hung on the tank's metal frame. "Nobody can see the future. There isn't that kind of hope in the world."

I watched him. The bruises my swamp man had nipped onto my buttocks began to pain me again, but still I lay on the couch and called to Rolando. Rolando kept his back to me. Perhaps it was true, he said, that a woman and a man could never really be friends, that they would always keep secrets. "Or maybe your sister's just crazy after all."

"No," I finally said, not so much because I wanted to reveal my secrets, but because I was desperate for Rolando to make love to me. "She's not. I do see things. There's very little I couldn't see, if only I wanted to look."

"But why don't you, then?" Rolando folded his arms across his slender stomach and said, "Show me. I don't believe you."

I sat up reluctantly and told him the dates of his birthday, his mother's birthday, and his father's birthday. I concentrated and described his parents in what Rolando said was miraculously accurate detail. I saw that Rolando had been born at Mercy Hospital, listed the names of his parochial school teachers, and recalled just how and with whom he had lost his virginity. I saw him working as a short-order cook at a truck stop near Lake Okeechobee the summer after his high school graduation and was about to speak of two other married women with whom he had carried on, three and then two years ago, when Rolando cried out, "That's enough!"

I let his past slip away from me. "Please don't be afraid of me now," I said, reaching out to touch him. He moved away and stood before the open window. "Rolando?"

When he turned, he was smiling, and as I looked into his eyes a march of visions was again revealed, visions I did not like and so refused to acknowledge as premonition. "Ruby, you could have the world. I knew you were special. Will I be rich some day? Will I be happy?"

"I won't look that far ahead," I said. "The future frightens me."

Rolando took up my hands and, after studying my

grimy nails, kissed each finger so devoutly I was again bewitched. "You said you'd marry me, and that's my future."

"But I won't look. I don't want to know anybody's future. Especially not mine. Let's quit talking about this now." I put my arms around his waist, but again he pulled away.

"Can you read my mind all the time?"

"I wouldn't try to," I said.

"Ruby," Rolando said, pacing back and forth. "We could go to the races—think of the money we could make."

"I'd be punished if I used my gift for that." I was struck with the sudden fear that the unsympathetic God of my childhood might be crouched in the bathroom or kitchen, looking out at me.

"You don't seem so puritanical when it comes to other things," said Rolando.

"I didn't want to fall in love with you," I said.

"Yes, you did." When Rolando kissed my cheek, I shivered. Even while I insisted that this affair had been some sort of accident, a difficult and romantic destiny, I remembered all those men with whom I had been madly in love for an hour, a day, a week, or a year. "Did you put a spell on me, Ruby?" Rolando asked. "We Cubans believe in those things, you know. Are you a witch?"

"I can't put spells on people. Jesus, Rolando, I shouldn't have told you anything about myself."

"I think you must have put some kind of spell on me, because I'm so obsessed with you." Rolando pulled me into the bedroom and made love to me so sweetly, hotly, and inventively that I cried and said that in all my life I had never wanted anything so much as to be with him. I forgot everything when I became lost in that landscape of bone and flesh.

Before the opened window of the dark bedroom we sat, I on his lap, his chin on my matted, soaked hair. We sighed at the wonder of the moon and at how we two had managed to find each other. I wondered at his beauty, and he wondered at mine, at my light-brown hair, which tangled between his legs, at the shape of my eyes and the curve of my hip in shadow.

"And there's music when we make love," I said. "Our bodies fit together perfectly."

Rolando said softly, softly rubbing his chin against my hair, "We'll be married soon. And nothing will ever hurt us."

"Nothing," I said. "Not a thing in the world."

10

Late that evening when I unlocked the front door and called out to my swamp man that because of his intervention I had spent a glorious evening with my lover, I heard a loud noise in the kitchen. When I pushed at the kitchen door, I felt a pressure, as if some one or some thing were leaning against its other side. I shoved against the door with all my weight, and as in a scene in a slapstick comedy, the door suddenly gave way, and I stumbled headlong into darkness. A figure rushed past me, and nimble fingers gave my hair a nasty pull. When I turned on the kitchen light, I cried out in dismay at the broken dishes, globs of strawberry and grape jelly, and puddles of ketchup and mustard.

"What message is this?" I asked. I worked for an hour or more, cleaning up the kitchen. From time to time I heard running footsteps and thought I heard my name being called in a melancholy voice. When I crept into the hall, however, I saw not a soul. "Don't be afraid of me, Eugene. I like you," I said.

A terrible groaning answered me.

"I don't understand you," I said. "Do you want me to

be happy or unhappy? What do you want me to be?"
I tried to discern my mother's shade, perhaps rumbling about the house with the swamp man. On the floors above me I could hear clattering sounds, like the noises of objects being knocked over and broken. When I ran upstairs to my bedroom, I saw that Artie's good pajamas had been laid out on the bed. I began to cry and cried all the while I was in the shower.

A tray with hot cocoa and some cookies was on the bed when I peeked out, frightened, from behind the bathroom door. I wiped my eyes and laughed and, tying my terry-cloth robe more securely, got into bed. I felt very comfortable and talked toward the door and hall while I ate. "So you're on my side, good. It isn't that I want to hurt Artie, but you know women have a tough time these days. I know why you put out Artie's pajamas, and you're right, he's the best. He's always wonderful," I said, and I lifted my husband's pajama shirt and sighed. "But when I look at Rolando I could cry, he's so beautiful. Who am I really hurting, Eugene?"

I waited and then said, "It's easy enough for some women to be good, because nobody wants them, anyway. I never meant to fall in love. But how could I have turned away Rolando, swamp man?" I left my bed and placed a nice warm blanket and a plump feather pillow at the foot of the second floor stairs. "I think you're my favorite person," I called. "And I'm going to help you whatever way I can. You can trust me, Eugene."

Artie called that evening around one o'clock. At the sound of his voice I immediately began to weep and told him many times I loved him. Rolando called shortly after that, and I wept once again and insisted I loved him.

"It wasn't my fault that I fell for you," I said.

After I had hung up the phone, I heard a crashing

sound in the hall. When I looked outside the bedroom, I saw that a vase had been knocked from its stand and dashed to pieces. "It isn't that I don't love you, too, Eugene," I called, turning the door bolt. "But a lady needs her privacy."

That night I dreamed that my mother stood above me, an uncharacteristically kind smile on her face, caressing me with firm and what I can only call guiding hands. At the last moment, however, she pulled on my nose, and I cried out in fear of losing my beauty. When I awoke in the morning I saw a grubby hand snatch away from my stinging face and a small body dart through the sunbeams that angled into my room between the white curtains.

My swamp man dashed through the opened bedroom door and vanished somewhere along the corridors.

"Breaking into my room" I cried, stalking along a hall, where I caught a glimpse of myself in an antique mirror: the image in the warped glass was distorted, but I could see that my nose was bruised and swollen. "You are in big trouble with me, Eugene. Why do you want to ruin everything?" I rushed down the stairs, and in the wide front hall I bounced against Janet Monsterville's big stomach.

Janet gasped and then giggled as she touched my nose. "Who hurt you?" she asked, in a voice so gay I was annoyed. From her purse she snatched her knife, sprang out the blade, and wiggled the sharp polished steel as if she were boring a hole into an unlucky intruder's arm. "Who might be here with you?"

"My mother's swamp man," I said. I told Janet Monsterville about my meeting Eugene in the swamps with Lillian and complained about the damage he had done to my kitchen and my face.

Janet shook her head, wiped the blade on the side of

her knit pants, and returned her knife to her purse. "What's running around here," she said, her gold-capped teeth catching and winking light, "is a little ghosty. He ain't trying to hurt you." She walked very slowly to the kitchen. "Little ghosties get put into houses to warn folks. My grandmother had one, and she called it a banshee." From the freezer Janet took some ice, wrapped the cubes in a dish towel, and said I should hold it against my nose. "My great-grand-mother had a banshee, too. And my mother used to get numbers to play from a ghosty living with her on the farm in Georgia. It's your mama," she said, "your poor, crazy mama trying to help you and warn you to settle down."

"I don't want her help," I said, flinging myself into a chair. My nose had begun to bleed into the dish towel, and I thought I could not possibly leave the house and face Rolando. I watched as Janet Monsterville re-moved her street clothes: first the yellow polyester pants, then the faded sleeveless shirt cut off from an old Easter dress, and at last a new corset, which she said she had worn last night beneath her tight red dress.

"I found a new boyfriend last night, only he chews tobacco. I don't want him spitting on my nice rugs, but he promised to come over tonight and give me sixty dollars. I've sure come a long way," Janet said softly. When she was a little girl, she said, she used to pick cotton with her mother for eleven cents an hour. "I've come a long, long way."

I rummaged through Janet's purse until I had found her cracked tortoise shell compact. When I looked into its mirror, I grimaced. "I look like a troll. Eugene wants me to be ugly so nobody will love me."

"That ghosty is just trying to set you straight. I knew there was a ghosty in this house," Janet said. She pulled on a pink housedress and slippers and laughed as she ran hot soapy water into the kitchen sink. "I ain't afraid of him, though. He knows I'm good."

"How are you so good?"

"I just am," Janet said. "The little ghosty is going to give me a number to play."

"He isn't your haunt, he's mine. Once I thought he understood me."

"He understands you all right," Janet Monsterville said, pointing a fat finger at me. "One thing fooling around and another thing getting carried away. I know you. You probably went and told that boy you'd marry him, just like you did the others."

"I always meant it at the time," I said.

"And those lousy men calling up here all the time, getting Mr. Holloway all upset. He knows what you're up to, and still he stays."

"He doesn't know anything about anything," I said. "He's so jealous, he'd kill me or leave me if he ever knew."

"He knows. Why he puts up with you I ain't never going to understand. Fooling around with that crazy Cuban. Get rid of him before he ruins you. You keep up with that boy, you ain't going to have a soul left in the world to talk to."

"You go with Alonzo, and still you keep your extras," I said. "Don't you think I have needs, too?"

"You need too much is your trouble."

I continued to study my nose in Janet's compact and then plucked at my thighs and stomach. "Not only do I look like a troll, but I'm getting fat, too."

"You ain't fat. You must be afraid," Janet said. "Afraid, afraid. But I'll stay with you always, no matter what. Till I'm ready to die, anyhow. When I'm ready, you got to promise to send me to my mama in Georgia."

"You're not going to die."

"Just because you say so! I ain't going to be around

here all the time just to help you out. I drink and I got diabetes and maybe even cancer."

"You don't have cancer. And if you're not supposed to drink with the diabetes, then don't drink."

Janet bulged her eyes at me and banged a jar of cleanser on the kitchen counter. "I like to drink," she cried. "I'm going to keep right on drinking. I think I'll get a drink right this moment." She stalked from the kitchen to the living room bar; when I tried to take the bottle of Scotch from her, she threatened to hit me. "You're just about the most spoiled woman I ever saw. Caring only about yourself—it's a sin." She took a deep swig from the bottle of Scotch and was about to return it to the bar when, glaring at me, she threw back her head and took another swig. "Spoiled and stupid, that's you. I ain't listening to any more shit about this crazy Cuban. If I was you I'd be happy instead of running around making myself miserable. It's your fault you woke up ugly this morning. That ghosty is going to fix you. Going and getting carried away, hurting my poor boss."

"Oh, what do you know? You and my aunt Catherine O'Connell—Christ, you don't know what it's like for me." I ran up the stairs to the bedroom, tried fixing my nose with makeup, and at last gave up and left my eyes bare, too. "I'll just go ahead and be ugly," I said, pulling on a pair of torn, baggy jeans and one of Artie's old shirts.

Janet Monsterville swept up and down the hall outside my bedroom and then stood in the door with her hands on her hips. "Shit, you look like hell." When I opened my mouth to reply, she said, "You shut up for a minute." Then she told me a story about a Haitian woman who lived in the apartment next to hers. "The man beat the child right out of her womb. That fool's had four miscarriages. Every time she gets pregnant he beats her up and throws her out the front door. The fool stays with him, don't know when to quit," Janet said, shaking her head.

"Rolando loves me—he wouldn't dare hit me," I said, but Janet pushed out her bottom lip and related three more stories that demonstrated the same moral lesson.

"Messing with fool's fire," Janet said, widening her round, heavily shadowed eyes. "I'd be doing you a favor if I took my knife and cut up that Cuban sausage."

"You fuck everybody you meet," I said.

"But I don't run round saying I love everybody I meet. At least I know the difference between needing some company and being in love. I admit I get lonesome, but only fools get backed into corners," Janet thundered. "That boy don't love you. He ain't got an idea in the world who you are, and you ain't got an idea in the world who he is. I'm your friend. I'm telling you like a friend."

"You're just jealous, because you're old and fat and your boyfriend Alonzo won't even marry you. You sell yourself, and you're judging me. Just don't get involved in my life anymore." I shoved past her and ran down the stairs.

"That boy is dangerous to you," Janet called softly. "You shouldn't wreck things with your good husband because of him." When I turned, I could see her wiping her eyes, and I heard her sob. I wanted to tell her that I was sorry for having shouted at her, that perhaps she was right, but I could not.

When I walked into the shop an hour later, wearing my sunglasses, as if they would help hide my throbbing nose, Lillian gasped and covered her mouth with her hands. "Ruby, what happened to your face?" my sister cried.

"I ran into the wall. Where's Victor?"

"I'd like to know. I pay him and he shows up for work only when he feels like it. You should be more careful where you walk, Ruby," Lillian said. "It's a good thing Victor hasn't shown up here. He'd make you miserable about your nose."

While I sat behind the counter, chain-smoking and running tapes through the adding machine, Lillian kept annoying me about my nose. "Nothing that happens in life is an accident," she said. "Someone wanted you to walk into a wall. Thank God your nose wasn't broken. It wasn't, was it?"

"No," I said.

"Your nose is bigger than mine now." She laughed gaily and leaned over to pinch my still bruised arm. Then she noticed a rip in my jeans just above my knee and saw in this lapse of grooming the signs of a deep and far-reaching depression. "I'm afraid I should have insisted that you take me into the swamps again. You can't hide from your destiny forever, Ruby."

When Rolando came into the shop, he squinted at me and then quickly averted his eyes. I said not a word to him, nor did he speak to me. He sat in a corner with Lillian until late afternoon, laughing and playing with her while I waited on customers, who kept asking me what had happened to my nose. When Lillian had at last disentangled herself from Rolando and shut herself in the tiny bathroom off the stockroom, I walked to the table where he sat and banged my fist before him.

"Do you want to see me tonight or what?"

"Of course, I do, Ruby, of course," he said, although he still would not look at me.

That evening he kept staring at my nose and suggested I ought to bandage it. He said my nose reminded him of the photographs in a book he owned about botched plastic-surgery jobs. Rolando showed me a picture of a woman whose nose had been stretched into what resembled the trunk of an elephant.

"My nose is not going to be like this forever."

"Of course not, darling," Rolando said. He kissed me so sweetly I thought it was time to remove our clothes. But when I began to unbutton Rolando's shirt, he said, "Don't. If we rub together, your nose will swell some more."

We spent that evening watching his clothes spinning round and round in the washing machines at a hot, mosquito-infested Laundromat. Rolando spoke of various mutilations of which he had heard and asked me how I could have been clumsy enough to walk into a wall. I sat brooding in a collapsing lawn chair, and when I refused to help Rolando fold his clothing and put his shirts on hangers, he took my hands and said, "Ruby, what's wrong?"

"You don't care about me." I looked with despair at the middle-aged women who filled the Laundromat, and imagined that next year, or perhaps the year after that, my hips would become very wide, and I would be moved to passionate discussion of diets, childhood diseases, home improvements, and the annoying habits my husband had cultivated. "You don't give a shit about what's inside me, Rolando. I am the same as I was yesterday."

"And I love you as much as I did yesterday," Rolando said.

When we arrived back at his apartment, I did something I had never done with any man: I begged Rolando to make love to me. "I want you so much," I said. I unzipped my jeans, opened my shirt, and lay waiting for him on the couch.

Rolando kissed me and then clutched his stomach. "My stomach hurts," he said. "I don't feel well. Take my temperature, Ruby."

"You're not sick. You just don't want to make love."

"I want to," Rolando insisted. "But my stomach aches, and I'm anxious. You won't leave your husband, when I love you so much."

"I think you don't want to marry me at all," I said. "I think you want to marry my sister."

"No—that isn't true," Rolando said. "I just feel like a shit next to your husband."

"You're marvelous next to anyone." I grasped his neck and tried to pull him down, but again Rolando clutched his stomach and moaned. He stayed in bed all evening, fully dressed, the sheets pulled up to his chin, his face as pale and lifeless as overcooked breakfast cereal.

Early the next morning Eugene somehow unbolted my bedroom door, crept to my bedside, and poured honey all over my hair. He gave my nose another hard twist.

"Get out of my life!" I shouted. I had to rip my head away from the pillow and left much of my hair sticking to the flowered cotton. I walked into the kitchen sobbing, cursing my swamp man and my mother, who had sent him to torture me. I flung a steaming pot of oatmeal Eugene must have prepared for me, and watched the hot cereal drip down the wall and onto the stove. "I'm not eating anything you cooked for me— you hate me."

I drove into town staring far more often into my rear-view mirror than at the road; not only was my nose so sore and badly swollen I feared I would be forever ruined, but my once beautiful light-brown hair stuck out in peculiar clumps all over my head.

Lillian walked around me that morning, clucking and shaking her head, and said that at least her life was going very well. "I feel so pretty! I'm certain Rolando is in love with me," she said, adding that this must be so, because although she had been working very hard in séance, her contact spirits were suddenly silent, as if she had to prove herself in a loving human relationship before she could make progress in the spiritual world.

"Have you seen our swamp man?"

"No."

"What about Mother?"

"Lay off," I said.

"Your hair looks dreadful," Lillian said. "Really, Ruby, your grooming."

Rolando sauntered into the shop that afternoon with a bouquet of flowers for Lillian. She gave him a frank, friendly kiss on the cheek, which he returned. But over my sister's shoulder he shot me what I interpreted as a conspiratorial glance, and once, when my sister might well have seen him, he stroked my thigh, as if he wanted me to be wet and ready for him later. After he left, Lillian said, "He's going to the bar at the corner of his street for a beer. Then he'll go home, fix dinner, and watch the news. After that, he'll repair typewriters. And then," she said, all the while watching the large orange wall clock, "he'll visit his parents. When he comes home, he'll call me. In the morning he'll clean his apartment, and come here when he's finished. You see how well I know his schedule," she said. "I always know when he's going to walk through that door."

Lillian did, too. Every day about five minutes before Rolando arrived, Lillian told me that he was on his way. He paid a great deal of attention to her and ignored me so that my sister would not become suspicious of our relationship. Lillian was already looking through *House Beautiful* and planning where she would like to go on her honeymoon.

"You haven't even slept with him," I said.

"No, but I'm going to have him, Ruby."

"I don't think he's in love with you."

"You're jealous," my sister said, "because your husband is away and your face is a mess." Every time I spoke to Artie during his absence, I begged to know if he still loved me and woefully asked if the women in Curaçao were beautiful. When Artie said, "I haven't had time to notice," I thought his reply was a ruse, and that lying beside him might be a husky, brown-skinned island girl.

"Come home," I said. "My life is terrible without you."

"And my life, sugar doughnut, is terrible without you," Artie said.

"Your face really is a mess," Rolando said each evening when I arrived at his apartment. "Ruby, you used to be so beautiful."

I said that beneath my bruises I was still pretty. "Don't you love me anymore?" I asked him often. Each time I indicated that I wanted to make love, Rolando complained that his stomach hurt, or remembered that he must do laundry or fumigate his bedroom.

"Don't you want me?" I asked.

"Yes, of course," Rolando always replied, and he might kiss me, or put a finger inside me, but without lust or soulful longing. Often he peered out his window with large, frightened eyes. "What would you do, Ruby, without me?"

"I'd die, of course."

"Your sister says the same thing. What are you looking for?" he cried when he saw me peering out the same window through which he so regularly stared.

"Nothing." I had been suddenly struck with the thought that my swamp man Eugene might, if he wished, follow me into town, but I was unable to see his slight figure beneath the streetlights. He must have been peculiarly rooted to my mother's house and the Everglades outside. I thought perhaps I need not go home to be tormented by him, but a sense of having been unjustly treated compelled me to return there and attempt to explain my actions—to make Eugene understand how life was for me.

I stood in the hall outside my bedroom with every light blazing, alert to the possibility of the imp creeping up behind me in ambush, and addressed the apparently empty house. "I don't know what you'd have me be," I said. "My sins are common sins on earth, Eugene. I know I have a spirit, but I'm flesh, too. I admire biblical standards as much as anyone, but we aren't living in biblical times."

"Have faith," came the severe reply.

"In what?" I cried.

I went to the library to prepare myself for my arguments with Eugene. One evening I cited the statistics on married women who had carried on affairs. "Sixty percent admit to doing what you would punish me for," I said. The next evening I offered the swamp man the authoritative quotes of psychologists as proof that infidelity was inevitable in modern society. "And even if it weren't inevitable, I have passion, I'm not immune to loneliness. Lillian once told me," I said, unable to quell the wail in my voice, "that in another life I was burned at the stake for being an adulteress. But that's nonsense," I said, rallying.

Why, I asked, should I be made to feel guilty by the eccentric likes of him?

"Everybody else does it," I said.

Still, Eugene remained unmoved. Each evening he took something belonging to Artie and placed it on the bed, as if to confront me with my sins. Each evening after I had talked to Artie and cried myself to sleep, Eugene somehow slipped the door lock and pinched me gently enough so that I still slept, but viciously enough so that I was terribly marked.

The night before Artie returned from Curaçao, when

I was thumping up the dark stairwell toward Rolando's apartment, a broad-rimmed straw hat pulled low on my forehead so that my bruises might be veiled by shadow, I was greeted by a horrible shriek. Rolando stood at the top of the stairs in front of his apartment door, wearing a new suit and clutching an overnight case.

"My life is becoming a nightmare," he cried. "Your mother has moved into my apartment, Ruby. Don't go in!"

When I turned on the apartment lights, I gasped. Rolando's collection of animal skulls, of which he had been so proud, was in splinters on the living room floor. Each window in the stuffy room was bolted, and when I went to open one, Rolando cried out, "Don't touch anything!" He tugged at my arm, weeping. "Drive me to the mental hospital," he said.

"No," I said. "Look around, Rolando. My mother isn't here. Has Lillian been talking to you about her?"

"She says you're haunted by her—I saw your mother."

"Ghosts can't hurt you," I said. "They're more bluff than anything else. They just like to hover and frighten. I'm sure my mother isn't here."

"You have a gift—get rid of this ghost for me, Ruby!"

"All right," I said. I went through an embarrassing little charade: in each corner of the apartment I made the sign of the cross, said the Lord's Prayer, and threw down a handful of salt. "She's gone now," I said. I sat on the couch and pretended great weariness. "You can put away your overnight case and sit with me."

"No. I'm too angry with you. Take me to your sister. She loves me. You don't."

"My sister only loves you because she thinks I might," I said. "She's always been competitive that way. She only loves you because she thinks you might love me."

"That's not true," Rolando said, "that isn't true. She would marry me. I know she would. She wouldn't let me be alone and miserable. She's braver than you, and better. You're a coward, Ruby. If you love me, why won't you leave your husband?" When I remarked that Rolando and I no longer had sex, he shouted, "Because you've drained me of passion." Rolando ranted and raved for a long time about married women: "All they want is strange cock," he said.

I was deeply hurt and cried, "That's not true—they want other things as well."

"It is true. Your big complaint is no sex. If you loved me, you'd marry me anyway."

"None of this makes any sense," I said. "I think I'd better leave right now, Rolando."

"No, don't." Rolando moaned and flung himself on the couch beside me so that his head was in my lap. He rubbed his chin against my thighs and told me that he would give me the most wonderful life. He would not, he said in a mournful voice, take a penny of my divorce settlement—he would accept only what I wished to contribute, as a loan, toward his college education or any number of businesses he might start. "Maybe I'll become a lawyer just like your husband," he said. When he sat up, sniffling into his hands, he looked like a terribly frightened boy without sex, heart, or pluck. "Don't leave now. Every time you go home you're running from your true feelings. I was born on a warm island—I am passionate. If you don't leave your husband this time, I won't be responsible for what happens."

A rush of jumbled information made me dizzy, and it seemed I could hear my mother, the banshee, warning me. "What did you do? You've done something already," I said.

"I've done nothing—nothing. Go away now, Ruby. I can't do anything for you tonight," Rolando said.

"Don't hurt me tonight, please, Eugene," I said when I got into my bed. That evening he did not pinch me but lulled me into comfort by singing in the corridors. At three o'clock in the morning I awoke to the sound of some sweet spirit picking out a lonely tune on the piano downstairs. In the morning I found a note upon my stomach. The message read: "Please let's still be friends. Don't send me away. I don't want to be alone. Your friend, Eugene."

I could hear a dry coughing coming from the hall, and cautiously pushed a bottle of vitamins just beyond my bedroom door. "Stay well. I won't leave you—stay well, swamp man."

That morning Victor Riley graced the shop with his elegant, silver-haired, lilac-polyester presence. His eyes widened at my face, but he said nothing, indeed seemed rather sad for me, and brought me a cup of hot tea. He chattered so nicely with Lillian that she forgot her distrust of him. She told him all about the man she hoped to marry and asked him whether she should furnish her new home in modern or Early American.

Rolando came into the shop just before lunchtime, splendidly dressed but pale, and talked for several minutes with Victor about baseball and poetry. Then Rolando and Lillian went off to lunch together.

"I don't like to see her with that guy," Victor said. "I know him. He doesn't care about Lillian. But maybe he's getting money from her. Is she giving him money?"

"I suppose," I said, wincing.

"I think this is my fault. Your sister is a very vulnerable, loving woman. I shouldn't have treated her so lightly. I'll fix it now," Victor said, "before she runs off with that jerk and ruins her life."

"He wouldn't have her," I said. When Victor replied that Rolando might marry Lillian just to torment her, I cried, "I know for a fact he wouldn't."

"And how do you know that?"

"Never mind," I said. "Never mind."

When Lillian and Rolando returned, Rolando smiled at me in what I thought was a perfectly innocent manner. But Victor's expression darkened, his finger inadvertently twisted itself into the air, and he took my arm and pulled me into the stockroom.

"So!" he said. "So! I think I see very clearly what's been going on here. You and that sluttish boy have conspired to make a fool out of your sister. You're not the woman I thought you were, Ruby. I don't want your love—keep it."

"I don't love you," I said.

Victor was silent for a time. He sat on a wooden crate, his face in his hands. "I guess I'm getting old," he said. "I'm less attractive, but I still have the feelings of a young man. I can still be hurt."

"Don't," I said. "Please don't."

"This isn't the life for you, Ruby. I live it, so I know. You're essentially good. Prove it now. Be nice to your husband. I don't want to see your life ruined by that fellow out there. Your sister is liable to kill herself over him," Victor said. "I hate to think of what that guy will do to her."

"Is it possible that you love Lillian?" I asked.

"No," Victor said. "It isn't possible."

Lillian sang behind the counter all afternoon. Near closing time she pointed at the clock and said, "It's time for two beers and a game of pool. Then Rolando will go shopping for dinner. Tonight he'll have fish." Lillian was full of sweet, spicy cheer until Victor Riley caught her in a corner of the shop.

"Fooling around with that kid when you love me," he said.

My sister did not notice the urgency in his voice. "When I loved you, you wouldn't love me," Lillian said.

"What if I said I love you now?"

"It's too late. I wouldn't believe you."

In a twilight remarkably similar in quality and shade to the first evening he had waited for me, Rolando approached me as I locked the shop door. He was wearing his old clothes, the tight, faded jeans I had found so glorious, and a torn, faded T-shirt. "Ruby," he whispered, clutching his motorcycle helmet, looking so thin, so awkward and wasted with disconsolation that no amount of wishful thinking could transform him. His sad, dull eyes seemed to catch and then destroy the first light of the moon and stars. Rolando touched my shoulder and then my hair. "Ruby, come away with me tonight. We'll get married in Mexico. Come away with me now."

"I can't," I said, stepping back. "Not tonight."

Rolando gasped. "You're angry with me—you have no right—I won't be responsible. Don't talk now, Ruby." Together, he said, in a soft, dull, rapid voice like that of a child repeating a memorized rhyme, we could erase all our troubles, our loneliness. We would live in a dream. "Don't talk!" he cried, wrenching my arm so hard that I was frightened. The sidewalks were deserted, and the street seemed to melt into the diffused lights and shadows of the park. If I had to scream now, I thought, no one would hear me. "Look!" Rolando said. "Look how your hair blows in the wind." He caught and kissed a strand, and I felt battered and sick and foolish. "Will you come with me now?"

"I told you I can't," I said.

"I'm not worried." Rolando was twisting his head about, as if something dreadful were standing in the edges of the shadows, or waiting for him behind the battered trashcans in the alley. "You said you wouldn't come before, but you did. I know you're my angel, and that I can be your angel, too. Don't talk! I'll be waiting."

11

As night approached I fell into a profound horror of seeing Artie again and of being seen by him, and like a ghost I trailed up and down the front porch in the long Victorian nightgown my husband had bought for me. I had painted my eyes and lips and had creamed and perfumed my skin, but my bruises were as vibrant as if they had been freshly planted, and my nose was still swollen and sore. Through the open windows of my house I could hear the little noises of my swamp man and could see his shadow in the center of the living room.

"Why'd you have to do this to me, Eugene?" I asked.

Eugene whimpered.

In the distance the alligators bellowed, and the woods seemed to vibrate with lonely noises. My aunt Catherine O'Connell must have been fishing from the riverbank, a solitary and mysterious figure in the shiny evening mist. I wondered how she managed to live in such terrible, adult solitude. "You know my aunt, don't you, swamp man?" I waited and then said, "I think you do know her. You could go live with her, if you disapprove of me so much. I might never change. There's no need for you to stay around here and make me unhappy. You've done enough. Can't you make my bruises disappear?" When I did not immediately hear Eugene's whimper, I said, "Don't leave me now."

Eugene groaned.

I felt as lost in myself and my confusion as the very last dinosaur must have felt, and having said that, I began to dwell on the subject of dinosaurs—on their enormous, important lives and their undignified extinction. "I'm much smaller than they were—that's certain—but I need as much. Do you have any monsters on your planet, Eugene? Do you know any monsters?" Eugene made a beeping sound, and I said, "I expect you do know monsters. If you come from another planet, I expect that humans look like monsters to you."

I took it as a sign that my husband, who had fallen asleep last year on a bench at the Museum of Science, arrived home also preoccupied with just how the last great reptile had felt. Even while Artie was getting out of the car he was talking about the subject, like an adolescent boy moved by shyness to chattering. "I had a good flight—I read an interesting book about dinosaurs on the plane," he called, resting his gaunt cheek for a moment against the car door. "Do you know how many pounds of vegetation they needed each day to stay alive?"

"Hundreds of pounds," I said. "That's the reason they couldn't survive." I leaned over the porch railing. Even from a distance I could see that the muscles of my husband's face were slack with some grave disappointment, and for the first time I thought that in his eyes flickered the light of a soul much like my own. "What's wrong, Artie?"

"Nothing," he said. "You look lovely in that nightgown."

"My face is messed up. I fell. Can't you see it?"
Artie walked up the creaking wood steps into the
bright light of the porch with a bundle of office mail.
"Are you all right?" he asked softly. "Did you see a
doctor?"

"No, I didn't. The bruises will fade, but I look so
ugly."

"You look beautiful to me." Artie sighed deeply and
said he felt all worn out. "Go upstairs, baby, it's late. I
just have to sort through my mail. I've got to get caught
up—I have an early appointment tomorrow." At the
door of his study, Artie caught me gently around my
waist. "Am I going to be a father yet?" he asked.

"Not yet," I said. "But I'll get pregnant any time
now, Artie. A woman knows these things."

Artie nodded, patted my stomach, and closed his
study door. An hour or so later he came into the bedroom with his dinosaur book. He lay quietly on the bed
beside me and thumbed through the illustrations of
monsters battling and lying in decay by the lush sides of
primordial ponds. He said, "I've noticed from the
checkbook you've been spending a lot of money lately.
Did you buy some pretty new clothes?"

"Yes," I said. "A pink silk blouse, and a white silk
blouse. A lot of other things. I won't buy any more
clothes now, Artie."

Artie held up a picture of *Tyrannosaurus rex* and said if
he had it to do all over again he would become a pa-
leontologist. "Listen to this, Ruby," he kept saying. I
wanted to touch him while he read aloud, but I was
afraid and ashamed.

"When I was a little girl," I said, "I had a whole set of
dinosaurs. They were made of plastic."

Artie closed his book. "A long line vanished, wiped
out," he said. A zenith could only mark the beginning
of a decline. "Take a man, for instance," he said, "a

man about to achieve the dream that had given him direction all his life . . ."

"Maybe we can learn new dreams," I said quickly. "What happened in Curaçao?"

"Everything is fine. We'll probably sell the land in the next couple of weeks and make a killing—I wish you could see how beautiful the land is, Ruby. I almost wish I could keep it."

Artie switched off the lights and began to make love to me the way he had when we first knew each other: slowly, gently, without straining or acrobatics. We went limp at the same time, and smiling sadly and shyly as we waited for sleep, we said that what we needed now was a good bedtime story—if only we could think of a story to tell.

Artie said he felt lonely. "I wish I knew someone and that someone knew me."

"We know each other," I said.

"Do you think so?" Artie asked. "Poor Ruby, you're so battered." When I touched his face and kissed his sad eyes, he swallowed hard and moved to the far side of the bed.

Sometime during the dark hours of the early morning the lights were turned on, and a large manila packet was dumped on my stomach. I could see my swamp man well enough as he darted from the room. He was wearing an old, paint-covered pair of my jeans, rolled up at the cuffs, and a pair of my torn sneakers. His frame was so slight he resembled a twelve-year-old boy, and his mud-caked hair was straight, light brown, and earthlinglike.

"Artie," I whispered, so fascinated that I was unable to look away from the doorway through which Eugene had just ducked. When I reached for my husband, my hand touched only cold pillows and sheets.

I opened the envelope the swamp man had dropped

onto my belly. The packet, which had been ripped in several places, was addressed to Artie at his law office. What I removed were the two strong-smelling pairs of silk bikini panties that Rolando had been using to decorate his fish tank.

I stumbled into the hall, choking, and saw a light burning at its end. As I passed the staircase I looked up and shrieked, "Eugene, you are with her!"

"With whom?" my swamp man asked, his hands flying to his mouth. "Who am I with?"

My husband knelt in a room used for storage, rummaging through boxes of papers and mementos, of high school, college, and law school yearbooks that an affectionate aunt had saved and sent him several years ago. Artie had never before looked at the stuff, but now he was wearing his old letter sweater and a University of Michigan scarf. He seemed to be preparing to blow into a battered bugle when he saw me and stood.

"What's wrong?" he asked, his voice and face still remarkably full of concern. "What are you doing up at this hour?"

"I saw a ghost in the hall. I saw my mother, and I'm more frightened than I've ever been."

Artie removed his scarf and put his arms around my shaking shoulders. "I'll protect you," he told me.

"Maybe you can't," I said. I sobbed, but quickly dried my eyes.

"Poor Ruby. You were talking in your sleep again last night. I guess I've been leaving you alone too much."

"It isn't your fault. I'm not a child," I said.

"I guess you're not," he said, with infinite sadness in his voice: he sounded as sad and alone as my swamp man had sounded running through the swamp and saw grass. Artie said harshly, "Don't apologize for anything—I couldn't stand it now." He turned away from me, trembling, but when he turned back he seemed to have collected himself. "I've decided to give up my law practice. I'm not going to work anymore."

"You're sick," I cried. "Or angry, or both."

"Why should I work? I'll have enough money, and I have you. You're all I need in this world." This my husband said without a trace of irony. "I have it all figured out—we'll travel with our baby."

"You shouldn't give up your law practice because of me," I said.

"I have to do something. Don't you know how much I love you?"

"I didn't know—I don't know why. Why should you have loved me?"

"Because you seemed to need me, and that made me feel important. Why should you have loved me?" he asked.

"Because you loved me." I picked up one of the high school yearbooks and thumbed through the stiff pages until I came to Artie's senior class picture. His very blond hair was plastered to his head, and I saw that he had been captain of the debating team, class vice-president, and a sweetheart of some girls' club. "I've got to tell you, Artie," I began, but he held two fingers over my lips.

"No. Don't. I've left you alone too much, I told you. I'd deserve to lose you, Ruby, but I don't want to. I really don't." Artie took off his letter sweater, folded it carefully, and returned it to its box. He said that he had wanted to look through his old things to see how much he had accomplished, to see how far he had really come. He held up a deflated soccer ball and smiled. "I guess I have come a long way by some standards, but what I've accomplished doesn't seem important now."

"It's all important," I said. Resting in one corner of the dusty, cobwebbed room, amid a pile of boxes, suitcases, and stacks of magazines, was an ancient black trunk in which my mother had stored many of her keepsakes. If people were haunted because they wanted to be haunted, and if people unwittingly arranged the circumstances and details of their haunts even while they tried to flee what horrors they saw or heard in their houses, then I had wanted to see my swamp man with my mother. "I'm very proud of you, Artie."

Artie said that he, I, and our baby would have the most wonderful life. We would take our baby all over the world. In the mornings, when we stayed in Venice, we would take our baby to Saint Mark's Square, and in Rome the baby would be blessed by the pope. "I guess people will ask me if I'm the kid's grandfather, but I won't mind. My kid will be proud of me. My kid is going to remember me."

"Remember you! Artie, the baby and I will take care of you."

"You," Artie said, smiling. "You can scarcely take care of yourself. No," he said then, "I'm wrong. It's just that I don't want you ever to have any bad surprises, Ruby."

He rubbed his eyes and held a wet finger to the smoky shaft of light angling in from the dusty window behind us. I hugged him, and his tears felt like grace and broke my heart, and I was filled with a wonder I had thought was forever lost.

"What did you want to be, Artie, before you wanted to be a lawyer?" I asked.

Artie laughed and looked ruefully at his narrow chest and thin legs. "When I was twelve I wanted to be a heavyweight boxing champion. What did you want to be when you were twelve?"

"Six again," I said. "When I was twelve, all I wanted was to be six."

...

Because he meant to set into motion immediately the dissolution of his law practice, Artie left for work early. I went into the bedroom and threw away all eight hidden packages of birth control pills and tried to imagine that the shame I felt was the beginning of relief. I was in too much horror of myself to be angry with Rolando for having let Artie know about me: he had told me he was mad, and I had thought his madness fun.

Janet Monsterville arrived unusually early that morning. Her eyes were red and swollen, and she wore faded and mended cottons, as if to dress had required great effort. As she staggered across the kitchen she fell over a chair, and I had to help her sit. I poured her coffee and she bent her head to sip it without picking up her cup, her hands holding the sides of her face as if she were nursing a terrible toothache.

"You're not going to die now," I said. I put my arms around her shoulders, but she shrugged them off. "Let me take you to a doctor, Janet."

"I got a headache is all." Janet's broad face crumpled with a secret misery. Each time she sipped her coffee she moaned and held her stomach, and at last she pushed the cup away. "I saw the Lord last night, Ruby, just as plain as I see you. He was standing at the foot of my bed." Janet told a long and confusing story of how the Lord had come to her in a miraculous, long-awaited vision, and of what dangers He had warned her about. She mixed the implications of the vision into tales of her family, her husbands, Alonzo, and her other boyfriends. She had decided to give up men, she told me, and was going to save her money to go home to her mother in Georgia. "I ain't got a thing here. Stupid old man Alonzo ain't even called me in two days. He got me sick. How'd he know I wasn't lying dead on my floor? He don't love me."

"He ought to love you. You'll hear from him soon."

"No. The Lord says all that is over. I've been fooling myself. If the man wouldn't marry me for eight years, he ain't never going to marry me. The Lord says no! He told me about you, too," she said. "He told me about your ghosty, and He told me about your Cuban sausage."

"I know about Rolando," I said quickly. "I'm going to drive over there and finish things up. Maybe life can be easy, if only you do the right things. Eugene—he let me know. Artie loves me. I think he's always known about the other men, and he still loves me. I think I wanted him to know."

Janet gently pried my hands from my face. "I wanted Alonzo to know about my men, but it didn't do me any good. I was lonesome anyhow."

"My father left me lonely," I said, "and my mother did, too. But maybe they couldn't help it."

"The light spreads," Janet said, rocking her face in her hands. "It's God speaking through you now. I'll change, too." She heaved a great and weary sigh. "I better change. Last night I was finally saved."

Janet told me that when her postman had arrived at her house at three o'clock in the morning, she had told him he could "shove his fifty dollars, kiss my ass, and tell me how it smells. I need his money to go home, and I want affection, but I saw the Lord." Janet rose with a cry and fell against the table. Her cup and saucer crashed to the floor. She leaned heavily against me, dazed and shaking her head. "I wonder how much longer I can work and save my money."

"I'll send you back to Georgia," I said, but Janet said it wasn't quite time. I peered into her eyes. "Don't you want to go home and get into bed? When I'm through talking to Rolando, I could bring you some soup. And after work I could stop by and bring you more soup."

"You never brought me soup before when I was sick,"

Janet said. "I ain't staying in bed with nobody to talk to." She must have suddenly recovered her balance, for she rushed for the broom, the dustpan, and a sponge and began cleaning up the splattered coffee and broken china. When I tried to help her, she said, "I don't need you. The Lord's my power—I got the Lord now." She flipped her apron above the garbage can so that the pieces of broken china fell neatly into the container. "I got the Lord now," Janet said again, "and I know what that means. I'm free. I'm going to choose my time and place."

Janet followed me upstairs to the bedroom and talked while I showered and dressed. We heard the tinkling of the piano downstairs, and Janet hummed along to the Christmas carol the seasonally confused Eugene played. "Now ain't that nice," Janet said. But when the music stopped, she thundered grievances against her Thursday, against Alonzo and all the men she had known, and railed about her diabetes, her obesity, her last hospital checkup, and how all of this related to the Lord's having spoken to her.

"You're going to be fine," I said, and then, because I was unable to bear the thought that she might not be fine, I chattered on and on about the baby I would soon be expecting. "You could come to Europe with Artie and me, and help me take care of my baby. We could try to be happy. What do you think, Janet?"

Janet Monsterville was crying. "I think nothing," she said, wiping her face on her apron. "I'm just old and foolish and I talk too much. I got no friends in this world."

"I'm your friend," I said. Her cheeks were unusually dry and cool beneath my lips.

"Then how come you never listen to me?" she asked.

"Because I've been lonely myself, I guess."

"You got a good husband," Janet muttered. She was rummaging through the perfumes and creams on my makeup table, dusting the crystal bottles with her apron and then holding them to the light to admire them. "You must've been so pretty, the day you were married. Young and pretty and in love."

"No," I said, stepping into a pair of old jeans. "I don't think I loved Artie then, not really. I think I only wanted to know someone would have me. But I've learned to love him now, and that must be the best kind of love." When I turned Janet was staring sadly at me and holding out a lipstick and some rouge. "Let Rolando see me the way I am," I said.

"You want me to tell that Cuban for you?" Janet asked.

She made me smile. "I guess I have to do this myself."

"You be careful over there. First get back the money he owes you—you running around with trash! Where the hell was your head?"

"It's been lost as long as I can remember," I said.

"If that beans and rice wants to fight you, you know where to kick him. God ain't going to mind you kicking him where it counts."

"Maybe it'll all work out. He doesn't love me. Maybe he won't even mind."

"And maybe," said Janet, stumbling against me, although once again she insisted that she was as well as could be expected, "I'll wake up tomorrow blond and white. Well, we fall and we rise, fall and we rise up. Listen there!" she said, clutching my arm. "There's your swamp man—my ghosty."

Eugene was wailing somewhere on the third floor, and my mouth opened, and I wailed loudly with him. "He's sad," I said. "Why should he be so sad now?"

I let my imagination run wild as I drove toward Little Havana. The morning had darkened and a chill drizzle fell, slickening the dangerously narrow road. If

Rolando and I discussed our relationship without anger, without reproach, we would agree that it had been a dreadful mistake. It would be Rolando who would say I belonged with Artie, because Artie loved and needed me.

"Your husband is a good man," I thought he would say. He might even remark that Artie had been an example to him, and that he had given him hope. "I'll be all right. Go to your husband. I knew you didn't want to marry me—I pushed you into saying that. I'm leaving town now. I want you to feel safe."

"Maybe he'll go to Alaska," I said, twisting up a madly inventive finger.

This pleasantly painful scenario never took place. On the wet sidewalk in front of Rolando's building I ran headfirst into Lillian. I stood rubbing my aching nose and staring at her in bewilderment.

"You're in a hurry—no wonder you always bump yourself," Lillian said. She was smiling sweetly and striking silly poses in her flounced and ruffled eyelet frock that matched her lacy white umbrella. Her red hair had been prettily curled, and my sister, who rarely painted or powdered or plucked, had made up her face with a generous, hopeful hand. "You almost messed up my dress, running into me that way."

"What are you doing here, Lillian?"

"I was about to ask you the same thing. You don't look well, Ruby." Lillian put her hand to my forehead and said she thought I was running a temperature. "I'm always in a fever myself now," she said, laughing and flipping out her skirt. "I was coming to see Rolando. I've found my man at last." She kissed my cheek, and for a moment, when our eyes met, she looked sad. But then she whirled around, and her face was joyous again. "He's so romantic. We had the most wonderful time last night." Rolando, she said, had ridden her on his motorcycle to the beach, where she had run through the woods according to the guidance of yellow arrows painted on trees and dug in the sand until she unearthed a jar in which Rolando had captured moonbeams especially for her.

"And then we made love by the ocean. He's so sweet," Lillian said, "and vulnerable. I've tried with him, Ruby. I know now it wasn't just luck that you had a good marriage. I have a chance now, too." Lillian frowned at me. "Didn't you know about us?"

"I didn't know," I said. I bit my lips to keep from crying, and then I could taste my own blood. "You're certain you're in love with him?"

"We're both certain. You're still not smiling. I thought you'd be happy for me."

"I'm happy." I could not help staring up at Rolando's window, where the curtains were slightly parted, and even with my terrible hatred I remembered with a sudden, violent aching his touch and the way his eyes had looked above mine.

"I'll be back at the shop soon," Lillian said. She gave me another benevolent, triumphant kiss. "He asked me to marry him, you know, and I've accepted."

I watched Lillian go up the stairs toward Rolando's apartment. I started to follow her, but I could imagine no way to right this. I turned and wandered down the sidewalk, crying quietly. At the first phone booth I could find, I called my father.

"It's Ruby," I said. "I want to come over."

"Don't, unless you have my plane ticket."

"Stop this game! You love me," I insisted.

"I do not love you. Why should I?"

"Because I'm your daughter, and you have to love me."

"You're very wrong," Sam said. "I don't have to love you at all. You're a high-strung, selfish woman, just like your mother. You're no concern of mine. You should've sent me my money. Then maybe I'd have reason to love you."

"And if I gave you reason and you ran off again, what then? You're an evil old man, and I've been tricked."

12

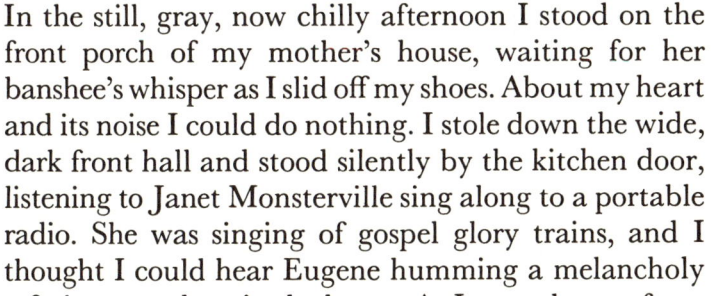

In the still, gray, now chilly afternoon I stood on the front porch of my mother's house, waiting for her banshee's whisper as I slid off my shoes. About my heart and its noise I could do nothing. I stole down the wide, dark front hall and stood silently by the kitchen door, listening to Janet Monsterville sing along to a portable radio. She was singing of gospel glory trains, and I thought I could hear Eugene humming a melancholy refrain somewhere in the house. As I moved away from the kitchen, Janet's wet, glistening neck and scarved head jerked at what she might have thought was the wisp of a spirit fleeting through this still incomprehensible house.

Upstairs I unlocked and opened each of my bedroom windows. Among the dark treetops and black-and-silver thunderheads I looked for the shadow of a flying, cackling witch. I pondered the distance from the second-story ledge to the ground below, and then, remembering my husband and my baby, got into bed with my clothes on. My skin hurt all over, and to breathe seemed annoyingly tedious. All that was vital seemed lost: I was certain that death crouched in a corner of my room, and I wondered if my mother was happy at my pain.

"Ruby?" My swamp man appeared at the opened bedroom door, his small, dirty hands clutching his face. "You haven't helped me at all, Eugene," I said. My swamp man fled down the hall with small steps resonant of varnished wood and alien fear.

Moments later Janet Monsterville scuffed into the room, her transistor radio held against her ear. She groaned, bending for the clothes I had thrown on the floor that morning.

When she straightened, our eyes met and she said, "You! When did you get here?" She switched off her radio and, leaning over, tried fruitlessly to remove my shoes. I curled my feet beneath me. Janet cried, "It's bad luck to keep your clothes on in bed."

"I have to keep my clothes on," I said.

"What the hell happened to you this morning? He beat you when you told him?"

"I never had the chance to tell him anything. I've been tricked—go away, Eugene, will you?" I turned my face into my pillow, but a dreadful, shocking alertness kept me seeing. "Rolando," I said, "asked Lillian to marry him, and she accepted. He wants to torment us both, and there's nothing I can do about it."

"If I was you," Janet said, at last slipping off my shoes, "I'd remember what I said about loving my husband. That boy ain't going to marry your sister."

"But he is." I wished I could be rid of that terrible alertness, for I could see a frightening change in Janet's eyes and posture. She was crying and rubbing her plump chin and muttering something that sounded like a prayer. "Please don't cry," I said.

"Why does your sister want to do this to you? I warned you about her, and I warned you about that boy." Janet handed me the dish towel from the waistband of her apron and told me to cry, if it would make me feel better. From along the dark hall outside my room I heard my swamp man whimpering again—poor, melancholy sprite. Janet's head jerked toward the door. "Your sweet little ghosty tried to warn you, too. Well, it's your pride hurting you now. You thought they loved you because they said so? Ain't none of us big shots. I've been alive a long time, and I've seen lots of things. My mama in Georgia loves me, and maybe that's all. Ain't none of us smart. Think about the Lord like we did this morning."

"But this morning," I said, wiping my eyes and nose with the dish towel that smelled of garlic, "I thought I would fix all my mistakes so nobody would be hurt."

"We fall and we rise," Janet moaned. She waved her apron as if she were warding off a devil's bull: she mumbled about my troubles as if they were hers, and I blinked at her in astonishment. When I sat up and began to scratch away the paint of the wall behind me, Janet cried out that I should not pay attention to evil ghosts, but ought to think about the Lord.

"I'll kill them both," she said. She rumbled around the room, dusting the furniture with the palms of her hands. "I ain't got nothing to lose by killing them. A prison ain't keeping me more than a few weeks. I'll kill them before I go back to Georgia, if you tell me to." Janet turned, her eyebrows arched, as if she were merely waiting for the word.

"Don't say that. You saw your Lord," I said.

"But I want you to be pretty and happy."

"I feel like I'm dying," I said.

"You're going to live, fool. You're just thirty-three."

"But I know what's going to happen to me. I can see it all."

"If you could see it all you'd know I was going to die

soon, and you won't admit that, will you?" I shook my head. Janet pushed her face so close to mine I could smell the tuna and Scotch on her breath. She shouted, "I ain't put on this earth to serve you. How come you know so much and you won't know I'm going to die soon?"

I smiled at her and said, "You're going to live until you're eighty. I can see everything."

"You see nothing. Get up from bed now. Forget about yourself for a change." Janet said she would help me bathe and pick out a pretty dress for me to wear. Oh, she said, I could wear nearly any color and style, while she had to watch what she put on. "And your beautiful hair," she said, a sly look in her eyes, as if she could put one over on a woman who knew what she had done to her life and to the lives of her husband and sister. I had the gift of vision and could see years ahead.

"I don't want to put on a pretty dress. I'm sick. I'm dying," I said.

That rainy Tuesday night Artie stood above my bed with his hand on my cheek. "You feel warm. You better stay in bed a few days," he said. He was pale and tired with the strain of having told his law partners he wanted to leave the firm. "They think I've gotten romantic notions," he said, his small mouth twisting.

Although my husband appeared convinced that I showed all the subtle first symptoms of the highly infectious type-B influenza that had killed a thousand people in 1960, he did not urge me to see a doctor. Instead, he cheerfully remarked upon my ashen face and glassy eyes, and brightly explored the possibility that I would require a long convalescence.

"No work for you for a while. I was supposed to go to Curaçao Thursday to see about a proposed land sale, but I won't leave you if you're sick." When I laughed, my husband's cheeks reddened. "Maybe you should see a doctor after all," he said.

At once I became grim. "I'm afraid to see our doctor." I rolled to one side so that I could stare out the windows at the autumn storm. Outside the wind howled through the brush and shook the walls of the house. I said that my mother had been correct after all in her last estimation of men. "Most hate women. They want to make love to a woman one moment and kill her the next."

Now my husband backed up to the doorway, a funny, stooped, Chaplinesque figure in his elegant clothing and white socks. A look of melancholy surprise contorted his face. "Did I put that idea into your head?" he asked. "When I warned you about men, I didn't mean for you to hate them all."

"I know what most men are," I said.

"You don't sound like yourself," Artie said. "You used to trust everyone."

"That was when I was still a child. Oh, come here," I said, wiping my eyes. As he crossed the room my husband tugged at his hair and ears and seemed afraid to look at me.

"I don't know you when you talk like this," he said.

"Let's make our baby," I said.

As we made love I whispered every obscene word I knew, so that several times Artie lifted his head and gazed at me with sorrow. My eyes ached and watered. I remembered the color of Mitchell's eyes, the curve of Jake's mouth, and the warm, musty smell of Rolando's bedroom. I couldn't help thinking of those things while my husband made love to me.

Afterward I cried, looking into Artie's face. "I feel awful."

Artie stared at his hands and then at an empty corner of the room.

"Look at my eyes, Artie," I said.

Artie peered into my eyes and, after a moment, drew back. He sat at the edge of the bed with his hands clasped between his knees. "I guess you are sick," he said. "I guess I better call Janet and ask her to come every day until you're better." Before he stood he wrapped a blanket around his waist. "Would you like me to call Lillian? Maybe she could come over and cheer you up."

"Please," I said.

Artie left the room to make the telephone calls, his hands grasping the blanket around him. When he returned, he was wearing a pair of rumpled shorts he must have plucked from the laundry basket. "Lillian says she can't come," he told me.

"I didn't think she would. She's getting married to that Cuban fellow, you know."

Artie grew very red in the face. "She just told me—it's wonderful." When I burst into tears, he said, "Be happy. It's for the best." He sat beside me for a few moments and then remembered something—a leaky faucet or a stuck window—to which he had to attend downstairs.

After he had left the room, I set to work on the wall above the bed, and while Artie worked downstairs, I removed six layers of paint from a surface at least six inches in diameter. I thought I might expose whatever strange dream my mother had attempted to make real so long ago with a swamp man who had not come to her but was now residing in my house. Finally, Artie came quietly to bed and slept on its edge. All night I looked for my mother's shade in the lovely light and shadows cast from curtains just barely illuminated by the cool November moon.

I hate this gift, Eugene, I whispered to the figure crouched beyond the bedroom door. I stroked my sleeping husband's cheek, but my fingers sprang back, as if they had no right to touch him so tenderly.

Very early Wednesday morning I awoke from familiar dreams with tears on my face. When I saw the tray of pancakes and coffee set upon my bureau, I laughed and cried at once.

"What's wrong now?" Artie asked. "I love you. Why won't you be happy? You always seemed happy before."

"Let's make our baby," I said.

"I don't feel well," Artie said, but I was already working with my hands and mouth. When I whispered a few obscenities, he said, "Don't," and covered my mouth with his. I could taste myself on his tongue and didn't like the staleness.

Afterward I said, "I think we did it this time, Artie."

Artie stood and fumbled with the strings of his pajamas. "You better eat something. You don't want our baby to be undernourished."

"I'll eat something later. I still feel sick."

Artie blinked rapidly and tucked in the blankets all around me. "I'd call the doctor if I thought he could help you. But he can't, can he?"

"No, I guess not. But I'll be all right soon. You're good," I said. I smiled away and thought about the old gospel tunes that once seemed to shake the earth beneath the white wood revival church to which my mother had infrequently taken Lillian and me. I tried to think of my baby and me climbing the marble stairs to heaven. "Artie, where should we take our baby first? Tell me again," I pleaded.

My husband set down his appointment book and knotted his tie with nervous, jerking motions. His face was still fatigued, as if sleep had not revived him, and his voice sounded tired. "What's closest to heaven?" he asked, frowning at his watch.

"The little grape arbor in Montmartre, near Sacré-Coeur," I said.

"Montmartre was where you rushed off with that

drunk artist. I remember Paris, and I remember Rome." Artie swallowed hard and said that he expected the next days to be miserable. "Dissolving this practice so that I don't lose out is going to be difficult. I'll be late."

All morning I leaned back, smiling, against the pillows and so vividly imagined my death that I was convinced God was going to take me and so save me. The sweet quiet was broken only by the occasional ringing of the telephone, Janet's voice downstairs, my swamp man's whimper as he scooted back and forth in the hall, and the gentle flipping of the curtains in the Everglades breeze.

When I refused the lunch Janet brought me, she said, "It ain't your turn, I told you." All afternoon, while I watched and cried over soap operas with great relish, Janet staggered in and out of the room with cookies, hot breads, and tea she said the ghosty had prepared for me. "Open wide," she said, trying to stuff a spoon into my mouth. Her dark, wide eyes were as revealing as a nickelodeon—there in miniature were her mother's farm, her mother, her cousins, a preacher, black mourning crepe, and viscous, brown-edged flowers.

Some time later Janet came into the bedroom, smiling slyly. I smiled slyly back at her. "The boss just called," she said. "He wants you to pack him a bag for Curaçao. Here—get up now."

"I can't pack a bag," I said. "You know I can't pack a bag. I'm not leaving this bed on my feet. The only way I'm going is straight up through the ceiling."

Janet's dusty toes wriggled angrily in her crushed pink slippers. "Then what the hell are you talking about your baby for?"

"I don't know," I said.

"Here!" Janet shouted, rushing toward the bed as if she meant to beat me. But when she peered into my eyes, she gasped and took a step or two back. "You going to be in bed when Mr. Holloway gets home and nothing wrong with you? You ought to be ashamed of yourself, worrying the boss this way." Her eyes widened and grew wet, and she turned abruptly and went downstairs. When she returned she smelled of whiskey, and she shook her head angrily when I asked if Lillian or Rolando had called. "I'm dying," she said, pointing her finger at me, "and I ain't staying in bed all day long. Look how I'm working for you." She looked as if she had been crying very hard. "I'm the one who's dying. Ain't you dying."

"Maybe we're both dying," I suggested. The screen of the open window glittered beautifully in the hot sun; flies landed on it and then took off. If I rolled to the edge of the bed and lifted my chin onto the windowsill, I could see over the Everglades for miles, could look down on the front porch roof and its cover of blossoming flame vine, and could watch the purple bougainvillea that grew around the white porch railings sway in the wind. I saw no silver ships that might, instead of God, carry me to another world and another life. But acres beyond the house, standing by the pole fence, I saw the figure of my sun-bonneted aunt. Her long dress was blowing in the wind, and I imagined she stared toward my window with a disappointed expression in her eyes.

In the warm sunlight that fell over the bed, I slept. When I awoke I felt a heavy body against mine. I turned my head into Janet Monsterville's creased, sweating neck. She was snoring lustily and still clutched in her fat fingers a dirty yellow sponge. Her feet hung over the bed, and her slippers dangled from her big toes.

As soon as I kissed her, she awoke, and she blinked at me as if she could not remember where she was. I thought it was very companionable and gracious of her to come sleep beside me, she who said she was dying also, she who had seen the Lord two nights before and had spoken with Him. "Both of us are heading out, aren't we?" I asked.

Downstairs the vacuum cleaner was running: sweet Eugene was helping two women in distress.

"Not you. Me," Janet said. She got up quickly and left the room on feet too rapid and vital, I thought, for her to be really leaving at the same time as I.

That evening Artie came into the bedroom carrying a boxful of fresh doughnuts. "Look here, Ruby," he said, smiling gaily, and flipped back the lid of the box.

"I'm not hungry. I'm sick," I said.

Artie sat at the side of the bed, his curly, cloudy head hanging, his hands clutching his stomach. "I'm going to cancel this next trip to Curaçao," he said. "I haven't been feeling well myself. I think I'm coming down with what you've got."

"Maybe we're both dying," I said, but then, for dying people, we made a splendid effort at growing a baby.

The next morning Artie remained in bed with me. Together we moaned and clutched our stomachs, and together we looked with great anxiety out the bedroom windows. We were wonderful elderly companions, and we quarreled only once, over the television. If we got better, we said, we would take our baby to the Virgin Islands in the winter, as babies were prone to colds and the weather there is splendid always.

Artie spoke several times to his law partners about the dissolution of his firm.

"I think it's a mistake," I said.

"It's no mistake. After I'm paid my share of this deal, I won't need to do any more business. I better not do any more business."

"You aren't your father," I said.

When Janet arrived and saw Artie stretched out beside me, she cried out, "No." Casting me many dirty looks, she plumped up the pillows behind his head, begged him to drink some juice, and then drew the curtains so that the boss could sleep a few extra hours. As soon as Artie had dozed off I sat up, threw my pillow to the floor, and began scratching at the wall behind me. I imagined that in a few weeks I would have bared each wall of the house down to its original paint. I would rip up all the carpeting, the tiles, the parquet dining room floor, until I understood my mother's dream.

While I worked on the wall, I watched Artie. In sleep he spoke of his dead uncles, his dead cousins, and his dead father, and in sleep he cried out with anguish that I was certain was my fault.

"I don't ever dream," he told me, when he awoke. "It was you dreaming."

Around lunchtime Janet came into the room. She slid her apron over the furniture she passed and glowered toward the stairs. In the hall I could see the slight shadow of my swamp man, but I knew that someone else was in the house. "You still feeling bad, my boss?" Janet crooned, bending to pick up a crumpled Kleenex from the floor beside the bed. She put her hand on Artie's white forehead.

Artie groaned. "I'm a very sick man," he said, fumbling for my hand. Although his index finger rubbed a hot, signaling circle in my palm, his eyes looked listless, as if he were indeed quite sick. "I've caught what my poor Ruby has, only worse. Ten times worse."

"He's very sick," I said. "He's not leaving this bed."

"There's a man waiting downstairs to see you—I'll run him out now," Janet said, starting toward the hall. She cried out in anger when the old man squeezed past her into the room. His black eyes glittered as he looked about, and his gray lips seemed unrelentingly merry. Artie immediately pulled the sheets up and over the gold-spangled nightgown I was wearing for him. "My wife isn't dressed," he said, his face very red. The old man smiled and turned his back while Janet brought me a robe. "Didn't you get my message? I told your secretary I couldn't make this next meeting. Ruby and I are very sick."

"I'm sorry about that," the old man said. "But you've got to come with me now. It's time to jump."

"We really are sick." Artie crossed the room slowly, holding both sides of his head as if he were dizzy.

"If it were any other time, Arthur," the old man said, "I could have gotten along without you. I remember once, on a similar business proposition, your father had to travel with a hundred-and-six-degree temperature. But I guess the old stock was a little tougher, eh?" The old man, the Judge, said that he had been offered a price he really could not refuse for the land in Curaçao and intended to exercise his option to sell it. "I need your signature. The papers are being drawn up, and eight million dollars has been transferred to a Curaçao bank."

For a man who had been waiting for this moment all his life, my husband seemed remarkably uninterested. He coughed into a Kleenex and then examined the tissue. "I'll fly down in a week or so," he said.

"No. The deal either goes through this week, or it won't go through at all. We made a bargain," the old man said. "You come with me now, sign a few papers, and in a few days you'll return a very wealthy and happy man." He put his arm around my husband's shoulders and drew him into the hall. The men stood away from the doorway, speaking in hushed tones.

Janet Monsterville, who had been rearranging shoes

in the closet, now wiped the windowsills, her eyes directed toward the hall. She sang loudly. When she bent over the bed to tuck in the sheets, she whispered, "What the hell's happened to my good boss, bringing trash into the house?"

Janet had not seen Artie returning. Now he frowned at her. "Nothing has happened to me. Go downstairs and make my friend a drink, will you?"

"Don't want to," Janet said, smiling sweetly as she passed.

Artie dressed rapidly. I watched him for a time and then began to pick at the walls with my broken nails. He leaned over the bed, his tie half-knotted, and caught my arm, saying, "Don't. I'm afraid I'll have to call for a painter to come now, Ruby." His eyes were very bright, and his lips were full of spasms. As soon as he released my hand, I was back to removing paint from the wall.

"Well, you're getting what you wanted. You must be very happy," I said.

"I am," Artie said. His eyes were full of tears, and he said that he had the feeling that his father was looking down upon him this day and was very, very proud. Artie sat on the bed and put his trembling hand in mine.

"What's wrong, Artie?" I asked.

"I have a pain in my chest." Artie wiped his face with a handkerchief. He packed, unpacked, and packed again a small suitcase, kissed me many times, and walked to the door, all the while issuing instructions: I must keep the doors locked and note the emergency telephone numbers he had written on notepads all over the house. "You're sure you'll be all right? If I thought you were really that sick, Ruby, I wouldn't go today."

"I'll be fine."

My husband paused for a moment, his head leaning against the door frame. Behind him passed Eugene, whimpering, and Artie's head jerked, but not in time: my swamp man had already vanished. "I have a pain in my chest," Artie repeated, as he turned into the hall.

"Could you fix me a cup of tea?" I asked Janet some time later, when she came into the room angrily muttering about the old man who had removed her poor sick boss from her care.

"My boss is good—why'd he want to mess around with that kind of trash?" she cried.

"He wants what he can't have. Could you call Lillian and tell her to come see me?" I asked.

"Call her your stupid self. She knows you're sick, and I ain't no slave." Janet left the room with her hand over her heart.

I dressed quickly and crept down the stairs with my boots in my hands. While Janet's back was turned and she was muttering at the tea kettle, I stole past the kitchen door and ran down the porch steps.

Deep into the woods I ran, skidding in mud and moss, and thrashed through small brackish creeks. I walked and paced in a circular clearing for hours. A butterfly darted too close to my face and was too quick and beautiful. The beauty of the butterfly and of the jungle made me cry. I was not going to die after all.

I felt very young and full of rich, quick blood, so quick and so rich I was afraid of going mad. "I have ruined my life," I shouted at an egret flying high above me, "and God isn't even going to make me die."

Rolando and my sister had conspired to humiliate me and would be torturing me at the shop if I were there, would be wrapping their tongues and licking on ears and perhaps making noisy love in the storage room until I rushed for their throats.

"I'm never going back there," I said. I climbed high into a tall pine tree, scratching my hands and face and ripping the cuffs of my jeans. If Rolando had thought he had suffered from nightmares before, I would make all the world a nightmare for him. I inched my way out onto a long, thick limb and bravely, carelessly—I was my mother's daughter—threw both my legs before me.

I screamed and repositioned myself. "Why did you make me this way?" I shouted. "You gave me a gift and dreams and made me too stupid to use them."

Below me I heard a crunching that stopped suddenly, and then I saw my frail little swamp man standing in the clearing, his head twisting this way and that and finally lifting toward the sky. His mouth dropped, and his eyes widened.

"What do you want from me now?" I asked. "Who sent you? Was it my mother?"

Eugene nodded. As I stared at him it seemed that visions and words were struggling to form and break free.

"Run!" I called. "Go back to the house. Stay low, Eugene! I won't leave you, I promise." Eugene darted away obediently, the ragged tail of my old shirt flapping, my old sneakers squishing water and sliding against his pink heels.

Well, I thought, smiling and shifting my position, except for the impediment to free movement, this was quite a pleasant place. Tucked below me in the branches I could see a nest from which came the softest, prettiest peeping. To my right I could see the river and how it curved and blossomed with lavender orchids, could see all the way to the cabin where my aunt Catherine O'Connell still lived and worked. Far away I could see a tiny airboat cutting a path through the waving saw grass. Vines of wild hibiscus grew as far up the tree as where I sat, and down below a line of plump, quality quail passed, bobbing and wagging.

"Why should I be earthbound?" I asked but at once hit upon the answer and twisted a clever finger into the air: even I could not imagine my arms into wings. I began to sing a song I remembered from my childhood but stopped when I heard the rattling in the brush. "I told you to stay at home, Eugene."

Far beneath me the branches parted, and my aunt Catherine O'Connell approached the lazily running creek. Even with her lameness, which required her cane, she sprang over the water as nimbly as a frog.

Although she was far below me, my aunt did not look small. "How come I'm running into you so much all of a sudden?" I called. "For years I never saw you. Did my mother send you around, too?"

"Think what you want, but get down from that tree right now, Ruby," Catherine said. Her voice was cracked and husky, her face wrinkled, and her red hair full of gray, but still I was jealous of her beauty. She leaned on her bumpy cane, her eyes so fixed and direct that I thought she could see straight through to my brain. She stretched her long, brown arm toward me as if it were a length of rope. "You've got business to finish. Get down from that tree. I can't come up after you, obviously." Catherine lifted her cane toward me, swayed, and then set it down again, grasping its top with both hands and looking for all the world not like the witch of the woods, as my sister called her, but rather like its keeper.

"I was just coming," I said, my eyes full of relieved tears. My aunt was smiling at me now, was shaking her head and calling for me to be careful as I inched backward along the limb and wound my arms and legs around the trunk. "It's a good thing I'm strong, isn't it?" I cried, sweating and hurting, my knees hugging the tree as I pulled myself down the rough bark. The scratches on my hands and face burned from the sap. I fell away at the last seven feet or so and rolled over and over on the pine needles, so that the sky seemed of earth, and fragrant earth of towering blue sky. I lay breathing hard, just inches from my aunt's heavy brown shoes.

"Stand up, will you, Ruby?" Catherine said. Her face was gaunt and strong-boned—there was certainly nothing pretty about it except for the beauty my imagination put there. "I can't pull you, you know. I'm telling you that you've got to finish things up."

"I wasn't really going to kill myself," I said, shuddering. "I was only resting by thinking I might. Eugene made me forget that I wanted to jump."

"Your mother would've stopped you anyway."

"No," I said, shaking my head. "My mother is the one who sent me up there." I said that I had fulfilled her prediction after all. I had ruined my life. I had ruined Artie and Lillian's lives.

"People don't ruin so easily. You won't get your mother back that way. Don't ruin yourself for her, Ruby. That isn't the way to make things up."

"I wasn't," I began, but my false bravado broke as soon as my aunt put her arms around me. "I don't think I'll ever find what she took when she left. I've forgotten so much. If I could've forgotten you, what else have I lost?" I cried until my tongue was thick and the swollen feeling inside my breasts subsided, and then I changed again and kicked a stone. "I don't see why I should try. I can already see what's going to happen. I have this awful gift, and she gave it to me."

"Look around you. You've hardly ever used your gift," Catherine said. She stood very still and seemed grave: only her eyes, lifting often to the sky, were merry.

"You're crazy," I said, wiping my eyes and lifting my intelligent, analytical finger. "Crazier even than my mother was, and that's traveling some. One of the troubles with you is that you don't remember what it's like to feel passion. That's your trouble—or your luck. My feelings break me, but you wouldn't know about that, would you?" When I looked into my aunt's eyes, I saw that this was not true. She had great passion. "Tell me I can't have something and that's exactly what I have to get. What good has Eugene been to me?" I asked. "I was happier before he came."

"If that were true, you wouldn't have had him move in with you. Go back to work," Catherine said. "You can't stay here."

From the tangle of palmetto, tall grasses, mossy vines, and berry bushes came a rattling of leaf and branch and a rasping breathing that must have sprung from my strangely hurting swamp man.

Oh, Eugene is so good, my aunt and I said, he is so precious and good.

"Aunt," I said, stepping forward, "once you said you had great hope for me. You said that a long while ago. Do you still?"

Catherine smiled and gave me her hand. "I have great hope. Go home. I'll see you again. You have a gift. Forget about yourself and look with it."

"I'll try," I said. I turned and bent to duck below a thick limb that blocked my way to the path that would lead me from these woods to my house. When I looked over my shoulder again, I saw that my aunt was gone; she had vanished as quickly as if she had been just the light and air of apparition in the approaching dusk, just the echoes of memory that always filled the last warm light.

As I walked back to the house I could hear the comforting crunch of my swamp man's feet. The cypress and the pines formed a dark, brooding border against the spectacular sunset, the flamingo-colored heavens and the top of the earth meeting in paths and lines small, narrow, and bright.

Janet Monsterville was dozing on the front porch

swing, her head resting against her plump shoulder, her hips bulging beyond the green slatted seat. The creaking of my feet on the porch steps made her start up. "Where've you been?" she demanded, rubbing her eyes. Her scarf had slipped down on her forehead, and the fireflies stirred around her head like little angel lights.

"Just walking."

"You must be feeling better then." Janet rose with difficulty. She bent to put on her scuffed bedroom slippers, but I swept them up and slipped them onto her swollen feet. "You see any bad witches out there?" she asked.

"No. No witches."

"You see your poor crazy mama?"

"I don't know," I said. "Maybe I did."

Janet shuddered, looking over the porch rail at the hugeness of the swamp, and at its darkness. "You want me to pray for you tonight?" she asked.

"Please," I said. "I'd like that very much."

13

My sister's three husbands had been more alike than most brothers, with a similarity of flesh and spirit that my sister said was revealed in the most trivial ways: in how they ate a piece of corn (methodically, from left to right), for instance, or how they slept (on the stomach, one leg up, foot bent, as if they were about to scale a wall). Each had been penniless or nearly so, excitingly volatile, and had possessed handsome, dark looks that were to Lillian a promise of a sensuous life. Although these three marriages and subsequent estrangements had the same absurd slapstick quality, my sister had loved these men and indeed had been deeply hurt by them. Although her pain over these failures was the pain typical of any failed love affair, her joy over the inventive ways she managed to resurrect her pride was delightfully unique.

Lillian's first husband was an Italian cornet player who fractured her left arm during their honeymoon in a North Carolina cabin because—as much as I could gather from her cheery explanations—he was bored in the country. Some time during this short-lived but lively union my sister contracted a venereal infection from Salvatore and contrived to get even by breaking the fingers of his gifted right hand in a car door, slammed at an opportune moment. Lillian, who wept for her husband's pain and nearly fainted in the emergency room, delivered her intention to get a divorce just after the doctor had told her groggy husband that his index and fourth fingers would always be stiff and difficult to move.

"He'll never play the cornet again. I always get even," my sister told me.

Her second husband was a waiter from Afghanistan, a quiet, retiring, wildly superstitious young man whose temper was no less fierce than her first husband's but was most often expressed in cruel, crude, barely intelligible jibes at his wife's physical and moral flaws. Lillian remained charmed by his Moslem rigidity and instruction for just one year—a year that included several wonderful battles and glorious reconciliations—and then sought to even the score. She began leaving around the house weird evidence that she had been delving into black magic while Abdoul slept. Half-melted candles, locks of black hair, a monkey's paw—these she scattered about the house, and whenever she was questioned about her midnight absences from the connubial bed, she smiled serenely and said that Abdoul would soon know everything.

The crisis had come after an unfortunate gaffe at the dinner table, Lillian told me, when she accidentally spilled a crock of hot gravy into her husband's lap, and he sprang up from his chair and slapped her ears in front of the company. Soon after she had sent him running and screaming to his car by planting beside his sleeping face a dead frog done up in pins, and then pinching him. "He deserved it," she said later. "He went too far, hitting me in front of my friends."

Her third husband, a traveling salesman who hailed originally from Haiti and wore chains to protect himself from lingering island curses, believed Lillian was a witch, though a good, gentle one, when he married her. Except for his extreme dislike of her pets, a moral lapse that made my soft-hearted sister cry, he seemed well suited to Lillian: he liked to roughhouse but shied from breaking bones, and he flirted just enough with other women to excite without actually straying. Lillian was in love for two and a half years, until she came home after our mother's funeral, convinced of the fine moral destiny awaiting her, and found Roger beating the loyal dog Lillian said was the reincarnation of the terrier that had lived with us for two years at the Orange Blossom Tourist Courts.

Of the curse she put on this husband and of his subsequent automobile accident, Lillian only said, "He deserved it. I always get even."

In the months of contrition and grand revelations that followed her third failure at marriage, Lillian remembered that I had seemed doubtful about the disposition of each of her three husbands. She vowed that if she ever again planned to marry, which she did not, she would make certain to choose a man of whom I approved. "My life is going to take a different direction now—the noble swerve," she had told me.

When, shivering not so much from the cold, salty bay winds as from my own anxiety, I walked into the shop the day after I had seen my aunt in the woods, I intruded upon just the sort of courtship scene in which my sister had played her part so many times. Lillian, dressed in a stained cotton blouse and a wrinkled shirt, her nails painted a vicious secular red and her cheeks flushed with cheery petulance, stood behind the counter with Rolando, returning his shoves with slaps and pinches, taking his abuse with a woeful smile and hurling it back as if she were engaged in a net game. They had apparently not heard the buzzer as I crossed the threshold, so engrossed were they in their love-making.

Rolando wore a white linen suit and several heavy gold bracelets. His hair was lustrous and his teeth were immaculately polished, but his eyes were weary and rimmed by dark circles. He appeared to be pointing out the physical disparities between himself and his fiancée. "You're a mess," he said, lifting a lank, unwashed strand of Lillian's hair. He ducked quickly to avoid her fist. "You'd ruin my life if you could."

"I wouldn't," shrieked Lillian. She stamped her feet and muttered an ominously unintelligible phrase.

"You were mumbling over me last night while I was asleep," Rolando charged. Lillian smiled and said nothing. "As if I don't have enough trouble with nightmares." When Rolando saw me standing by the door, he gave a stiff little bow. His dark eyes remained fixed on me as he kissed Lillian's neck and smoothed her tangled hair. "Lillian, look who has come to see us," he said. I could see his fingers dig hard into Lillian's waist, just before she escaped and rushed to greet me.

She hugged me for a long time and then, stepping back, her eyes sparkling behind her glasses, said that she was glad I was feeling better. "I was afraid, all things considering, that you weren't happy for me," she said.

I could smile and feel gentle if I thought of my good aunt Catherine, of my good swamp man Eugene, and of my good husband. "You're my sister—remember how we said we never ought to forget that? If you're happy, I'll try to be." I bared my teeth at Rolando.

Lillian insisted that Rolando hug me. "Kiss the woman who's going to be your sister-in-law," she said.

Rolando stepped forward and, his hands playing in my hair, kissed me full on the mouth.

Lillian slapped a ruler against the counter. "That's enough," she cried. Explaining that Rolando loved to tease her, she hooked her arm into his and giggled when Rolando licked her ear. "It was lonely here without you, even with the man of my dreams," Lillian said while I grinned and nodded away. "We're going to be married in two weeks, on Thanksgiving Day, because this is a new life for me."

"And for me, too," Rolando said, in a soft, fearful voice.

"I couldn't be happier for you both," I said. Even with my terrible sadness, I was able to smile, and that seemed to disappoint and fluster Rolando: he moved away from Lillian and stared toward the bright, windy street. "So, Thanksgiving Day. You've made all the arrangements, I suppose?"

"We have," Rolando said, glancing uneasily toward Lillian, who smoothed with coquettish hands first her hair and then her rather too small and unironed skirt. For just one moment, when our eyes met, I thought that perhaps she really did love me. "Lillian wanted to wait for your advice on the flowers and dress, but I had to dissuade her. I've never seen two sisters so close." Rolando kissed my sister hard. She might have stood moaning and pressing up against him all day if he had not broken away and wiped his mouth with an impeccably starched and ironed handkerchief. "Go brush your hair, will you? It's a mess. And the animals in back need feeding."

My sister frowned and appeared uneasy. "Let Ruby feed them," she said. "She has a better way with animals."

"I said for you to go," Rolando replied. "And wash your hands afterwards."

As soon as my sister had rushed away, I walked calmly toward Rolando. He looked up from the sports pages spread over the counter—he had marked several races at Hialeah—and cried suddenly, his hands flying to his perfect face, "Don't hit me! I told you I wouldn't be responsible."

When I looked at him I could not remember what trick of my imagination had made me fall in love with him. I could only feel a shocking emptiness clamoring inside me. "You're not worth hitting, for God's sake. You're too easy. You're a tart," I said, looking toward the back room, from which floated the faint sound of my sister's conversation with the monkey and baby alligator in the courtyard.

"*You* were easy, *you* were the tart."

"I admit I was easy. But don't do this, Rolando, please," I said.

"Do what? I give her what she wants, which is cock, and that's all."

"That's the least of what she wants," I said. I felt as if all my bones and muscles would disconnect and I would fall into a dry heap on the floor.

"You," Rolando said, his face reddening, "don't think I can make any woman happy, do you? Well, I can. Your sister worships the ground I walk on. By the way, you're going to be in the wedding. Lillian insists upon having a big one." As Rolando paced he was careful to avoid brushing the dusty shelves and kept rubbing his fingertips together as if even the air might soot the perfect whiteness of his suit. "We're going to Paris on our honeymoon," he went on. "We'll rent a car from there and tour Switzerland and Italy. I've always wanted to spend more time in Rome. It's my favorite city. We discussed such a trip ourselves, remember?"

"I remember," I said. I watched him come toward me. "Don't touch me!"

"Your sister likes my touch—you think I couldn't make love to you anymore, but I didn't want to." Rolando's voice was small and full of self-loathing. "She—your sister—wants to pretend now that nothing ever happened between us. She's managed to convince herself. Ruby," Rolando moaned. When he said my name his smug expression broke, and once again, for a second, he looked like the frightened, lonely boy with whom I had imagined I was in love. "You can still stop this, you know. She really won't be happy with me. Every night she threatens to kill herself, for one reason or another. When I make love to her, I have to pretend she's you." Rolando smiled oddly and placed his hands on my shoulders. I could still hear Lillian's muffled voice in the courtyard. "You still want me, I know."

"I don't want you. You're a dead man, Rolando."

He recoiled. His eyes wandered toward the window, as if on the bright sidewalk or among the wind-shaken palms he saw again the woman, my mother's ghost, who stalked him in nightmares. His beautiful eyes widened. "Lillian will do anything for me," he said hoarsely. "If I told her to shoot herself she'd do it." His face was earnest and sad, as if he were awed and dismayed by his power over Lillian. "I could put her on Biscayne Boulevard in trade, if anyone would have her. Anything I want she gives me. I'll ruin her."

"Maybe she'll ruin you," I said.

Rolando's eyes looked full of nightmares as my sister approached, her voice as bright and gay as a crystal bauble. She held up her scrubbed hands for Rolando's inspection. "Can you imagine?" Lillian said. "I'm the first woman he's ever really loved, and I know he's the first man I've ever loved. It's as if we're virgins again." At once she let loose her grip on Rolando and stood with her face pressed against the streaked front window.

"Have you heard anything more about the aliens, about Relga?" I asked. From the drawer beneath the cash register I took a pile of receipts and the ledger and stared at the columns of figures. "My sister has a fantastic gift," I said loudly. "Better even than mine."

"She's given up the outer-space alien. I had to insist,"

Rolando said. "Rushing after all those foolish dreams!"
"It was my choice. I don't need the aliens anymore,"
Lillian said. "I was searching for perfection, and now
I've found it. I don't need any alien to save me."
Rolando stooped beside me, fetched a cowboy hat
from beneath the counter, and placed it at a cocky an-
gle on his shiny black hair. "It's madness, believing in
those aliens. Your mother was mad—there is no swamp
man. And your sister doesn't need to learn charity," he
said, picking up Lillian's purse. "She's one of the few
generous women I've met." I saw Rolando take many
bills from my sister's wallet; he counted the money,
placed two dollars back in the wallet, and threw it into
her purse. "Lillian has put all her money into a joint
account for us both. Didn't you, darling?" Lillian
nodded. "I intend to quadruple that amount by the
end of the week."

"Rolando's lucky at the track," my sister said, casting what I imagined were timid looks at her fiancé and
me. "I give him the horses to play every afternoon."

"If I played your combinations we'd be broke by
now. You have no talent," Rolando said.

"If you don't apologize," Lillian said, her arms
folded smugly, her face and voice threatening, "I'll
make certain you have nightmares every evening this
week. I'll get you."

Rolando was cowed. "I'm sorry," he cried. The sports
pages folded beneath his elegant arm, he kissed my sister on her order, and then he stalked from the shop.

"He's a little nervous," Lillian said, standing at the
front door. Cold air rushed into the shop and made her
cheeks glow. Some woman, she said, had done something dreadful to Rolando, and the experience had
made him afraid. "I understand what it is to have hard
times—you don't, Ruby. I can't tell you the number of
times he's said he'd kill himself for me."

"I can guess," I said grimly. "I bet he wanted you to drive him to the mental hospital for the greatness of his love."

"So, you really are jealous, aren't you?" Lillian said. "He's a gorgeous young man, and any woman would be moved by him, but you'll have him as your brother, and that's enough, isn't it?"

"The three of us will be in heaven," I said.

As if he had been lurking in the alley waiting for Rolando to leave, Victor Riley now strolled into the shop. His silver hair was combed down on his forehead, his mustache was perfectly trimmed and waxed, and he wore his finest clothes: red trousers, a purple-and-red-plaid shirt, a jaunty red silk scarf, and purple patent leather shoes. With a magician's flourish he swept a bouquet of fragrant carnations into Lillian's hands. "For the beautiful bride to be," he said. He laughed then, but his laugh sounded melancholy, and its tone seemed to surprise Victor as much as it surprised me: he cleared his throat and laughed again, and this time seemed pleased. While Lillian stared at the flowers, he nibbled the back of her neck.

My sister swatted at him with the carnations. "Get your dirty, filthy lips off me," she said. "I belong to someone else now, and you know it. I'm nearly a married woman. Tell him, Ruby," she said.

"She's very nearly a married woman, Victor," I said. "Lay off."

"Still carrying on the competition, eh, Ruby?" He gave Lillian the most maddening wink. I tried to think of Artie, my swamp man, and my aunt, to soothe myself by the richness of my life, as I watched Victor walking around Lillian, exclaiming how wonderful she looked. He preferred her out of the caftan, he said, with all her voluptuous curves displayed to make a man go wild. "You really are lovely. Won't you come out with me for one last drink?" He dared to place his hand on Lillian's shoulder. "I've got to talk to you, Lillian."

"What could we possibly have to talk about?" Lillian asked.

"Our relationship," Victor said. When Lillian replied that they had no relationship, Victor scowled and said, "Your wedding present, then. I want you to help me pick out your wedding present."

"I don't remember inviting you to my wedding." But already Lillian's nose was buried in the carnations, and her nostrils quivered, and her eyes became soft and dreamy. She had excellent, charitable eyes. When Victor remarked that her cheeks were far brighter and sweeter-smelling than any flowers, Lillian laughed and said that he was absolutely shameless.

"I'm going to be a faithful wife," she told him.

Victor replied that her words were a knife to his heart. He flung himself into his chair by the magic table in dejected repose, as if to indicate he was in great need of being comforted over his loss. "Do you think I have no feelings at all, Lillian? We were very close, I thought. I imagined," he whispered, gazing at my sister with his mouth slightly open, smoothing his silver mustache and then his bright hair, "that we had love in our relationship. Didn't we, Lillian, or was I so wrong?"

"I thought so," Lillian said softly, "but I didn't know that you thought so. You confused me, Victor." When Lillian stumbled toward him and gave him a gentle kiss, Victor sighed and said she had truly broken his heart by not waiting for him.

"Tell your sister how I feel, Ruby."

"You tell her." I was trying to think of my swamp man, my aunt, and of Artie, but my temper had risen considerably. "Now that you're getting married, you've become attractive to him again. What the hell are you trying to prove, Victor?"

"Oh, shut up, Ruby," Lillian said, laughing and touching her carnations to her cheek. How pretty, she said, receiving flowers made a woman feel.

"Does your young man bring you flowers?" Victor asked. "Does he make love to you as nicely as I did?"

"He makes love very nicely," Lillian said.

Victor, whose face had become very red, said that he thought this marriage was a terrible mistake. "But let's ask Ruby," he said. "How would you rate, by imagination of course, this Rolando, compared, say, to your husband?"

"I wouldn't know," I said. "You have a pathetic way of trying to fix things, Victor."

"Ruby, we're all friends here," Lillian said. Hugging her flowers to her breasts, her arm around my waist, she told Victor the exact manner in which Rolando had proposed: he had been staring out of his window, frightened of some vision he had seen in his sleep after love-making; the vision was of a woman very much like our dead mother, proving how close, how absolutely intertwined were their souls. He proclaimed that Lillian was the only woman who could save him from a life of misery. "I have my ways with him," Lillian said.

Victor seemed to be growing more and more distressed. "I thought that this Rolando was more Ruby's friend. I do recall a conversation with him during which he said—don't pull on your eyebrows, Lillian— that he had never seen a lovelier woman than Ruby."

Lillian's head jerked toward me, and her lips compressed in dismay. "Ruby is a lovely woman," she said. "But your conversation with Rolando must have taken place before he and I got together."

"I do believe," Victor said, his hands clasped over his belly, his legs stretched and crossed at his feet, "that I spoke with Rolando about this not five days ago. But who can keep track of time during these happy hours?"

"Ruby was always the lucky one where men were

concerned," Lillian said. She had begun to pluck apart her flowers. "Men always fell for her." Lillian stared at me with mournful eyes, and her mouth opened several times, as if she wished to say a great many things. "It's true, isn't it, what Victor said? You slept with Rolando just yesterday—I can feel it in my bones. No, wait!" Lillian shut her eyes and held up her hand. "You tried to seduce him, but he said he was in love with me." Hurling her bouquet into my face, she rushed into the stockroom, bolted the door, and sobbed loudly and harshly.

"How could you do this, Victor?" I cried.

"Never mind—I'll fix everything," he said. He knocked several times on the storage room door. "Lillian, come out with me now. I'll make you feel better. Lillian." Victor's voice was high and confident and sweet. "What would you want with that lunatic boy, anyway, when you could have me?"

"You're old," Lillian screamed. She flung open the door and gave Victor such a mighty shove that he fell backward against the counter. "All you are is sixty years old."

Victor's face was as stiff and white as if it had been starched. He stood and carefully brushed off his clothing. "I'm young enough," he said quietly. "I have an appointment in a half hour with the most gorgeous seventeen-year-old. You'll never be seventeen again," he told my sister, who began to cry. Why, he said, in a petulant voice, this beautiful young woman had broken off her engagement to a star college football player in the hope of coaxing him into marriage; and she stood outside his house nights, staring at his windows and calling his name, so that he feared his mad wife would kill them both; once she had hid in his car all evening, had slept naked on the back seat so that he might have the joy and surprise of finding her; and she had been a virgin, too, had not allowed the football player to make love to her, but had let Victor Riley; she was nearly nymphomaniacal in her passion and would do anything at all for him, would spend twenty-four hours a day in bed with him if he let her, if he didn't insist that she have some respect for her parents. "She's little more than a child, and all she wants to do is fuck and suck."

"Why are you telling my sister lies?" When I gazed across the room and into Victor's eyes, I could see such huge horrors I wanted to scream. "She's not seventeen. Closer to fifty, I'd say. She wears a brown wig, doesn't she, Victor? The last time you were in bed with her, no, in the back of her station wagon," I said, closing my eyes, "she complained about the—"

"Shut up with these parlor tricks!" All the cords on Victor's his neck strained, and his eyes seemed full of shocked tears as he backed toward the door. "Parlor tricks—I'm a magician, too, you know. Spying on my life! I'm telling you she's seventeen years old—twenty at the most—and that she likes to fuck me twenty times a day."

After the door had slammed behind him, Lillian wiped her eyes and smiled shyly at me. "He isn't as bad as he sometimes sounds. He just doesn't know very much about women. I'm afraid I've hurt him very much." When I said nothing, she tried to take my hand. "I'm sorry. I'm a little nervous about the wedding."

"I really don't think I should come to your wedding, Lillian," I said. I kept my back to her and banged the ledgers and boxes of old receipts. "Let's just call it quits right now. We can't fix anything now."

"We can't call it quits, and everything can be fixed. You know that, Ruby." Lillian's eyes were full of sorrow, and she said that her wedding would not seem festive if I were not her matron of honor. "If you're not there," she said, kissing my cheek with such tenderness I was confused, "I wouldn't feel hopeful. And my wedding is going to be so beautiful." She said she was going to wear a pink gown, because Rolando thought she looked like a dream in pink. She said she had chosen the most glorious flower arrangements, and in minute, artistic detail described the flowered canopy she had ordered to be erected above our mother's grave.

I laughed in horror. "You're going to have your wedding at the cemetery?"

Lillian's eyes were sparkling. "Rolando's afraid of that, but I did want Mother to be there."

"She's dead."

"Not in my memory. But why are you crying?"

"Don't you know?" Lillian shook her head. "You're only marrying him because you hate me."

"I don't hate you," Lillian said. "I love you. You don't understand, do you?"

"I understand that you couldn't love him."

Lillian said that I had imagined I loved Rolando. "That's why I know he's good. You picked Artie."

"No. Artie picked me," I said.

"It's all the same, isn't it? You haven't made the mistakes I have with men. Please don't tell me Rolando is a mistake," she said. "Even if I did believe you, I can't stop loving him now. I can't suppose the worst of him. Don't tell me he isn't good."

"Then I won't," I said. "I want you to be happy."

In perhaps wishful poetic imagination we said that we had conceived yet another spiritual bond. Toward closing time, after we had talked and fretted over a number of urgent issues and had sought and failed to explain ourselves and our lives, we grew rowdy and light-headed over our failure and fell at last to holding up our hands, just as we had done when we were mystical children outside on an immense and starry night, imagining that we saw God's work in our fingers.

14

In the two weeks before Lillian's wedding, I was certain I was pregnant. I was pure-minded and blissfully optimistic, and favored full blouses, loose trousers, and flat shoes. Mornings I was unable to drink my coffee or look at an egg without retching, but I was ravenous for pasta with clam sauce at the crack of dawn. I gloated over my aching legs and arms and attributed this symptom to early-pregnancy water retention. My cheeks were unusually high-colored—one might say that they glowed—and my modest-sized breasts seemed to have grown beguilingly swollen and tender.

Ripe, slow-moving, and carelessly groomed, I studied children in the supermarket and in my shop and became easily enamored and thought I would like my child to have that baby's energetic eyes, or the red hair or silly smile of another. If my baby was a girl, I hoped she would be strong and independent. I hoped she would never lose her gentleness, and I hoped she would never be afraid without reason. She might become a Supreme Court Justice, with her father's genes, but if not, no matter; she would be pretty but not dangerously so; she would have faith and charity; and she would know that she was loved.

At work I eschewed coffee and drank only herbal teas. Most often I was alone in the shop, with the monkey from the back propped on my lap, its head nestled between my breasts, for company. Victor kept irregular hours, showing up only to recall his friendship with Lillian, whom he now pronounced a fine, sensitive, and intelligent woman, and to wonder where he had gone wrong with her.

Victor told me that he had given up all of his girl friends, including the twenty-five-year-old who had wept hysterically and then had mailed him a silver watch. "The Fox is getting old, Ruby," he told me.

"Sixty isn't old. It isn't young, but it isn't old."

"My wife may be mad, but she needs me. I realize that now. When she has her lucid moments, she loves me more than her life. Too bad she never got any better. I thought, when I married her, that she was going to get better. Do you understand how things have been for me?"

I felt luminescent with understanding. "Of course," I said. "Of course."

"What are you going to do about Lillian?"

"Nothing. I'm going to do nothing."

"She's going to ruin her life," Victor said.

"No, she isn't. She hasn't been ruined yet."

My sister was running all over town, choosing china patterns and a proper trousseau, and came to the shop just once, to have lunch with me. Then I kept my marvelous secret, so as not to steal her thunder, and listened serenely while she laughed about her complex methods of encouraging Rolando's nightmares, in which he always saw our mother in such pose and dress as Lillian would describe just before Rolando fell asleep.

"He looks terrible," she said, grinning.

One morning I drove into town and straightened all

the stock on the shelves, brought the books up to date, advised Posy Adams, Lyla Zimmerman, and the Thurnwood sisters about a suitable wedding present for Lillian, and then sent them into the park with meatloaf sandwiches.

"He's coming," I said. "Your Relga is coming, and Lillian will be back with us soon." I assured the women that Lillian had not deserted her cause but had merely forgotten the dream for a time, as once I had done also. "We can't lose faith now."

In the afternoon I drove all over town looking for Christmas trees. The lots were not yet open but were receiving their first shipments, and from an enterprising truck driver I bought two large and perfect Scotch pines. The first I decorated in a corner of the shop, and sang a carol or two as I strung the tiny pulsing lights, looped the silver foil garlands, and hung the wonderful wooden miniatures. At five o'clock I hung a sign in the front door advising customers that the shop would be closed until January, and I drove home with the spider monkey curled around my neck.

That evening after I had finished decorating my Christmas tree in the living room and had turned out the lights to admire its shape and silver shimmers, I saw a bent shadow at the other side of the room, and then flames sprang up in the fireplace for the first time in many years.

"Happy holidays, Eugene," I said. He stood up quickly, as if he were going to bolt, but I said, "Don't go. I won't come any closer. I won't turn on the lights."

I sat on the couch, and after a time I could hear Eugene picking out Christmas carols on the piano. He began to sing in a mournful voice, his melancholy turning tender every word, every note. It hurt me grandly to listen.

"You're nice," I said. "I think you're one of the few things in the world I'm not afraid of. I wish I could do something for you, but you won't even let me touch you."

I came to learn that if I sat in the darkness in the living room with the tree lights shimmering soft colors into the dark and silver icicles, Eugene would creep downstairs and start up a fire. He would sit on his heels before the snapping, glowing logs as long as I did not approach him. But when Artie called from Curaçao and I switched on the lights to cross the room, Eugene bolted, as a fairy boy must.

"You mean I'm going to be a father?" Artie cried after I had told him the news. "Are you certain, Ruby?"

"Fairly certain." My recent illness, I said, must have coincided with conception, for some women became lethargic immediately after becoming pregnant. I was nauseated in the morning, I said, and my breasts seemed to be swelling. "You have wonderful sperm," I told him.

"I always suspected as much," Artie said. "Drink milk now, Ruby. I'll be home just as soon as I can. There's been a delay in the land sale."

"Who's delaying it?" I asked.

Artie said in a proud, stubborn voice, "I am. I won't be under anyone's thumb."

He called me several times a day to discuss the subtle, but, in retrospect, very significant physical changes he had noticed in me before he had left for the islands. My eyes had appeared glassy, he said, and I had shown an inordinate interest in discussing our baby's future. The more he thought about the matter, the more certain he was that I was pregnant.

Janet Monsterville recalled the three times she had been pregnant and said she believed in a mother's intuition: she had always known the moment she had conceived. "Only my babies always fell out dead. But this one's for both of us. You'll share the baby with me," she said, smiling.

"Yes. I'll share my baby with you."

"That's nice. Then I don't have to die right away." Janet patted my stomach, which was still flat and firm, and then went up to the bedroom where I had slept as a child. She would pull the old crib from the storage room, she said, and paint it a cheerful color. "I feel like a mother," she said and then, staring down at her swollen legs and feet, said, "I'm just as puffed up."

A week before Lillian's wedding she replaced the bedspread in my old bedroom with a yellow organdy coverlet, her present, she told me, to our baby. On the coverlet she put some new stuffed animals, and in one of the bureau drawers she placed an exquisite sweater that had been given to her at her own first baby shower. She smiled to think that my swamp man had been sleeping in the baby's room. Often, she said, when she entered the room she could see an indentation on the bed, and sometimes Eugene left one of the stuffed animals on the floor in his haste to flee. "I heard that music box you put in there just playing and playing," Janet said.

One evening I came across Eugene sleeping in a corner of the hall. I bent to put a blanket over him and was unable to resist touching his cheek, which was remarkably soft. Eugene jumped up immediately, and although the hall was too dark for me to make out his features accurately, I could see that his eyes were shining with tears.

"Don't touch me!" he said.

"Where are you from?" I called as my swamp man scampered down the hall. He paused for a moment at the stairs to the third floor. "My sister says you're from outer space. She'll remember how she means to catch you one day," I said, teasing.

Eugene cried, "Don't let her. Please—don't let her." The next morning, wondering at my poor sprite's fearfulness, I drove into town and bought him what I thought would be the correct size clothing for a thin boy, about five feet tall. These clothes I placed at the foot of the stairs leading to the third floor. Some hours later I caught a glimpse of the new red woolen sweater, and when I cried out how grand Eugene looked, he screeched angrily, as if to insist upon his independence.

"Don't be angry. I know I need you more than you need me." In the dim light I could see Eugene hanging over a railing, looking down at me. "Will you stay with me forever? Forever and ever, Eugene?"

"Forever and ever," he replied. When I gathered up the courage to mount the stairs, meaning to embrace him, he was already gone.

Early each morning I walked through the chilly woods to the river where a festive mist rose and swirled. There I hoped to meet my aunt, whose house I was still afraid to enter. What I feared I was unable to pinpoint; but always, as I approached her cabin, I was compelled to turn around and make certain Eugene was with me. He darted through the brush, singing strange and pretty tunes.

"You are the loveliest creature," I called. "I want to keep you always."

Janet Monsterville, queerly subdued, moved slowly through the house. I watched her and tried to feed her vitamins and help her with her work.

"You don't be helping me—you sit," she said, finally planting me in a kitchen chair. "We ain't going to ruin our baby. Working too hard was how I lost mine." Janet crashed the dishes together in the sink and said that my sister had called her. "She wants me to come to that stupid wedding of hers, but I ain't sitting in no cemetery. I'd like to set her some place and light a torch to her."

"Lillian doesn't deserve that. What's wrong with you?" I asked.

"First the Lord came to me and I got rid of all my men so I'm good and alone and sick. Now I keep dreaming. I have these dreams about seeing my mama in Georgia, and they scare me. My mama loves me. I only get the kind of love I want from men in dreams, but I dream sweet. God can't hold my dreams against me."

"I'm sure He wouldn't. Last night," I said, "I dreamed of my first kiss. It was so lovely, Janet. But then I saw my mother, either saw her or dreamed her—"

"Don't know which, either, in this crazy house," Janet cried, her eyes bulging, her large body suddenly erect, as if she had become all of the spirit and fire of a wild boar. "Don't know which or what."

"That's right. But why should I still see her?"

"You must want to," Janet said. "I walk here and I ain't never seen her. You must want to love your mama, like I want to love mine. Lord, I sure want to run back to her. I will, too, some day."

"I thought you were going to die," I said, smiling, although when I peered into her eyes, I winced. I kissed her suddenly. "I'm glad you've decided to live."

"What—me die, when you about to be coming down with morning sickness, throwing up every hour? No," Janet said, her eyes bulging, her large body suddenly erect, as if she had become all of the spirit and fire of a and take care of you and the boss and the baby. After a while, when the baby is grown, I'm going to go on home to Georgia. And you can send me pictures of my godchild. In the meantime, I can practice being a nice nurse with the ghosty. Here, little ghosty," Janet called. She slugged chocolate syrup into a glass and filled it with milk. She placed the glass in the hall near the stairs, and when next we looked, the milk was gone. "Oh, I just love that boy. He's too good for this earth. He scares me sometimes, he's so good."

Oh, he's good, we both sang, he is so very good. "He helps me with my work because he knows I'm sick and I'll feed him something nice," Janet said. "He's helped me, too. He inspires me. My trouble has got to be past now," I said. Still, nights I saw my mother, and still, she looked angry with me.

Artie did not return home until the day before Thanksgiving. I was sitting in the kitchen drinking hot tea when I looked up and saw him leaning in the doorway with his luggage at his feet. His dark suit was as rumpled as if he had been sleeping badly for days in it, but he grinned proudly, impishly, as he crossed the kitchen to kiss me. He had brought me flowers and several books about raising children, and he was so excited about how important our lives were to become that he seemed to have forgotten all about his business dealings in Curaçao.

"Oh, that," he said, in a mild, cheerful voice. "The deal was delayed, and so I sold out to the Judge. Don't look so surprised, Ruby." Artie said that the old man thought he was foolish, particularly since his had been the only objection to the land sale, which was bound to go through any day. "We could have gotten twice the money for the land—it was the principle of the matter," Artie said.

Soon, he said, the world would know what kind of man Arthur Holloway was. "I think I've got everything figured out," he said, twisting up his finger. "The stock market is down at the moment. I made twenty thousand above my original investment in Curaçao, and I might do very well to invest in Coca-Cola while the prices are still down."

"A captain of Wall Street!" I said, smiling.

"Do you think I'm stupid?" Artie asked. "Do you think I was crazy to sell out at the last minute?"

"No," I said. "I think you did exactly the right thing. I'm proud of you. But when did you decide to sell out?"

"Two weeks ago," Artie said, "when the Judge came for me, and I had a pain in my chest. I'm a man with everything to look forward to now. Let the others kill themselves in the islands. I'm satisfied with what I got. Have you been to the doctor, Ruby?"

"I don't need to go. A woman knows about these things. Besides, it's too early for a test."

Artie stood entranced before the nursery door and admired the yellow organdy bedspread Janet had bought, the stuffed animals, and the newly painted crib. He unpacked many gifts: teething rings and silver rattles, a very soft blue pillow shaped like a fanciful fish, a soccer ball, a bonnet, and a solid gold spoon.

In Copenhagen, he said, we would take the baby to Tivoli, where our alert and intelligent baby would watch the acrobats and ride in a boat shaped like a dragon; in Vienna the baby would attend the children's opera on Saturday and afterward eat ice cream at the Stadtpark. "Don't you want to do this, Ruby?" Artie asked.

I was staring at my stomach with astonishment. "I have cramps," I said.

My husband's mouth turned down. He said softly, "It doesn't mean anything. Women have cramps when they're pregnant, too." In Venice, he said, the baby would sit in a stroller at St. Mark's Square and watch his father feed the pigeons; his child would some day marry and have children, and then he would be a grandfather many times over. He would not have made much of a tycoon anyway, he told me, because the men in his family did not take success well. "I think I'd do well to stick to law. I'll start a new practice when I'm ready, and keep it small. What's that?" Artie stepped into the hall and looked up and down. "I thought I saw something dart away."

"That was my swamp man."

Artie laughed. "Why haven't I seen him before?"

"I guess you had no need to."

Artie slept restlessly all afternoon and into the evening, and I slept restlessly beside him. We bolted from our pillows at the same time, and at the same time shuddered and complained of nightmares.

"I saw my mother again," I said.

"And I saw my father." Artie looked defiant as he glanced around the room. "He was pointing his finger at me, no doubt because I left Curaçao early, and he looked older than he should have. But I'm not afraid," he said. "Don't you be afraid either."

"I'll try," I said.

We tossed in bed and watched the clock and wondered how the weather would be for Lillian's wedding. We did not feel like going to a wedding at a cemetery, we said, but supposed we must. We drank hot milk and rearranged our pillows, until at last Artie said that he had an idea that would lull us to sleep. "I'll tell a story. Once upon a time," he began, but stopped. "I can't think of a single story. You try."

"Once upon a time," I said, "lived a very good king."

Artie immediately interrupted me. "Where did he live?"

"Where would you like him to live?"

"It's your story," Artie said.

I said, "He lived in Germany."

"Not Germany," Artie said. "For some reason I don't believe Germany."

"How about Scotland?"

"France. France is better. Is the king young or old?"

If the king was too old, he said, the story might lack possibility, and if the king was too young, Artie might feel he had nothing in common with him. We fretted over the king's age until dawn, and when I stood to pace away my confusion, Artie pointed at the sheets.

"Look," he said. He tried to catch my arm as I rushed into the bathroom. "Why be upset this particular month?"

"Because we were ready."

"I can wait. I'm not going anyplace," Artie said.

"Do you promise?"

When I left the bathroom, Artie was staring at a tray of food on his dresser. "Somebody was just in this room," he said. "I was pulling the sheets from the bed, and when I turned around, I saw the tray. I do believe this house is haunted after all." He touched the coffee pot, as if he wanted to make certain it was real, and lifted a piece of buttered toast to his lips. "I have it," he said, smiling proudly. "We'll make the king young-hearted, and take it from there tonight."

"I love stories about young-hearted kings," I said.

15

After his first good deed that morning Eugene was a terror, like a child who had awakened cranky and spiteful. While Artie and I were getting dressed, he began howling as if he were dying. After having completed an unsuccessful search for a wounded or dead person, we returned to our bedroom to discover the contents of our bureau drawers dumped on the carpeting.

"Your swamp man, Ruby?"

"Yes, my swamp man."

"I didn't see him, but I could hear him," he said.

At first I was unable to find the purple hat that matched the hooped purple dress Lillian had sent to the house; I found it beneath the bed along with the shoes I had meant to wear, the heels of which had been deliberately broken off. "Eugene," I shouted, shaking my fist at the empty hall. "He doesn't want us to go to the wedding," I told Artie.

Artie walked to the door and stood there for several moments. "I never believed in ghosts before, but I think I see a strange shadow at the end of the hall." He went to the dresser to choose a pair of cuff links, but was unable to locate his jewelry box in its customary corner. "Where could I have put it?" he said, scratching his head. After much searching he discovered that the box had fallen beneath the bureau. His wallet and keys were also missing, and these we pulled from beneath a couch cushion in the living room. "Maybe I'm just becoming forgetful," Artie said. He laughed when he saw me dressed in my ill-fitting frock and put his arm around my shoulders. "We're both getting older."

Artie's car would not start, and he had to tinker with and cajole the engine for a long while, spotting his trench coat and hair with grease, before he found that an essential wire had been disconnected. "One of the ghosts," he said. "Is it possible, I wonder, to be haunted without even knowing it?"

"Ghosts are tricky." I shivered in the cold morning air. Buzzards flew in shrieking broken circles over the mist-obscured trees, and I pulled my white shawl more tightly over my shoulders. My river and my aunt's cabin would be nearly hidden in the fog. "My swamp man prefers us to stay here."

"I won't be under your swamp man's thumb," Artie said. "Get into the car, Ruby."

As we drove away, I saw Eugene creep onto the front porch—just a gray shadow in the chilly gray morning. The saddest, silliest beeping noise escaped his lips as he watched the car bump along the dirt lane and turn sharply into the woods.

"Artie?" I said, during the long, quiet drive east. "I'm afraid to be so close to my mother's grave."

"She's dead—she can't hurt you now," Artie said, although his voice was full of uncertainty.

Many cars and people moved along the cement drive of the cemetery in which my mother had been buried. On that Thanksgiving morning we passed three funerals, and I remembered how angry Lillian had been when I had neglected to cry over my mother's casket. The last funeral we passed was hugely attended, and even in the car I could hear sobbing. Rubbing a clear spot on the misted window, I saw a woman in black collapse on the wet grass and watched a man—he was wearing a red baseball cap—stoop to help her.

"Sometimes I miss my mother, Artie," I said. "I know I didn't feel anything when she died, except for fear, because she said she would haunt, and I knew her word was iron. But just recently, I've begun to miss her. I don't even know why."

"Sometimes I miss my father, despite everything."

"Despite what? You loved him and worshipped him."

"That's right," Artie said, and his eyes locked far into his past and grew dull with memories I could easily decipher.

"My captain of Wall Street," I said, patting his hand.

Artie pulled the car up against a mound behind Victor Riley's small car. Across the grass and beyond the trees I could see a gaily decorated canopy, and from its edges blew crepe-paper streamers of pink and white. Beneath the canopy roof was my mother's grave.

"Rolando isn't going to show up." Staring up into the cold, gray sky as if I were looking into the depths of the future, I said I knew he was going to jilt Lillian and run off with all her money.

"Maybe things will work out for your sister." Artie frowned and rubbed at a spot of grease on his trench coat and fussed with his hair and tie. "People know a man by his appearance," he told me.

I giggled, looking down at my purple dress and its huge, pink silk roses, which covered my bosom with mermaidish modesty. "No," I said, "Rolando is absolutely not going to show up, and Lillian will just die then."

Artie seemed not to hear me but strode on ahead. I followed him up the wet, grassy slope, and beyond the canopy of white and pink roses—my mother's favorite flower and mine—and behind a row of crypts topped with trumpeting, heavy-lidded angels, I saw Lillian leaning against a cold wall. Her hooped skirt stood out like a huge pink balloon. Clamoring around her with brushes and hair spray were her psychic friends: Grace and Clara Thurnwood in identical gray suits, Lyla Zimmerman in a yellow lace dress, yellow gloves, and yellow hat, and Posy Adams in green and white.

"Only Lillian would think to have her wedding here, and although I admire her originality, I think this was a poor choice," Victor Riley said, coming toward Artie and me. Behind him, near the chairs arranged to the left and right of the wedding canopy, were several middle-aged men and women talking in hushed Spanish. Apart from them was a stony-faced group of women, well dressed and fashionably made up.

"His family and old girl friends," Victor said, nodding at Artie. He shivered beneath his heavy woolen coat and shook hands with my husband with a kind, pleasant-uncle expression. "I don't like this. I don't like this at all. If I weren't such close friends with Lillian I would have stayed at home with my sick wife and watched the football games."

"You'll be home soon enough," I said. "It's obvious that the shithead won't show."

At once Victor's eyes slid to the left, and I saw a white-suited figure lurking in a despondent posture behind a tree.

"I've been meaning to ask you a legal question," Victor said, putting his arm around Artie and drawing him away.

Rolando wended his way through the tombstones

like a gorgeous but pale and sullen vampire; his dark eyes glowed, his black hair curled beautifully on his forehead and around his ears. He nodded and walked past me slowly, as if he were merely rambling on a fine day, but then he reached back and touched my arm. "You lose, Ruby."

"No—you lose, Rolando," I said. I rushed to my husband's side and put my arm into his. I watched Rolando talk animatedly, first with his relatives and then with his old girl friends. "I want to go home," I said to Artie. "I'm not feeling well."

"You'll be all right," Artie said.

Victor said, "It isn't such a happy occasion for your wife. She never got along with that fellow. She told him several times she thought he was just using Lillian. Ruby was very brave."

"Don't be sad, then," Artie said, smiling. "You've done everything you could."

I choked. Victor squeezed my arm and shook his head very slightly. When Rolando approached again, Victor stepped in front of me.

"Nice setup here," Victor said, rolling his eyes.

Rolando smirked and stared past my husband at me. "Lillian forced me to have the wedding here. I was against the idea, but sometimes I'm powerless to change her mind." When he gazed about, my eyes followed his to the tombstones, the metal markers, the brown-edged flower arrangements, the rattling, damp trees, and to the crypt beyond which Lillian wept. Not more than twenty headstones away from us, a funeral party approached an open grave, and when the crowd parted I caught a glimpse of the casket, and I sobbed aloud.

"Ah, Ruby, you always were sentimental," Victor said, smiling at Artie, who looked stricken with fear each time he glanced from Rolando to me.

"And how do you feel?" Artie said in a faint voice, clapping Rolando's shoulder. "Nervous?"

"No more than a dead man," Rolando said, wandering away.

"I told you the man is perverse," Victor said. "Ruby, you're a good judge of character. Still, you shouldn't let him upset you. Go to Lillian now. I see the preacher coming, and I'm sure your sister wants to talk to you before the ceremony. Poor Lillian is ready to jump out of her skin."

When I approached the side of the crypt where Lillian leaned face forward against the marble, Grace and Clara Thurnwood let out a cry in perfect unison, as psychic twins would in troubled times. Their blue eyes seemed ablaze with worry over Lillian, and they touched her arms and smoothed her crimped, curled red hair.

"Don't cry, Lillian," I said, putting my arms around my sister. I turned her around, took her hands from her face, and told her how lovely she looked.

Without her glasses, her eyes seemed as ethereal and misty as the cemetery. Her face was pale, except for her cheeks, which were red and hot to my touch. "I don't think Mother is happy with me today, Ruby," she said. She clutched me awkwardly, for the width of our skirts made sisterly caresses difficult. She said she had sensed Mother's anger the moment she had arrived. "I've neglected the work I promised to do. I'm frightened."

"I'm frightened, too, but it's all air, it's nothing," I said, snapping my fingers. Not far from us, I could see Rolando in solemn conversation with the preacher. The peculiar maniac beauty of his face now struck me with the same force as it had the first day I saw him wander the aisles of my shop. That had not been so very long ago, but in the mist of the cemetery I felt as if a hundred years had passed.

Lillian stared toward him, too. "He's got his old girl friends here today—he thinks he's going to make a fool of us all, that skunk. Do you still love him?" she asked. Her cheek was wet against mine.

"No," I said.

"I love him. I know it's crazy, because he wants to ruin me, but I do love him. Nevertheless!" Lillian smiled suddenly and proudly, as if she had a triumphant secret. She stepped forward when the preacher neared. "I'm ready now," she said. Her face contorted between the clouds of red hair. "We won't be afraid, Ruby," she said, staring toward the canopy, its fluttering pink and white streamers, and beneath, in shadow, our mother's tombstone.

"Whenever you're ready," the preacher said. "First your sister, and then you. Have you got the ring?"

"Yes," Lillian said. She watched the preacher depart, and then she pushed me gently. "Go on," she whispered. "I promise you it'll be fine." Then I was walking alone toward the canopy. My feet moved remarkably well, I thought, over the wet, short-mowed grass. My purple silk skirt rustled around my legs, and its hoops knocked against the chairs and legs of those who stood and smiled uneasily.

Rolando stood smirking to the left of my mother's tombstone—an elaborately scrolled marker Lillian had chosen many years ago, full of granite eyes and fruit-bearing trees in whose branches genies perched. "You lose," he whispered again.

A voice, an unbearably kind and tender voice echoing my mother's mood and spirit before she had known much disappointment, before she had experienced the dread of what she had imagined was final failure, seemed to play around my ears. I imagined Lillian also heard the voice as she walked down the aisle, for she turned her head, and sobs escaped her lips. As she reached the canopy her bouquet of lilies of the valley fell from her hands, and I stooped and returned the flowers to her.

"Ruby," Rolando groaned. I caught a single glimpse of Artie's distraught face, saw Victor place his hand on my husband's arm and whisper in his ear, before I turned toward the preacher again.

I gulped cold air as the preacher's voice droned, and my skin hurt with the voice that continued to rise like a splendid and sad concerto from the ground. My heart contracted with fear, sorrow, and pity at my mother's life. Nearing the middle of the ceremony I imagined that my mother was sitting up in her casket and scratching to be let out, as if she could stop what I had been unable to prevent myself.

"Look down at the ground, Rolando," Lillian suddenly whispered. Her eyes were triumphant and still fixed upon the preacher, whose only indication of having been interrupted was a barely marked quickening of his speech. "Look down, and tell me what you see."

"You're crazy. Witch!" Rolando was compelled to gaze at the tombstone. His black eyes bulged, and he shook himself as if he were trying to awaken from a very sound bad dream.

The preacher had just completed asking the first vow and was smiling as he waited for his answer, although a deep wrinkle had appeared in his brow. My sister punched Rolando's arm with a force that caused him first to stagger and then to fall flat on his face against the very place he so dreaded, near the woman who had so persistently and horribly haunted him. "I said for you to look down," Lillian repeated.

Rolando's screams filled the cemetery and rocketed past the iron gates. "That woman—your mother. When will she leave me?" His fingers clawed the grass, and Lillian muttered what I recognized as a nonsensical curse, a mere limerick of the occult with which she must have taunted Rolando many times.

Still, Rolando got up with the help of the preacher and brushed himself off. "Let's get this over with," he growled.

"I'm not marrying you," Lillian said, in a clear, casual voice that must have taken enormous courage for her to summon.

"But Lillian—our love," Rolando cried.

Lillian wiped her fingers on her skirt to indicate her hands were washed of the entire affair. "Don't look so surprised," she said. "I told you and told you. I always get even. Frog and snake eyes," she cried. "Lightning strike and thunder rumble—blindness and living death!"

Rolando screamed and covered his eyes with both arms.

Even after Lillian had turned and run across the grass, our audience was very quiet, still waiting soberly and respectfully for a wedding and then the cake.

Rolando shouted, "You can't put any of your curses on me. I have curses of my own, you know." His murderous eyes slid from me to Artie, who had walked very near the grave site. "You're a fool," he shouted, stepping forward. Something, perhaps the sweetness of my husband's face, frightened him, for he quickly stepped back. "You're not a man at all. Do you really think I was the only one?"

"Yes," Artie said, his face so shockingly pale I thought I could read the candlelike flickerings of his soul.

Rolando had only to glance at the grave before he tossed himself onto the grassy mound again, weeping and screaming about a living death.

A pretty woman in a red silk dress rushed to his side. "My poor, darling boy," she whispered. "Annie will take care of you again—my poor, darling boy."

"It's true, isn't it, Ruby?" Artie said.

Victor Riley shoved through a knot of now wildly gesturing and arguing relatives to reach my husband. He said, "It isn't true. It isn't true at all. I've made several passes at Ruby, but she wouldn't have anything to do with me."

"Shut up, Victor," I cried. Artie stared at me. He looked like an old and palsied man. His silence and his wet eyes were monstrously eloquent. "What should I do, Artie?" I asked. "Artie, tell me what I should do."

"Nothing," he said. "Do nothing."

"Very often I saw other men make passes at your wife, but she rudely turned down every last one of them," Victor said, patting Artie's shoulder. "And if she wouldn't have me, after all, who would she have?"

Artie's punch took Victor by surprise and sent him staggering backward. An astonished and rather happy expression was on his face as he fell.

"Leave me alone now, Ruby," Artie said. "Just leave me alone." He walked away rapidly, and when I rushed after him, tripping and entreating, he merely changed his direction, as if he were being annoyed by a large insect.

Behind me Rolando still shrieked and wept with his face in the grass, while his lady friend sighed and tilted her head above him.

"Leave me—when will you leave me?" Rolando screamed.

"Poor Rolando," the woman in the red dress said. "My poor, pretty baby." Then I heard another voice rising above the others.

My mother's voice was sweet and tender, and her face was as I remembered it before she had known many indelible fears: I was sitting in the wide wooden boat beside my sister, watching Mother row us down the river with strong, perspiring arms.

"The first time I came out here to look at the land," my mother was saying as we made our way through the swamp that seemed to shake with miraculous life, "I saw a strange light, and I heard—I did but my Sam didn't—the kindest voice. It was a sign, that light and that voice. I knew it. I remembered my great aunt Naomi's dreams about a strange creature who was supposed to save her, and I knew then that he'd come to me here. The women in our family are chosen—listen," she said, her eyes big in the shade of her bonnet. "Hear that? Listen hard now, babies, look as far and as well as you can."

Lillian and I looked, and we listened. I could hear only the pumping breasts of frogs, the occasional bellow of an alligator, the sharp cries of egrets, and the sunny splashes of mercurial flying fish. "Snakes," I said, huddling closer to my mother. I was just then three. Sally was in her late twenties.

"Don't be afraid. There's a whole universe out here, planets, stars, all left for us. It's mysterious now, and scary. But all it needs is the light and the music set to the right words. We'll put them there, once he comes to us."

The souls of the kind dead flocked to these vast, empty lands, Sally said, and creatures that could not be found in any encyclopedia or storybook roamed the swamps. She said that half-men–half-apes, visitors of great charity from other planets, looked for magical kisses from beautiful and good women. In the Everglades were the memory of all times and the future of all life. Sally listened to her childlike elves hid in the mossy hollows of the ancient cypress.

"When I learn to love," she said, "as I'm supposed to—and I will, babies, because I want to—I'll be able to see everything in the world and around the world and light-years beyond the world. And then my Sam will never leave us—not ever. He'll stay with us always, and we'll live happily ever after, just like princesses in a fairy tale."

I remembered, my heart contracting and swelling, how she used to read to us and tell us stories nearly every night, and those stories, I knew then, were love. Some of her own stories were so wonderfully fanciful and joyous they made me cry, and I could not understand why my father would not stay with her.

When I reentered the present I found myself in Victor's car. He was driving slowly, carefully along the cemetery road. I saw an old man walking toward the gates, his pink head bent and flushed, his large gnarled hands spinning a black umbrella. When I saw him turn, I imagined he stared toward the canopy beneath which my mother still stirred and sent messages.

"Daddy," I shouted.

"Don't," Victor said, taking hold of my arm as I tried to open the car door. "Let me take you home."

"But my father," I said. I was trembling with life.

"Not now," Victor said. "Not this moment, Ruby."

16

As we traveled west toward home, a rain tapped the car roof with a sound as gentle as running swamp-man feet. The light had failed very early. The dark, orchid-rolled canals and the green-and-brown fields were veiled by afternoon twilight and mist, and the gloom signaled that the night would grow clear and colder, with stabbing stars and icy white moon. I wondered where Artie would sleep that Thanksgiving night, and I imagined that we had become profound lovers. I could have looked to see where Artie would go, but I still did not know how to use my gift.

Victor kept clearing his throat, and then, for want of anything else to say, I suppose, he related the story of how he had lost his virginity on his eleventh birthday with a butcher's thirty-five-year-old wife. "Her husband was very ill-tempered—that was the real attraction," he said in a tired voice. "I carried on with her for six years but had to stop when she wanted to be friends with me."

I hung my head so that my face was hidden by my hair. "Artie was very good today, wasn't he?"

"He wasn't when he hit me." Victor smiled as he touched his narrow jaw. "He'll come back, Ruby. I'm never wrong about these things. I can't imagine why he should love you, but there it is. He'll come home soon."

"I don't know what to say to him." I rubbed my cheek against the cold window and watched the canals and fields rushing past in the rain.

"All that carrying on at the wedding confused me," Victor said, pulling thoughtfully on his mustache. "I think perhaps you're all mad, you and your sister, your husband and Rolando. I've certainly never carried on the way all of you did today."

"You were nice at the wedding," I said. "You were trying to protect me and Artie."

"Only because the cemetery unnerved me, and I wanted to keep busy. I didn't care what happened. I don't care about much of anything. When you know all about life, very few surprises remain."

"I'm constantly surprised, and some say I have a gift," I said.

"Nonsense," Victor said, in a voice both sweet and instructive. "Take the word of a man who has figured it all out. You have no psychic gift, and no swamp man is going to fly into your house this evening to save you from the consequences of your mistakes."

"I feel miserable," I said.

"Do you? Tell me exactly how you feel." Victor's eyes glistened as he encouraged me to tell him of my most dreadful mistakes, which he thoroughly analyzed, and of my dreams, which seemed to him silly and wrongheaded.

We reached the house about three o'clock in the afternoon. Victor stood beside the car, looking up and about, and said, "I've never seen a house like this. I can't imagine—I admit my imagination fails me—why your mother would have built this place." When I looked at the house with new vision, I could see that

even in its madness my mother had indeed puffed a sort
of disorderly beauty into white wood railings, sudden
angles, bizarre additions, and dripping eaves, and so
had fashioned a reflection of her busy, lonely soul.

I thanked Victor for driving me home. "I guess your
wife will be holding Thanksgiving dinner for you." But
as I approached the porch steps, holding up my huge
purple skirt from the mud, I turned and saw Victor
standing in a forlorn posture very much like my swamp
man's. He sighed deeply, and behind his head dark
branches formed lonely, ventricular patterns that broke
and rattled in the wind.

"Would you like to come in?" I asked. When I opened
the front door, I was startled by the sight of Eugene
standing at the end of the hall, his eyes so mournful I
cried out, and what I cried out was my husband's name.

"Why did you shout so?" Victor said, his eyes roving
over my mother's paintings, her heavy brass fixtures,
her odd and beautiful space.

"I saw a ghost," I said. "He looked like Artie for a
moment, and then he ran."

Victor took my arm and helped me up the stairs,
insisting upon resting every few steps so that I could
gather my senses. At the bedroom door I balked. Victor
said, "Don't worry. I'm not going to try anything with
you now." He sat in the chair farthest from the bed and
said I ought to shower and crawl beneath the blankets
for a nice nap.

"You're very kind," I said.

"And you thought I wasn't human."

I cried for perhaps a half hour in the tub, and I
tried—but failed—to imagine that Artie heard my crying and was moved by it. When I came out of the bathroom in my flannel pajamas and flannel robe, my hair
pinned to the top of my head, I saw that Victor had
removed his coat and was sitting very straight in his
chair, staring at a tray with hot tea and sandwiches.

"Did you see Eugene?" I asked.

"I caught a glimpse of him when I was taking off my coat—he ran off as soon as he set down the tray. He's a stubborn fellow, isn't he? I asked him a question and he didn't even bother to answer."

"He's independent," I said, getting into bed. "He answers only when he wants to."

Victor held his tea cup elegantly aloft, one jeweled pinky precisely curved, and said, "I wouldn't keep a servant like him, Ruby. He has no manners. No manners at all."

From the bed I could see Eugene sitting in the gloom on the stairs. His head was slightly tilted, and his chin rested on his small, delicately formed hand and his arm on his thin knee. At Victor's words his head jerked, and he wailed aloud. I said quickly, "He has the best of manners, Victor. He's the gentlest creature I know."

"If he were gentle, he wouldn't howl so infernally."

"He hurts—he still hurts," I said.

Victor drank three cups of tea with sugar and ate four sandwiches, which, he called into the hall, were excellently prepared. Then he settled comfortably into his chair and stared at me for a long time. "I don't understand you," he said. "It wasn't sex you were after, because you turned me down. What the hell did you want?"

When I said that I was after the essential thing, which was soul, Victor looked startled and said he had never been ambitious enough to go after any souls.

"I'm alone," Victor said, yawning. "I'm quite used to it and comfortable enough, thank you."

"I'm not. Artie's gone—who's going to stay with me now?" As if to answer, my swamp man wailed, and although Victor started in his chair, he said nothing about the noise but nibbled casually on another sandwich as if no extraordinary banshee's cries drifted down a long dusty hall into the bedroom. That wonderful boy-creature cried so sweetly I wanted to lick his cheeks, and I thought my mother had been very loving indeed to send me such a grand and inventive present. Full darkness fell quickly that Thanksgiving Day. Victor nodded asleep in his chair, and I dozed in bed. We awoke at the same time. Eugene had apparently crept into the room and tucked a comforter around Victor's shoulders. Victor drew the blanket closer around him, murmuring, and then his head sank once again. I kept watch from my bed and could see the slight shadow cast by my swamp man as he crouched in soft navy light just beyond the door.

"Can't you make Artie come home now?" I asked.

By midevening a profuse, glistening sweat had collected on Victor's forehead, as if he were making up for lost anxieties. Even his mustache looked drenched. In sleep he whimpered like my swamp man, and in sleep he bolted upright from his chair like my husband.

"I had a dream," he gasped, looking around without focusing. "I rarely dream."

"It's this house." I reached above the bed to turn on the light. When I saw that Victor was trying to hide his weeping, I thought I understood, at least in part, why my mother had built this house: for all its rooms and veering halls, for all its empty wings and its towers, she had left no place in which a heart could forever hide. Victor was responding to her ghost. "Everybody dreams in this house."

"I'm not like everyone." Victor shuddered and sank once again into his chair. I murmured from my bed, but he cast me a livid glance. "I'm not afraid, and I don't need your comfort," he told me. When Eugene began wailing again, Victor rushed to the bed and sat beside me. "I don't believe in ghosts, Ruby."

"I know." I picked up a corner of my blanket and wiped his face.

"It was only a dream," he said, breathing more easily

then. "I don't believe in dreams, and I don't believe in ghosts. But I wonder, theoretically, of course, if ghosts did exist, if they would blame me. Why should there be ghosts?"

Although Eugene howled like a moonstruck beast, Victor pretended not to notice. I said I guessed the only reason ghosts came to the living was so that we would remember them properly. "What did you dream?" I asked.

"It's too terrible to repeat," Victor said, covering his face with his hands. When he looked up, a mask seemed to have fallen over his features, and there was Victor Riley the magician. He laughed and pranced across the room and appeared to snatch from midair a bottle of perfume that moments before had been resting on my bureau.

"You see?" he said, twisting up a finger. "Nothing hurts me, Ruby. Especially not dreams. I'm a very special person after all. You look silly in bed." He sat at my side, wrinkling his nose and smoothing back his glorious hair. His eyes glittered as he touched my arm; but then the lights went out, as if a fuse had been pulled.

Victor was thrust from the bed. I saw his lavender legs, lit by moonlight, being dragged across the white bedroom carpeting, and his fingers clawing first the bedsheets and then the bureau legs. "Help!" Victor screamed. Eugene must have found it difficult to pull Victor through the door and into the hall, for I could hear the door bumping against its hinges. But at last my swamp man's incredibly strong, though very thin, limbs pulled his victim free. I heard a great gasp, and then the sound of Victor Riley being dragged and then tumbled down the stairs to the first floor.

At first I was afraid to move, for all was so quiet I thought Victor must be dead. But then I heard him groaning, and when I reached the foot of the stairs, he was trying to sit up. He was calling for someone whose name I could not make out; perhaps he called for his mother, or his wife. When the lights went on, he sat up and probed a huge bump on his forehead. He cried, "It's true—you're mad—throwing me down the stairs that way!"

"I did not." Eugene started up his howling once again. "You're too heavy—I wouldn't be able to lift you if I wanted to."

"It was that inscrutable tray-carrying maniac then— first your husband and now him. I'll press charges." When I explained that Eugene had simply wished to prevent any more mistakes, Victor shouted, "How dare he meddle in my business? I don't even know him." Victor stood, brushing himself off with his fists.

"Well, he must think that he knows you," I said. "He must like you, too. He doesn't show himself often."

"He has a strange way of showing affection—poor, mad devil."

Explaining that my very moral houseguest had many times rebuked me in such a manner, I took Victor into the kitchen and held a lump of ice against his bruised forehead.

"This is very nice—you're like a sister to me now." Victor was smiling as we walked into the hall. "Pretty tree," he said, staring from the hall into the living room. The tree lights had been turned on, and the icicles shimmered, black and silver, red and green. From the back stairs, beyond the wall against which the piano was set, came a ragged-rhythmed plunking and the laughter of a sprite. The music stopped suddenly, and the piano bench toppled. "You'll have to get my coat," Victor said. "I'm not going upstairs again."

As I returned down the stairs with Victor's coat, I was surprised to see that he was not alone in the hall. Eugene stood very close to Victor, and although he looked like little more than a shadow, Victor must have been able to see my swamp man's features so clearly that even the contracting and widening of the creature's pupils would be visible.

I had only to resume my pace, to look down at my feet so that I would not stumble on the stairs, and the swamp man vanished.

"I think this house is haunted," Victor said. As he pulled on his heavy coat and plaid scarf, he gazed toward the curving stairs. "It's awfully late for me to catch such a mad belief." He was smiling again when he walked out onto the front porch. The night had fallen very cold, with stabbing stars and a huge, drifting icy moon. "What I saw!" Victor told me.

Some time later I cast a small spell to fire my imagination, and recalling my husband's eyes, the touch of his skin against mine, and his good and gentle heart, I tried by phone to reach him. On my fifth or sixth try I called the right motel and I begged his forgiveness and asked him to come home.

"I can't," Artie said. "Just leave me alone now, will you? If you care anything at all for me, you'll leave me alone."

"All right," I whispered.

I called my sister. "Are you okay?" I asked. "Would you like some company?"

"Not yet," Lillian said. "I've got to be alone now. I'll call you soon. I promise. Just let me be for a while, Ruby."

I wandered into one of my mother's towers, which cast a long shadow across the lawn. I hoped to see my mother there, but she was ages and ages ago gone. There, still, was what she had seen: the swamps, the river, the stars, that hollow moon, the horrid beauty. Even with the cold wind rushing into my ears I could hear the sounds of my swamp man on the twisting stairs below. I listened to him, and although I could not rationally order his voice, for the wind blew apart his words, I said, "I know. I do know, Eugene."

17

That night I dreamed very sweetly for a woman abandoned and disgraced. Eugene awoke me early in the morning by yanking on my toes and bumping against the bed like a cat wanting its milk. When I opened my eyes, he had vanished. I dressed rapidly in the cold air, knowing exactly what I must do and where I must go that day.

As I walked downstairs and into Artie's study, Eugene allowed me to catch my clearest glimpses of him yet: I could see the color of his eyes, a very dark brown, and that he had taken scissors to his straight brown hair, for it was considerably shorter than it had been the night I had met him in the swamp, and his scalp was laid bare in patches. He wore a pair of my old blue jeans rolled up at the cuffs, and one of Artie's shirts, which hung from his skeletal frame.

"You should eat more," I said, as I sat before Artie's desk. In a locked drawer were several one-hundred-dollar bills that I had been saving since summer for Christmas gifts, and having lost my desk key many months before, I wiggled my fingers and deftly picked the lock. From beyond the mahogany door Eugene laughed as I stuffed my pockets with the money, and I was grateful for his approval. "You came at the right time," I told him, or his shadow. "I may just make a splendid Christmas after all. Is it possible, Eugene?" I remembered how Artie had looked the day before and then his expression, ages ago gone, the night I had first met him. When I called his name now, I could imagine that he heard me, and standing on the front porch looking out over the cold, bright swamps, I remembered last night's tender and erotic dreams of him.

That early morning no living soul crossed the cemetery where my sister had meant to be married and where my mother had rested so badly. The wedding canopy had been partially dismantled: only the poles were left, and in the distance a pink crepe-paper streamer blew in the wind. I parked my jeep near the cemetery gates, strode quickly among the tombstones, and hid behind a crypt near my mother's grave.

About nine o'clock a stooped, well-bundled figure entered the cemetery through a side gate, paused to tug on his hat, and walked slowly along the lane. Beneath the old man's arm was a small bouquet, and although the sky was a hard, clear blue I could see he carried a bent, black umbrella. In his anxiety the old man twirled and flipped his umbrella with fingers that could only have belonged to a magician. When he crossed over the slope and met the first of the tombstones, he hesitated, adjusted the woolen scarf around his neck, and looked about, as if to make certain he was alone.

"Sally," my father called, as he neared her grave. "You never would learn how to behave with me, would you?" From beneath his arm he took the crumpled bouquet and hurled it against the marker. He stared at the ground as if he were waiting for the earth to reply to him and then placed the bouquet more carefully among the flowers Lillian had left the day before. "Why do you still come to me at night?"

A flock of birds, disturbed by the shout, flew from one tree to another, and the old man stared up at the sky and shook his fist at the heavens. His finger touched his lips, and I could see him smile as he rested his arm on the tombstone. "It's indecent of you to intrude upon me this way," he said, "when I loved you with all my heart. You cheated on me with hundreds, Sally—hot pants do not make for a respectable woman." He chuckled then and seemed to be waiting for an answer.

At last he sighed. "All right. Suppose, just suppose, I never loved you at all. Suppose I married you for your money. Was that any reason for you to kill yourself and haunt me, too? Be reasonable, darling." His lips very close to the granite, he said, "I'm an old man—don't taunt me! All right, all right, if you knew I never loved you, why make my nights miserable and send our daughter"—my heart flipped when he said this—"around so suddenly, after twenty-five years? Oh, you were always wicked, Sally. I rather liked your wickedness. But it's enough now, I'm tired. You can't blame me forever for not loving you. You knew before we were married I would never care. Great men," he said puffing out his chest, "cannot be owned—I cannot love a woman the way you would've had me love you. If you really loved me, Sally, you could send me some money or a plane ticket—if you can haunt, you can do that. I belong in Puerto Rico now. It's cold in Miami, and I have no friends.

"And yesterday!" he railed. "What would you have me understand by seeing Ruby and Lillian carry on? It's the reason I don't like women very much. You're always playing for higher stakes than I can manage. I'm very unhappy, and very, very, displeased. Won't you leave me, Sally?" he asked, with as much charm as an old man might muster.

His head cocked and his hand cupped to his ear as he waited and waited. He cried, "All right, I apologize—

I'm sorry! I wanted to love you—I thought maybe I could. Please leave me now," he said.

I coughed loudly then and waited for my father to straighten up and wipe his eyes and move away from the tombstone. By slow degrees, taking advantage of his every twist and turn, I darted behind crypts and monuments and trees, so that I appeared to be just arriving through the gravesites closest to the paved cemetery lane.

"You—you've followed me here," my father said, his cheeks growing very red. "Or else she told you to come. You want to argue with me again, about my being your father."

"No, I don't," I said quickly. "It was just a romance. Forgive me. I knew you weren't my father all along."

"I don't believe you," Sam said, although he smiled. "You're just saying that now so you won't feel any financial responsibility toward me. My daughter would've loved me enough, no matter what I said, to send me off to Puerto Rico, where I could live out my last days in peace." We both stared at my mother's grave and then both looked away. "I suppose you're wondering what I'm doing here—I wonder the same about you, Ruby. I came," he said, "to pay my respects to an old magician friend and just happened by this spot. Has she stopped coming to you yet?"

"Oh, she comes all the time. Does she still come to you?"

"I am a great magician," my father said, "and I've gotten rid of her at last. Nobody can hold me down for long, not Sam Bittner. Oh, it's cold this morning, but no matter. Some woman who loves me very much is going to make my life bliss. You see, Ruby," he said, smiling kindly at me, "I don't want a daughter now anyway. What would I do with you if you wouldn't do anything for me?"

"I don't know," I said. I cried out suddenly, as if I were greatly alarmed, and flung one arm so roughly about his neck that Sam lost his balance and his wit. Just before he fell I slipped, with the delicate touch he had taught me, five hundred dollars into his shabby coat pocket.

"So you've given up on me—women are fickle," Sam said, standing and brushing himself off. "That's the way it is now. But it doesn't matter. I'll be leaving this town soon." A crafty expression came over his face as his sensitive fingers slipped over his coat pockets to remove the leaves and dirt. When I bent to retrieve his fallen umbrella, I knew he looked into his pocket. "Well," he said, giving me his hand, "I expect I'll be leaving tomorrow. I want to thank you, though, for all the excitement you've given me lately. To think I might have had a daughter like you." He grinned. "I suppose you were very much like my daughter. Remember all the good times we had? You were a bright and talented child."

"We had some great times," I said, smiling.

"And you grew up beautifully. We do look extraordinarily alike, for two people who aren't even related."

"We do look alike, don't we?" I said. "Well, life is strange."

"A magician knows better than anyone else," said my father, tipping his hat to me. "Just when you think you've caught the illusion, understood the reality, snap!" and he plucked, chuckling, a silver dollar from behind my ear, just as he used to do when I was a child. "I'll tell you what," Sam said. "I'll adopt you. We'll pretend from now on that I'm your real father. When I get to Puerto Rico, I'll write you and let you know just how I'm getting on. Who knows, I might even marry again. Oh, but you were wicked, Ruby, believing I was your father and not lending me the money. But you see, some woman loves me and expects nothing in return. Well, I guess you've taken after your mother," he said, laying a finger aside a hazel eye identical to mine.

"Maybe I have," I said. I leaned forward and kissed his rough cheek, and the scent of the spicy after-shave he had always used brought back lovely and unthreatening memories.

"I shall adopt you out of respect to Sally's memory. You're a magician also—that makes us closer than if we were blood relatives, Ruby, because you did me the honor of taking up my craft. Perhaps you'll do me a small favor. Of course, when I get to Puerto Rico, who knows how long I'll live? But if Houdini thought he could return, Sam Bittner can return. Will you keep watch for me, Ruby?"

"Always," I said. I was crying a little then, and my father dabbed at my eyes with his handkerchief, and his lips brushed my cheek.

"I'll write, daughter," he called, as he wandered away, a spritely bounce to his walk. Just before he disappeared beyond a cluster of oaks and hibiscus hedges, I heard him whoop.

"Oh, Mama," I said, leaning against my mother's tombstone. "I guess neither of us could've kept him after all, no matter what we might've done. I guess you didn't really send him running—he was born with swift feet." I patted down a tuft of grass that must have been uprooted during the wedding ceremony the day before. "Who would've guessed? You sleep well now," I told her. "I'll miss you."

As I drove through the black iron cemetery gates I tried to imagine that beneath my thick sweater a brand new accumulation of cells was quivering and expressing itself in my belly. "I've got to rouse you up again for Janet, baby," I said. "She loves you so much."

I drove for miles through a run-down business district where Christmas lights and faded aluminum Santa Claus faces already swung above the streets. I turned down a narrow and pitted lane and parked my jeep behind Janet Monsterville's pink Cadillac. Beneath the sagging metal awning of the faded orange duplex were several dishes drawing flies, and a thin dog with rheumy eyes skulked off, shivering, as I stepped onto the cement-slab porch.

Janet Monsterville had hung a pink-and-gold Christmas wreath on her front door. I rang the bell several times, and finally the door was opened and its chain lock removed. Janet leaned against the splintering wood frame, her head scarved, her eyes red, swollen, and blinking at the cold blue day.

"What?" she said. She pulled her faded red robe together and barred my entry with her fat arms. "You had to come and get me? Shit, I deserve to be late to work once every ten years."

"I didn't come because you were late—I don't even know what time it is," I said, kissing her alarmingly warm cheek. The light in her beautiful almond eyes looked faint. "I was in the neighborhood, and I thought I'd stop."

"You're in trouble—there was trouble at the wedding yesterday," Janet said. "I'll take a knife to that Cuban and your crazy sister both. And then we'll run away and wait for you to have your baby—what did they do to you?"

"Nothing," I said. "Everything went very well. I just wanted to see your pretty place."

"Took you long enough—ten years—for you to come visit me. But I look so bad—I ain't even put on my makeup yet, and this robe is nasty." Janet led me into the dark front room and pointed at each piece of furniture and explained its history. To my right were a large, pretty, beige velvet couch and loveseat covered with plastic, which Janet had bought on time two years before at a warehouse sale; inches from them were two plush-upholstered chairs, for which she had paid cash with the money a gambler friend gave her. She had bought the chrome-and-glass china cabinet the year before with her Christmas bonuses, and the crystal salad bowl inside it had been a present from a former "Thursday." I had bought the wine glasses, if I remember rightly, for Janet's birthday seven years before.

"I bought the china lady—see her pretty pink skirt—and those little china dogs myself," Janet said. She leaned heavily against me, swaying as she pointed at each figurine. "And this is my stereo unit—only fifty dollars left to go on my payments. I did very well for myself, I think. Careful, don't fall," she said, frowning, when I tripped over a ceramic cat which lay on the beautiful, wheat-colored carpeting. "Falling is what killed my first baby, I think."

In the cramped space before the kitchen doorway was a large dining room table of well-waxed walnut with eight apricot-colored chairs. There she sat me, telling me with what difficulty she had prevented her dirty but generous truck-driver friend from spotting the delicate cloth with grease. "Some day, when I feel better, I'm going to give a big dinner here. I'll get you some coffee—don't come into the kitchen," she shrieked. "I only just got the yellow curtains I wanted, but I still need to put up some wallpaper." I watched Janet stumble around the tiny kitchen, chattering about the Thanksgiving dinner at her ex-sister-in-law's the evening before. She leaned for a moment against the bright yellow stove, holding her head as if it hurt her badly, and then, reaching up for some cups, called, "So, do you like my place?"

"It's beautiful," I said. "You ought to be very proud."

"I told you my furniture was nicer than yours. I saved up all my money and bought everything myself, too. I wish my mama could see how I made it all alone. I called her last night in Georgia and begged her to come for Christmas, but she won't do it." Janet was swaying as she carried a tray with coffee into the dining room. In the center of the tray was a yellow hibiscus in a jelly glass, and beneath her chin she held several napkins, which she placed on my lap. "Don't want you spotting up my furniture," she said. "My mama ought to come see me—I miss her. I told her all about you. You know how to get her down here?"

"No," I said. The coffee was wonderfully spiced with cinnamon, cloves, and orange peel, a trick Janet said she had learned from a doctor's wife for whom she had worked many years before. Janet sat beside me and let her coffee grow cold as she sighed over how many years had passed and how old and sick she was now.

"I'll be okay," she said, her eyes sliding across my face. "I just woke up on the wrong side of the bed this morning. Nasty old diabetes! But I better get dressed and stick myself with my insulin so the poor boss won't get mad at me. You going to tell him about my house?"

"Next time I come, I'll bring him with me," I said.

"You ain't seen my bedroom yet," Janet said, pulling me up. "Come on, we can talk while I get dressed. How's your pretty baby?" she crooned, looking down at my stomach as we paused so I could peek into her pink-and-white bathroom. "Your belly's still flat, but in two months—" and she puffed out her round cheeks and predicted her godchild would be both beautiful and smart.

"My godchild's going to sleep in here some day," she said. Her bedroom was decorated in red and black, the colors, she said, that turned every man's heart. The carpeting was thick and red, and the walls were red-painted. Her red velvet bedspread, piled with heart-shaped cushions, could be covered with a towel when the baby came to stay with her, she said. On the black Formica night tables she would put the baby's bottle and food. "Well?" she said.

"It's gorgeous. It's a love nest," I said.

"Was a love nest," Janet replied. On the long black Formica dresser were many pictures, including one of Artie and me on our wedding day; beside bottles of prescription medicines rested a vial of insulin and a packaged needle. "Can't be a love nest now, since I found my Lord. But I used to stretch out against the red—I look good, with my dark complexion, against red—and my postman and even old Alonzo used to drool and call me honey. That's right. I knew how to get them hungry. But now I got more important things to think about—our baby." As she rummaged through her closet Janet hummed a soft, honeyed lullaby; she swayed her big hips, took two tiny dance steps, and then her legs collapsed beneath her.

She sat hard on the floor. Looking up at me, she began to sob. Although it was chilly in the bedroom, sweat was beaded on her forehead. "Let me take you to a doctor," I begged.

Janet struck feebly at me, her eyes wild with fear. "What—and get me put in a hospital? I ain't going to no hospital, not now, when you need me. Used to be when I had company overnight, my postman or my truck driver or Alonzo, they'd give me my shot. I could make it all right alone if I just had someone to give me my needle. I'm sick, I'm sick." She was crying harder now. "I don't want to shoot myself up—and what," she asked, plucking first at her breasts and then her groin, "if I got that old cancer that killed my aunt?"

"You don't have any cancer," I said.

"I don't? Well, that's a relief. Nights, when I'm alone, I worry."

I took the insulin and needle from her dresser. "It's only the diabetes. Your aunt may have had cancer, but you don't." I lifted Janet with difficulty and said, "Let me give you your shot now."

"Don't want any shot—you just want to hurt me," she said, but she shut her eyes and explained how and where, and pinched an inch of flesh in her thigh. "Oh," she said. "You hurt me—you hurt me bad." She hugged me. "You're nice, you're my friend. I'm going to feel better now—you'll see. I got to, because you need me. Should I put on my pink uniform or my white? What?" she said, her eyes widening. "What's wrong with you— why'd you come here today?"

"I had this feeling," I said, sitting on her bed and clasping my hands between my knees. "I think you should go home for the holidays. I'll drive you to the bus station now."

"I ain't going," Janet said. "You want to get rid of me now is all. You want to send me away to die."

"You're not going to die," I said. I laughed as if her notion were indeed ridiculous. "And I wish you could stay with me forever and ever. I just think you should go home for a little while—you've been talking about going home for so long. After that, I want you to move in with me."

"What, and have no privacy?" Janet cried, although her lips parted with a sly smile.

"And help me take care of the baby in the middle of the night."

"I'm an old, sick woman—I need some rest. You're supposed to be grown up now, and look at you, crying like a child. Always counting on me to run your life—I ain't living just for you."

"I know that," I said. "So go on home now. Don't be selfish."

"I ain't never selfish. I'm good—you know how hard I try to be good. I guess my mama needs me." Janet stared at her feet. "I know she does. I dreamed about her the other night, and she was calling out my name. I wouldn't go up there just to die—that'd be selfish, wouldn't it? I want to die in Georgia, but there's time left for me. Right?" she asked, and in her soft, dark, dying eyes was terror.

"You could tell me," she said, leaning toward me. "How much time I got left?"

"You have lots of time. Years and years."

"Then how come you're crying?"

"Because I'll miss you. But your mother needs you now. She's old. She wants you home for Christmas. That's right," I said, nodding. "And listen. Artie and I are going to St. Croix for a couple of weeks. Here, he told me to give you your Christmas bonus." I took from my jeans pocket four one-hundred-dollar bills and placed them on the bed.

"You're lying," Janet said. "It tells in your face. You ain't going to St. Croix."

"I am so—please believe me," I said. Janet blinked rapidly and rubbed her face with her arm. "Will you let me do something for you? You've been my best friend— my only friend—for a long time. After the holidays," I said, taking her wig from its Styrofoam stand and handing it to her, "you can come back to Miami. I'll be big by then. You're going to be a godmother."

"I'm afraid," Janet said.

I hugged her and whispered that she hadn't a thing to be afraid about. I went quickly through her closet until I found her favorite pantsuit. She put her hands on my shoulders and grunted as she stepped into the trousers. "You're strong and you're good," I said. "Even our Eugene says so. Even he says you should go home for a while."

"If he says to go, I'll go." Janet pulled off her head-scarf and spent a long time before her mirror, putting on makeup and brushing her wig. "I wish I had pretty long hair like you, but I can still look nice. You can drive me to the bus station—that's the least you can do for me. My, I'm going to have to pack a bag now, and bring up some clothes for my cousins. I ever tell you about my cousin Jimmy, who's a faggot? He likes to wear my blouses. He's so sweet, though—I'll buy my mama and everybody some candy when the bus stops at Stuckey's."

"It's going to be pretty up in Georgia now," I said, looking about for Janet's purse. I found it lying atop a magazine rack—Janet thought it bad luck to place a handbag on the floor—and put the four hundred dollars inside it. When Janet opened her mouth to protest, I said, "You'll hurt Artie's feelings if you don't take the money. Now," I said, sitting on the bed while she packed, "you're going to have a wonderful Christmas. And we'll see each other soon, if you don't forget me."

"It's you who'll forget me," Janet said.

Together we checked to see that all the switches were turned off, the plants well-watered, and the windows and doors locked. On the way to the bus station Janet talked and talked. "I'm going to walk into that little house just like I never left. My mama, she's going to put down her head and cry when she sees me. I'm going to cook Christmas dinner, too—turkey, macaroni and cheese, and greens—I cook very well," she said. "All my men said I cook very well." When the bus stopped for the last time just outside Valdosta, she said, she would go into the rest room and put on some perfume and maybe change into one of her pretty dresses. "My family's going to shit when they see me," she said.

I carried her suitcase into the bus station and watched to make certain she purchased her ticket. Janet settled herself in the waiting room and then said in a sullen voice, "You go away now."

"The bus isn't leaving for two hours. I want to wait with you," I said. Janet looked very tired and very ill beneath the fluorescent lighting, and from time to time she still clutched her head.

"You go away," she repeated, staring straight ahead at the row of plastic chairs opposite us. "I'm afraid. Go way."

"Do you want me to ride up to Georgia with you? I'll go buy a ticket."

Janet slapped my hand. "No. You're going to the islands, right? My mama'd kill me if I brought you home without telling her—you go way now." She leaned back in her blue plastic chair and said she wanted to take a nap. "I can wait by myself—I ain't the baby here. You don't go getting into trouble when I'm away—you don't go getting carried away over some pretty stupid face."

"I promise," I said.

"And you drink lots of milk for my godchild, and don't drink whiskey. How are you going to get along without me?"

"You've been getting along alone. I guess I can try, too."

"You get into trouble, you call me. Don't go getting into any fights with my good boss." Janet's eyes flew open, and she laughed aloud at a child who was running up and down the waiting-room aisles. "Look how he runs!" She made a face at him, poked me when he smiled, and said how everyone loved her. "And don't lift heavy things, and don't mop no floors. You don't forget to tell my little ghosty good-bye—tell him I'll bring him something from Georgia. And don't," she said, looking up at me with a severe expression, "don't you go forgetting me while I'm gone."

"I couldn't if I tried—I love you," I said.

"You ought to love me, after all these years," Janet said.

I walked to the bus station exit. "Stay pretty," I heard Janet call. "You stay pretty!"

18

When everyone had been sent for a time from my life and it seemed that I had little human love left to lose, I wandered that part of my house my mother had built for her ghosts. As I walked through rooms cloaked in dust and shadow, trying to see what my mother had seen, I imagined that the footsteps of the dead knocked and echoed and struggled against the gray edges of my soul. In a corner of a large room, just inches from the ragged, rose-printed curtains, I thought I saw the spirit of the wailing and rocking woman my mother had often mentioned: the rocker my mother had placed here long ago did indeed sway with fretful energy, and the old woman sobbed, it seemed, for some lost loved one. Farther down the hall I gasped, seeing, or thinking I saw, the ghost of the young bride who had lost her husband on her wedding night. I pitied her as much as if she were flesh, and envied her, too, but when I reached out to touch her pale shoulder, she vanished.

I might have been left alone in the dark, with only vague, heart-scratching anxiety for company, except for my swamp man, Eugene. He scurried through the halls with me, whimpering, and by those small sounds prevented me from giving up. "You've done so much for me," I whispered. "Isn't there anything I can do for you, Eugene?"

"Don't try—I'm lost," he cried once, just a voice and the flashing of teeth in the dark. He seemed never to see any ghosts, and I thought how odd it was that my sublimely good swamp man should be as lost as I.

"How can you be so lost and have helped me?" I asked. "Oh!" I said, remembering my sister's theories. "Is it amnesia?"

"That's it," Eugene said. "You still like me?"

"Ah, yes," I replied. "I love you. You've changed my life, but now you've made me lonelier. Still, I do love you."

"But you don't know me—there's the trick." My swamp creature's melancholy laughter echoed through the dark and damp halls.

"I do know you. My mother told me all about you when I was very young. I know you. Let me touch you and know you're real."

Eugene cried, "Don't touch! Leave here—think about your husband."

"But he's left me," I said, sneaking closer. When I touched Eugene, he shrieked as if he had been scalded and dashed toward the door that would let us out onto the stairs. As soon as I reached the stairs my flashlight was struck away, and the door slammed behind me. I saw the key turn in the lock and watched it glitter like a falling star as it flew over the banister and into the darkness below.

"Don't touch me again," came a small, timid order. "Your aunt says for me to be careful."

"So you do know her," I said. "But I'm not dangerous, Eugene. I'd rather hurt myself than hurt you."

Many mornings I sat shivering on the riverbank near my aunt's cabin, waiting for her to return and help me map out my life. But Eugene always came for me, shrieking and howling, running off into the woods and then running back, as if it were a matter of life or death that I follow him back to the house.

"Artie's come home," I always said, but each time I returned to the house, all was quiet and peaceful. I called Artie at his motel on a Sunday morning and pleaded with him at least to meet me some place, to talk, but he refused.

"I've asked you to leave me alone now," he said.

In the second week of my watch for my aunt, when time had become confused and disordered and I was certain Catherine was purposely eluding me, I saw upon my return to the house that my sister's car had been parked in the drive during my absence, and that the front door was ajar.

Lillian was sitting quietly in the living room, wearing a white caftan. In full sight of her Eugene beeped at me and pointed—except for his grimy appearance and his odd clothing he looked very much like a human—but Lillian seemed to take no notice of him at all.

When I spoke, he vanished. "Lillian, I've been waiting for you. Are you all right?"

She nodded, but her eyes seemed vacant behind her thick glasses. She was gazing at a tray of hot tea and little cakes on the coffee table. Lillian said, "I think there's an evil spirit in this house, and that we must banish it."

"There's no evil spirit here," I said.

Lillian wandered the living room with eyes full of dread, chewing her red braids, her fingers touching those paintings of battling devils and angels upon which our mother had worked with such fierce passion. "I almost made another mistake, with Rolando," she told me. "If imagination counts, I did make the mistake."

"But you stopped. You broke your pattern."

"I broke my pattern," Lillian agreed, managing a wan smile, "but there's still more to do. You wouldn't help me find our swamp man before. You only took me to him once, and then you kept him for yourself. I'm not blaming you. I know I wasn't ready for him. But look at me, Ruby—don't I look ready now? Now that I have nothing else, I remember him, and so I'm ready."

Perhaps out of the most glorious and selfless pity, fearful Eugene slid into the room and brushed my sister's caftan as he made his way around the back wall to the piano and plunked several discordant notes. He twisted his shaggy brown head around the wall several times to see if Lillian would discern the miracle and then returned several times to the piano. But Lillian only gasped at his noises, seized my hand, and hurried me up the stairs to the bedroom. "An evil spirit is in the house," she said, "and now I'm going to have to say many prayers."

"But that wasn't an evil spirit. That was our swamp man, and he calls himself Eugene."

"His name is Relga, but that presence in the living room was not him. Are you trying to tell me he's right under my nose, and I don't recognize him? No, he wouldn't come inside this house," Lillian said, pacing the bedroom. "That's too easy. We have to work to find him. Tomorrow the rest are going to join us, and we'll have to search very hard. Then maybe he won't want to save us anyway. You see we've sinned."

In the hall Eugene threw up his small, good hands, as if he were in great despair.

Lillian went to bed still wearing her caftan and talked most of the night of how, where, and by whom she was haunted. All night long Eugene kept slipping into the room, switching the lights on and off, thumping shoes, and calling my sister's name. Lillian seemed not to hear the strange noises, nor did she understand the matter of the lights. "Evil spirits," she said. At last she fell asleep, and I slept beside her, dreaming sweetly and erotically of Artie.

Some time near morning I was awakened by a shout. Lillian leaned through an open window, shrieking, "Relga." I stood beside her and could see Eugene running back and forth across the lawn. "Look—there he is, Ruby, running from me. Oh, it's going to be hard to catch him—look how he runs from this place. But I've got to talk with him soon and make him remember who he is. If I do that before Christmas, everything in the world will be right. He's going to make me somebody."

"You already are somebody."

"No. See how you still don't understand anything?" Lillian's blue eyes were full of tears, and the tears must have badly blurred her vision. "I'm nothing without him," she said, getting into bed beside me.

I kissed her hot cheek and remained awake until I saw that slight shadow in the hall. Then I went to the bedroom door and whispered, "You heard her, Eugene. She thinks she's nothing without you."

"Without me—why? I'm nothing," my swamp man said.

Still, Eugene crept into the room as we slept and placed breakfast near the bed. Still, Lillian refused to believe that our outer-space alien who lived in the swamps would perform so homely a task as to make hot cereal and coffee for two mortal and sinful women.

"You're just trying to placate me, to make things easier. I've got to struggle to see the light," my sister said.

"Love isn't always exploding stars, Lillian. You ought to know that by now. You see that I've just gotten up with you." I rubbed my eyes and yawned to make my point. "So how do you think the food got here?"

"Janet Monsterville brought it."

"She's gone home forever," I replied. "Poor Janet."

"Poor me. If Janet didn't bring the breakfast, and I know Relga didn't, I'm not going to touch a bit of it." Lillian put down her coffee cup and obstinately refused to eat. She, who before had been so willing to believe what she could not see, now refused to believe concrete signs that the swamp creature had been living in the house with me. "There are many ghosts, evil spirits, who would try to confuse us, Ruby. If he was living with you all this time, how come he let us get hurt, and hurt each other?"

At nine o'clock that morning Grace and Clara Thurnwood, Lyla Zimmerman, and Posy Adams arrived. Just as Lillian sat everyone on the living room couch, the Christmas tree lights went on, and the piano began playing. While the elderly ladies gasped and said that surely the alien was in the house, that surely it was Relga who made music for them, Lillian paled and said, "Do not be deceived by imposters. I was deceived recently, and I know how the devil masks. Be careful when you look in the swamps today."

"When I see him," said Grace Thurnwood, patting her pale blond hair and smiling sweetly at both Lillian and me, "I'll call out his name, 'Relga,' and then wait to see what happens."

"He'll have a white aura around his head," Lillian said. I could hear Eugene's muffled, delighted laughter, although no one else seemed to hear.

"When I see him," said Lyla Zimmerman, "I'm going to ask him where my husband hid our money, and when he tells me, I'm going to hug him and hug him."

All the keys of the piano sounded at once, and the piano bench toppled.

"We'll all hug and kiss him," Clara Thurnwood sang out.

A tremendous shrieking made us all start. Lillian

looked about wildly until she heard the sound of a door banging. Then the wailing ceased. "You've managed girls," she said, "to banish that evil thing from this house."

"Oh, no," I whispered. A feeling of emptiness seemed to seep into the old house and wrap around it like a snake. The edges of the rooms no longer glimmered with my Eugene's special warmth, and I knew he had fled the house for good.

I ran into the hall and stood just outside the front door on the porch, looking around the empty lawn. "Eugene," I shouted. "You promised you'd never leave me."

I stood trembling on the porch until I felt my sister's hand on my shoulder. "What are you doing, Ruby?" Lillian asked. It was as if all her orifices that let in light and sound had been shut up, and now my sister was both blind and deaf.

"Nothing," I said, following her back into the house.

"Now," Lillian said, going to each psychic friend and kissing her cheek, "everybody spread out, and be careful. Posy, you take Lyla, since she doesn't see well, and keep guard on the area between the house and the fence. Relga ran across the lawn last night, and he just may do that again today." Posy Adams helped Lyla Zimmerman through the kitchen and out the side door. "Grace, you head west, from behind the house. Clara, you go south. I'll take the woods near the river. Ruby?" Lillian said, blinking and smiling tremulously at me. "I'm giving you space, because I know you're going to find him. I know that you can, if you want to."

All that day I searched for my swamp man, shouting his name until I was hoarse. "Don't be frightened, Eugene," I called. "They won't hurt you, and neither will I. I won't let any harm come to you—that I promise. I need you—you promised you'd stay with me."

When I returned home alone that evening, Lillian's

friends had already left the Everglades, and my sister was once again morose. "I'm useless unless I find him," she said. Her face was streaked with dirt, and her caftan was torn and muddied. She shuddered, looking into my eyes, and at last said, "I saw our aunt Catherine in the woods today."

"I've been looking for her," I said.

"Then stop," Lillian said. "I asked her to help me find Relga—I was desperate, Ruby—and she refused. All I want to do is worship him. Oh," she said, sometime later, sitting up in bed with her Ouija board on her lap, "I have so much passion for him, Ruby. All the passion I was throwing away on Rolando is now concentrated on finding Relga."

Lillian refused to eat anything that evening, nor would she eat the next morning, or the next; she was falling into an eerie state of exaltation in which she imagined herself dying and haunting, just as our mother had done. "Maybe that's how Mother joined him. Maybe dying is the only way."

Each night my sister fruitlessly worked her Ouija board for directions to her outer-space man, Relga. "It's got to happen by Christmas, or it won't happen at all," she said, standing by the always open bedroom windows and looking out over the Everglades.

I roamed the woods every day and half the night, calling for my swamp man. I knew he was close, for several times in the woods I came upon abandoned campsites with strange booty: a woman's hat, several pairs of boots, and empty cartons of milk. Why Eugene had left me—who was not a part of the others—I did not understand.

During these two weeks before Christmas, the newspapers often carried articles about rural residents being burglarized by a strange swamp creature. One evening as I returned to the house I saw my aunt standing on the porch with Lillian. My sister was screaming, "He isn't in trouble—he can't be. And he wouldn't steal, he's too good. He's better than you are, witch." Lillian rushed into the house and left me to the wrath of my aunt.

"You're selfish, Ruby," Catherine said, looking at me with grave eyes. "You cannot keep him to yourself—find him before these people he's been stealing from do."

"But my sister will frighten him away. She'll take him from me."

"Aren't you worried about him, Ruby? That child's alone out there. You worry about being alone so much—look for him!"

"I've looked and looked. I don't want to lose him—not him. Why don't you just go ahead and find him, since you're so smart? If you can see everything, and you do," I said, my knees buckling when I looked into her eyes, "why don't *you* find him?"

"Because he's waiting for you," Catherine said. "Look to save him—look to save him. I don't need to find him. I already know where he is."

"Then help me," I pleaded.

"I can't."

That evening Lillian smiled in her sleep, and I sobbed and twisted with anguished dreams. The next morning I arose before my sister, stole from the house, and headed, according to visionary dream, due north. I stayed in the woods that night and the next, in lean-tos my swamp man must have built: in each I found a blanket, and in the last one I found a gold watch. I wondered why my swamp man would steal a watch, for a goodly alien must always know the time, but then I remembered that he had forgotten who he was.

On my third day in the woods I came across a campsite that was still in use: tied to the trees were four cows, munching the lush undergrowth, and not far from the smoking fire I found a portable radio, still playing music, a large baby doll, several more watches, many boxes of dry cereal, and a pile of canned goods.

"What would an alien want with this?" I asked, picking up the doll. The doll made me think of babies, and babies made me think of Artie. "You're lonely out here, Eugene, I know. But what can I do to help you?" I brooded for several minutes, until I heard the crackling of brush and felt a generous, sweet hand on my arm.

Eugene, as dirty as I and very thin, so obscured by mud and so skeletal he looked but half-human, stood behind me. When he blinked and pushed back his matted hair, I saw his face clearly for the first time. Though stunted in his growth—who knew how earth food and earth air might have affected such a sublime creature— he appeared to be about twenty earth-years old.

"Why are you crying, Ruby?" Eugene asked. His earthlinglike lips were swollen with insect bites.

"I've missed you," I said, "and I've been very worried. Why did you run away?"

"I was afraid of those women. They wanted to touch me."

"You've touched me," I said, but when I reached for his hand, he stepped back.

"I don't want to be touched," Eugene said sadly. "I'm afraid. I've been out here too long and I don't remember who I am. Who do you think I am?"

"Somebody important. Come home now," I said. "You have a home with me."

"No." Eugene sat by the fire and rubbed his hands together. "You really do think I'm someone important, don't you? I'm sorry I had to leave, but people were closing in on me—your sister and her friends, and now the farmers. They're angry at me for stealing their cows. I can't go with you, Ruby."

"Then I'll have to stay with you. But who are you— are you human?"

"I guess I'm not," said Eugene.

"If you are human, you're going to get killed, surely, for stealing from these Glades people. They'll shoot you, Eugene, but you don't even care."

"Yes, I do, I do! I'm only borrowing. Someday I'm going to return everything," he said, now rushing about the site and putting all in order, as if I were indeed an important guest. Together we ate the last of the dried sausages I had brought into the woods with me, and then Eugene asked me once again who I thought he was.

"I told you," I said, frowning, "that my sister thinks you're from outer space. But you look so frail and so human that I'd swear you're just a boy."

"Never mind," Eugene said, apparently hurt. "Looks are deceiving. Can I fly?"

"Lillian thinks so."

"Someday I'll fly off a mountain."

"Please don't," I cried, but Eugene waved an annoyed hand.

"Can people hurt me?"

"I'd think so, but not according to Lillian. She says you can do anything by a wish."

"By a wish!" Eugene stretched himself before the fire and stared into the popping orange flames. "It would be wonderful to get what you wanted by a wish." His face then clouded. "But I think your sister doesn't really like me the way I really am." Now, when I stared closely at Eugene, I saw that he looked confused and melancholy, although perhaps that was just his expression, the subtle difference in the manifestation of emotions misunderstood by earthling vision.

"She wouldn't hate you the way you really are. Lillian's been looking for you so long. She wants to live with you, as I have. It was nice of you to show yourself to her. You've been wonderful. And mysterious and funny."

Eugene said that in his youth he had read a great many ghost comic books. "You made me mysterious. What's my name supposed to be?"

"My sister says you're Relga from Artarius. She thinks you can save her."

"Save her?"

I sighed. "She says she wants to die if she doesn't find you."

"She shouldn't want that," Eugene said.

"She thinks you can save the world. She thinks when she talks to you, and you tell her she's good, that the rest of the outer-space aliens will come down to earth. Then the whole world will be saved, and she will have helped," I said, still frowning, but still wishing.

"To save the world—now that would mean something," Eugene said. Lying on the ground, one leg flung over a crooked knee, his hands beneath his head and his dark eyes staring up into the sky, he pondered what it would be like to know such immense power and to inspire so much love. "I wish you could have somebody like Relga, Ruby. If I were him, I would do wonderful things for everyone, and I wouldn't ever let anybody be sad. I wouldn't," he said softly, one dirty finger in his mouth, "because I've been sad. I'd make people laugh all the time, and I'd make them wonder."

"That's because you're from heaven," I said, drawing closer to him and warming my hands over the fire. Night was falling. "You've certainly made me wonder. You've just got to be from heaven, Eugene. Oh, if my sister were here, she wouldn't want to die."

"I don't want to be touched, but I don't want your sister to be unhappy, either. I'm afraid."

"How long were you staying in the woods before you came to my house?"

"I don't remember—a long time, though. I guess I have amnesia," Eugene said, brightening little by little.

He snapped his sprite's fingers. "I don't even remember how or why I came to the swamps, except that I was afraid to be around people. But the first time I saw you, I knew you'd be kind and generous. What can I do for you?" he asked. "If I can do anything, just wish and I'll grant it."

"My wish is that you'd run away, or come back to my house—only get out of these woods. The people around here are very angry with you. Come back home, Eugene." I stared at him for a long time. "Borrowing to stay alive—you're liable to get killed out here."

"I can't be killed if I'm Relga," Eugene said. "You tell your sister and her friends to come here tomorrow. Poor Ruby." He touched my shoulder with what must have been for him enormous bravery. "You've done a lot for me."

"What could I possibly have done for you?"

"I've been living here alone for a long time. You made me feel human again. And now," he said, his chest puffing, "I feel important. Your aunt said you'd find me. She said you could see things."

"I can see only sometimes. Apparently I don't use the gift correctly," I said, poking at the fire with a stick.

"Do you see my future?" Eugene asked. He folded himself very small at my side. "Those farmers couldn't catch a man from outer space. Tell me they can't, Ruby."

His face pained me so much, and I was so afraid he would run again, that I said, "Of course they couldn't, of course."

"Now the world is just like we'd have it." Eugene smiled and walked among his cows like a dairy imp. "You are my best friend—never in my life, as much as I remember," he said, turning his solemn, childlike face toward me, "have I ever felt like I belonged around people. People hated me until now, until you. Bring your sister and her friends to me tomorrow. Let me be who I'm supposed to be," he begged. "I've always been, for as long as I can remember, nothing. If you love me you'll believe in me."

They came the next evening, every one of them, my sister and her friends, smelling of perfume and of insect repellent, so joyously bearing gifts that I was joyous, too. Eugene's clothing was wet from his pond bath, and although he shivered, he set me straight at once about alien vulnerability. "I don't need your sweater. A man from outer space does not feel the cold," he said, his lips dancing together.

Lillian let the beam of her big flashlight rove over him, and her psychic friends commented upon Eugene's jaw structure, the mole on his chin, and the fact that his eyebrows, like mine and Lillian's, grew nearly together. Lillian said that she could see an aura dancing around his head. "Relga," she whispered. "You're Relga!"

"But he's frail," Lyla Zimmerman said. "He's puny."

"Physical strength has nothing to do with the spiritual," Lillian said. "Are you Relga?" she asked. "Do you know me?"

"I'm Relga," Eugene said, "and I've been waiting for you, Lillian."

"At last," Lillian said, crying quietly. When she reached to take Eugene's hand, he let out a subdued cry and stepped quickly back.

"Nobody touches Relga," he said. Although he seemed frightened, he accepted with pleasure all the gifts offered him. Grace and Clara, both of whom had gone to the beauty parlor for permanents that afternoon so that they would look their very best for the outer-space alien, presented Eugene with a gold-and-diamond locket. Inside the locket was a picture of their dead mother as a child. Lyla bowed from the waist as best she could and placed in Eugene's hands a box of doughnuts she and Posy Adams had baked in my kitchen. She begged Eugene to speak with her dead husband at once.

"Tell him I need the money," she said. "Tell him he's got to remember where he hid our money."

Lillian had brought Eugene a silver jacket, which he immediately donned. "I am very touched," he said, and smiling gleefully and a bit wickedly, he passed his hands over all heads. "Relga is grateful."

"You don't know how long we've been waiting for you," Lillian said, still crying. Then she lifted her head and seized control: as Eugene must still be suffering some effects of the amnesia, believed felt she must coach him in the ways of being an outer-space king.

"Remember that your power is unlimited," Lillian said. "Do you know that all the earth belongs to you? Anything you want, you can have. And nothing can ever hurt you. Those farmers looking for you—why, if you just pointed a finger at them, they'd be turned into mild babies. You can have anything in the world you want."

"Anything?" Eugene asked.

"Lillian," I said, suddenly frightened.

"Oh, quiet! Anything at all, Relga. May I ask you a few questions?"

"Of course. Go on, Lillian," Eugene said, touching his silver jacket and smoothing his tangled brown hair.

For every question put to him Eugene had a prompt and glorious answer. He was astonishingly articulate about the splendor of outer space and the grand destiny that awaited us among the spinning purple globes, the silver and the blue globes, the awful, pure suns, the soul-soothing and soul-engulfing black. He promised that the other aliens would soon come to earth in space ships so bright the human eye would be unable to grasp their intricate, blazing glory and would call these vehicles large and beautiful stars.

"There's one now, I think," Posy Adams said, so that we all looked toward the sky and pointed at what looked like stars or windy angel eyes.

"My fellow aliens are going to look as human as any of you in this group. Indeed," and Eugene smiled charmingly, "they may not be as elegant. But you'll know them by their goodness—they might appear very ordinary otherwise. You might not always grasp their true moral nature—we're very subtle beings. And I would advise you not to mention to them that they're aliens—Artarians have a bit of a mania for secrets."

Eugene seemed astonished by the applause he received, and then, stepping beyond the reach of extended hands, promised all would be right with everyone. "My throat is dry. Could someone bring me a drink of water? And another doughnut?" He snapped his fingers, waited to be attended, and took a huge bite from his doughnut. A full five minutes passed before he spoke of his home.

"Artarius is very different from this planet. The plants, you see, are made of material similar to earth rocks, and the metal—even the metal—is alive. In the Artarian woods run animals very similar to earth elephants, except they're no bigger than my thumb. The miniature there is far more complex than here." Eugene said that on his very beautiful home planet, everyone treated each other kindly, and because communication occurred through thoughts alone, deception was quite impossible. "That's what I've come to teach you," he said. "The impossibility of deception."

"He's some orator," one of the Thurnwood sisters said.

"Don't book me as a speaker yet," Eugene said. "Yes, Lyla?"

"Tell my husband I need the money. Tell him I do need the money."

Eugene continued to speak with remarkable eloquence about the evils to which humanity was vulnerable—greed, treachery, and most particularly, the obscurement of the soul. "Aliens, of course, cannot obscure. Genetic evolution has made obscurement an anachronism. The word no longer exists in our language, except to describe physical phenemona." Eugene yawned then, and after requesting that he be brought the next evening a soft pillow and a transistor television set, he grandly dismissed everyone. "Tomorrow," he said, "I will tell you why nobody ever grows old on Artarius. Mrs. Zimmerman, perhaps I will have the answer to where your husband hid his money."

"He has my vote," Lyla Zimmerman said as she tagged after Lillian into the woods.

I remained behind and begged Eugene to come home with me.

"No, thank you, Ruby, why should I?" he said. "Nothing can hurt me now. Thank you for saving me. You've given me the world. And I've done some splendid things for you, haven't I? I'm more important now, right?"

"You were important as just Eugene." When he kissed my cheek with the most innocent and the most human lips, I sobbed. "Are you just a boy?" I asked.

"No. Once I was a boy, but now I'm Relga."

19

Every night we went into the swampy woods with flashlights, snakebite kits, and binoculars, and listened to Eugene make prophecies and describe the landscapes of other worlds. Eugene dressed for these evenings in a stolen tuxedo several sizes too large and told of such wondrous things I felt buoyant and later fell into sweet, reassuring dreams. He told me that Artie was coming home. He spoke of his fellow aliens, who lived among the constellations of bears and horned horses and who mirrored God with far greater accuracy than earthlings.

"Still, they'll look like you," he said. "Only by deed will you know them, but you humans are so confused you may not see the deed. I'd tell them to grow mustaches if I could," he added smiling, "but if you'll look at my face, you'll notice I have no beard."

We felt witness to a miracle, watching the always well-scrubbed Eugene, his shining brown hair falling over his ears, his milky complexion wonderfully illuminated, tell his stories and glory in having found us.

"I've chosen you all," he said, letting his gaze fall upon Lillian, "because you're so good and beautiful. I could not have had a more wonderful greeting from earth."

Eugene told Lillian that her soul was one of the most becoming he had seen. "I feel so pretty," my sister said upon awakening each day. He said that all the women were destined to receive much love and respect for their charitable endeavors. "Ruby, your husband will come home before Christmas. Lyla," Eugene said, passing his hands over the eldest woman's head, "soon I will tell you where your husband hid your money."

Lyla Zimmerman snorted. "Soon, soon," she said. "When are you going to fly for us?"

"In a day or so," Eugene said. "You might not see me do it, though—don't blame me because your earthling eyes are what the Artarian council pronounced as legally blind. And my powers are still recuperating from my long voyage. It took me one thousand years of wandering to arrive on earth."

"A thousand years of wandering—imagine," Lillian said.

I was elected to bring the outer-space alien hot meals during the day, and so I was the first to notice the rapidly increasing bounty around his campsite. For a time I thought how charmingly funny was the junk Eugene thought worthy of an outer-space king's attention: a single day's booty netted the boldening boy a wheelbarrow, three boxes of candy, a red telephone, a woman's wig, and several more suits. But when the cows tied to the trees around his campsite had increased to seven, I became worried again.

"You shouldn't," I told him. "It isn't safe."

"I need milk," Eugene said, abandoning untouched the picnic I had spread for him. "I've got to keep my health if I'm Relga. Also, I need the company." He flung his arms around his cows and called them each by name.

"But this is cattle rustling," I said, "and the people

around here shoot cattle rustlers. I don't want you to die." Still, Eugene smiled and refused to come home with me, reminding me that as Relga he had nothing in the world to fear. When I brought him as a warning the newspaper clippings about the mysterious swamp creature who had been stealing from rural county residents, he laughed.

"I'm getting a name for myself," he said. "When I approach a house, Ruby, I smear my face with mud and growl. I walk bent over like a monkey."

He seemed delighted with everything on earth, until Lyla Zimmerman again brought up the question of when Relga would fly for us all.

"I'm waiting for the right time," Eugene said. "It isn't easy being Relga, you know. I've got to time everything perfectly."

But Lyla Zimmerman began quarreling about the matter with everyone, for what proof did we have, really, that this was Relga? "I can tell stories, too," she said. "He might only be an imaginative boy."

Posy Adams became uncertain, too. "I don't see why, sir, you won't fly for us," she said. "That ought to be easy enough for you."

Although Lillian always begged for patience, saying that for all we knew Relga might already have flown for us, she cast the most yearning looks toward Eugene. He now fell silent whenever the subject was brought up and often turned on his transistor television set and watched, his back to all, the late-night news. "Girls, we must not doubt him. We must never doubt him. He'll show us when he's ready. Won't you, Relga?" Lillian asked. "Or have we—have I—done something to displease you?"

"No, you've been wonderful." By way of placating her, Eugene made another happy prediction, told another miraculous story. But soon it became clear, even to Lillian and the Thurnwood sisters, that Eugene was stalling, and that he didn't yet wish to make himself known to them because he didn't trust them or love them enough.

It was not, Lillian said, that her faith was flagging, but an inspiring sight could do much to revive the pilgrim's soul. "Have I been so abominable all my life," she asked one evening very close to Christmas, "that you won't show yourself to us at last? I'm only asking for a little miracle to keep me going." She burst into tears and declared that she was probably good for nothing. After she had been led away by the rest, Eugene paced before the fire.

"It's lonelier than I thought it would be as Relga. What can I do to show them how much I love them?" Eugene said that he feared that if he did not show these women some grand miracle soon, they would stop believing in him. "I don't want them to be that sad ever," he said. "I have to think of the biggest miracle in the world so that they know who I am, and how generous and good and powerful."

The next evening Eugene put forth the question, "What can I do for you?"

Lyla Zimmerman immediately cried, "Fly for me!"

"He needs time," I said, going to Eugene, whose head was lowered and whose sneakered feet kicked gently at pinecones and coral rocks.

"He's had quite a lot of time, don't you think?" Posy Adams said. "Isn't it possible, Ruby, you've mistaken him for someone else? He looks like a boy."

"He said aliens look like us. I believe in him." Eugene stood patiently while even the Thurnwood sisters shyly said they would accept any miracle at all—he needn't fly if he didn't wish to—and his patience convinced me that the possibilities my mother had envisaged did indeed exist, that the most miraculous and goodly light illuminated my swamp man's eyes.

"Go home now," Eugene said, his voice soft and a

trifle melancholy. "I'll think about all of this. I won't disappoint you."

The following afternoon as I approached my swamp man's campsite carrying a box of Christmas ornaments, a coil of silver garland, and a gold star for the top of a baby pine, I could hear Eugene softly crying. When I broke through the palmetto fronds I saw him sitting at the edge of the fire, holding his bloody leg. He explained through chattering teeth that his calf had been grazed by a bullet as he had run from a farmer's house. I ripped off the long tail of my shirt and wrapped it around his leg. We both stared as his blood seeped onto the plaid flannel.

"You're not supposed to bleed. Come home with me now," I begged.

Eugene shook his head, his thick eyebrows rising into his bangs. "I have to bleed when I'm on earth," he told me. He rose then and helped me decorate one of the small pine trees with the red and green glass bulbs. He placed the star at its top himself. "It's as beautiful as your tree," he said. "Ruby, you've been very good to me. Unselfish. You've trusted me."

"How could I do anything but trust you? It's you who have been good to me. And when you think I'm good, I feel good and kind and gentle. I only wish Artie were home," I said. "I miss him terribly."

"He'll come home, Ruby, I promise," Eugene said, placing his hand on my shoulder.

"Are you the outer-space alien my mother looked for? Tell me now and I'll believe you."

"I'm who you were looking for."

"I believe you," I told him. "I believe." I wanted to kiss his cheek but restrained myself from doing so. I was afraid he might still shriek with fear.

"All I need is your trust," Eugene said. He limped in a circle, one trouser leg rolled up above my flannel bandage, to admire his Christmas tree from all angles. But as the wind blew, Eugene sighed. "Can you see my future, Ruby?"

"I won't look," I said. "Not for you. Least of all for you—don't leave me!"

"I won't. But this is a command now, Ruby, from your Relga. If you believe in me, just tell me this. I won't be murdered, will I? It would be a great misunderstanding—I won't be murdered."

"No," I said, "nobody will murder you." My swamp man let me push back his hair and even caught and squeezed my fingers.

"You see, if I ever have to die, maybe in about two thousand years, I want to die bravely." Eugene laughed when he said this and hobbled around the campfire, a weird figure in a stolen tuxedo, his arm transformed by a wish into a thrusting, deadly accurate, and righteous sword. "No, I can't be killed by an earthling. I want people to keep loving me just as they've been loving me. But your sister—she's stopping, Ruby, and if she doesn't believe in me anymore, I won't be able to keep her alive. When they doubt me, I doubt myself."

"I don't doubt you. I'd never doubt you."

Eugene's sad, dark eyes wandered toward the misty horizon of trees, telephone poles, and radio towers. He threw back his head suddenly and laughed. "When you don't doubt me, I know I can do anything at all. On Christmas Eve," he said, "I am going to perform such a huge miracle that any of my followers who ever doubted will be forever convinced. I'm not telling you," he said when I implored him to reveal what miracle he would perform. "It's a secret. But I'll always be who you want me to be—I am he. You hoped I was special the first time you saw me, and now your wish has been granted."

That night as we gathered around the fire, Eugene

spoke with joyful, loving energy. "I am going to show you my great powers at five o'clock tomorrow, on Christmas Eve. Over there," he said, pointing toward a path that wound through the woods on the other side of the river. "Just follow the path until you see me. I want to reward you for being such good women." Eugene looked fondly at my sister, who was weeping. "You remember how important you are," he told her. "Promise me you won't forget."

"I promise," Lillian said. "Relga, you do love us, then?"

"Enough to make sacrifices," he said, his voice rising above the chorus of praise. The Thurnwood sisters hugged one another, and Lyla Zimmerman cried on Posy Adams's shoulder. "You've all made me very happy—happier than you'll ever realize. And that is important, no matter who I might have been. You are saved," and again he passed his hands over our heads, as had become his habit. "Now go home and wait until Christmas Eve. You, too, Ruby," he said, nodding anxiously at me. "Go home now."

For a moment, when I gazed at his thin, rumpled figure standing alone by the fire, I felt a terrible fright; I opened my mouth, but Eugene put one finger to his lips and disappeared into the brush.

My sister grabbed me around my waist, so joyful that all my fears dissipated. "He makes me believe in everything good," she said. "How could I ever have doubted you, or myself, for that matter?"

All the ladies sang praises to Eugene during the walk back to the house, and through the woods, hidden by brush and bramble, Eugene accompanied us for a time, his voice ringing out in praise of us all.

As we walked along the path toward my house, I thought I saw the figure of my aunt standing behind a huge berry bush, and I thought I heard her softly crying. But when I fell behind the others and beseeched her to come out so that I could speak with her, I heard her answer from her hiding place in the brush, "I can't—isn't it wonderful now, Ruby, and wasn't it sad before?"

"Wasn't what sad?" I cried, but only the wind rattled the brush and branch in answer.

"I don't think I'm haunted anymore," Lillian said that evening as we prepared for bed. She breathed quietly and happily, and truly a calm had come over her face, and all lines of anxiety seemed to have vanished. "It's so quiet, Ruby. Mother has sent me love through Relga, and I'm not haunted anymore."

"Nor I," I said, and in the morning we both remarked upon the peacefulness of our dreams: our mother had not appeared in our sleep to terrify or accuse.

Christmas Eve day dawned beautifully and crisply. Lillian spent a long while with her friends in the kitchen cooking up a splendid dinner, for surely, she said, Relga would be hungry after performing his amazing feat. "I knew that Christmas would tell, one way or the other," she said.

It took us most of the afternoon to reach the part of the woods where Eugene had told us to gather. First we had to go south along the river until we found a rickety bridge over which to cross. We had to rest several times before we reached the path Eugene had told us to take, for Lyla Zimmerman's legs were unwieldy, and the Thurnwood sisters suffered palpitations and moved slowly so their hosiery would remain unsnagged.

My eyes scanned the sky, looking for silver space ships Eugene might have called in glorious formation —or for a lone flying figure. As I gazed straight ahead at a radio tower that loomed like a mirage above the horizon, I could see a tiny figure dangling halfway up its height, and I broke into a run.

Even as I took the first winding steps of the tower, Eugene waved down at me, and his eerie sprite's laughter seemed to fill the woods. "Don't do this for us!" I screamed.

For every step I took, he managed four. Below, my sister was furious with me. "Leave him alone. Leave our Relga alone!" she shouted, and in the late-afternoon sun I could see her cheeks glittering.

"Just wait for me a minute, Eugene," I cried. I hurried my pace. Sometimes Eugene halted, and sometimes he quickened in his climb.

The women on the earth below were shouting at me to come down, to quit my interference.

"Eugene, just a moment of your time, if you love me," I called. At last my swamp man stopped climbing and held his hand toward me.

He was shaking with the cold high-altitude winds. His lips were blue, and he could hardly speak with the chattering of his teeth. "Why are you following me, Ruby?"

"I want you to come down before you kill yourself. Please climb down, Eugene. I don't want you to fly. I don't want you to leave me."

"I thought you believed in me," Eugene said. "I can fly. Or were you making up a story, Ruby? You weren't wrong about me, were you? I told you I love you—how else can I prove who I am?"

"I'm afraid."

"Let me be him, Ruby." Even while he stood crouched in the cold on the narrow metal steps above me, Eugene looked very proud. "You stay where you are, Ruby, unless you want me to die a thousand times over." When he pointed his finger at me and I looked into his dark, sad eyes, my muscles seemed to freeze and then go limp. I watched him climb farther up the tower to a small metal platform. From there he urged me down, and I clung to the cold metal rails and dizzily obeyed until I dropped to the ground.

I lay on the pine needles wailing like an infant. The other women looked curiously at me and then up at Eugene, who was a black, corona-edged figure in the late-afternoon sun.

This swamp man, this Eugene, and this Relga had begun to speak in those ringing orator's tones that had somehow replaced his first primitive howling.

"I am returning to my fellow aliens, to tell them of your virtue. But I promise you that I'll return—in five minutes, a day, a week, a year—and that the others will come with me. Watch for us! Remember me!" When he stopped speaking the wind seemed to pick up, and he made that characteristic blessing motion with his hands and then turned and resumed his climb.

At the tenth platform and at the fifteenth platform Eugene again paused, tinier, darker, his oversized suit edged with fiery light. Twice again he called down to us. "You are loved," he shouted. "Watch for me."

I was still crying and imagined that I could sense his human trembling in my own shuddering limbs. In the single moment I took to wipe my eyes, my swamp man vanished from my sight. He might have ducked away, might have managed to wind quickly around the huge steel girders to the far side of the tower and there hide, crouched—or perhaps he had indeed floated off into outer space. For aliens, according to Eugene's fanciful theories—or his accurate memories—would slip like silky light from earthling vision. While Lyla Zimmerman cried in a hoarse voice that she had been tricked, and while my eyes scanned each platform and every girder accessible to my vision, Lillian began shouting.

"I see him. Look, there he is, about thirty platforms

up." Her fingers touched her lips, upon which was the loveliest, the most serene smile, and her blue eyes were charged with a preternatural glow.

Grace and Clara Thurnwood, dark, embracing silhouettes in the light of the sinking sun, also perceived the extraordinary in remarkably similar, pretty manner.

"He's spreading his arms," said Grace, in a hushed, marveling voice.

"He's poised in midair," Clara said. "He's small, but he's elegant."

All the women gasped in unison, except for Lyla and me. Their eyes seemed to follow, from east to west and then straight up, a figure that now apparently made appalling and marvelous flight.

"This isn't a dream," Posy Adams whispered. Tears were streaming down her glad elderly face.

"I'm saved," my sister cried. "I'm saved." She stared often at the sky as she walked toward me, her eyes blazing with what I decided was a hysterical flight into fancy. "Did you see him, Ruby?" I nodded. He had not looked like a bird, she said, oh, perhaps a little like a white egret; he seemed more like a spark or a rapidly traveling star.

He had told us, the women whispered, while Lyla Zimmerman still shouted and sobbed that she had been tricked; he had said the aliens would look like the stars, and so he had, flying off into the sunset.

"I felt his touch," Clara said. "Even as he flew away, I felt his hand on mine."

Lyla Zimmerman, whose sobbing seemed unable to penetrate the blind good will around her, staggered among her friends, her hands over her eyes. "No hope," she screamed. "I want to die. I'm good for nothing. I'm too old. He didn't love me."

"He left you a message," I said, backing away. "Your

Relga left you a message. Look in the red suitcase in your attic—you'll find a bank book there." I rushed off into the brush, crying hopelessly myself, and ran around the far side of the steel tower. But I found no body, no footprints, and no boy whom I had seen bleed in the jungle.

By the time I reached the river, darkness had fallen, and I made my way through the woods toward my aunt's house with a timid, angry heart. The wind rattled the dark palmetto and stung my face and hands. The cows, and all of Eugene's booty, had been removed from his last campsite, where none of his footprints shimmered as an angel's ought. Only the icy wind blew through his tent, one side of which was collapsed. The wind creaked the tent poles and made the front flap lean fluttering out.

My mother had once said that on Christmas Eve, fairies and elves danced in celebratory rites in the woods. One had only to believe, she said, to see them.

"Eugene," I called, but not a living or a dead voice answered. Nothing stirred—everything seemed to be hibernating.

Over the frosty path along the river, which steamed and seemed almost to boil, I trudged, heavy-boned, my flashlight snapping here and there. My aunt's cabin was just down the river, beyond a curve in its belly where a wooden dock sloped toward the water.

"Where are you, Eugene? Come back now, and I'll believe in you." When no voice immediately answered me, I became impatient and knew that he was a fraud and forever gone.

My aunt's front porch was well lit. All along its wooden planks were potted plants covered with newspapers and towels to protect tender tropical leaves from the settling frost. From a nail on my aunt's door hung a red-ribboned wreath, and beyond drawn glowing shades I could see the shadows and colors of a small lit Christmas tree.

With dreadful anger I burst through her door. I stood blinking at a one-room cabin so immaculate I might have thought, if logic had not prevailed, that a sprite swept and cleaned for my aunt just as the fraudulent Eugene had swept and cleaned for me. In the center of the room at a long pine table sat my aunt in a faded blue skirt and sweater, working on her wonderfully intricate, ambitious maps charting never-before-charted portions of the swamps. My aunt frowned and sighed as she put down her pen. She rose, rubbing her hands, and walked slowly past me, as if I were invisible, to throw some wood on the fire.

"Who was that you had me believing in?" I asked. I was shocked by the gladness of her face. Catherine hummed as she returned to her table and there broke into song, her ugly, heavy shoes tapping time. "Don't answer me, then. I'll tell you. That was," I said, pacing and twisting up a cold and analytical finger, "some clever common criminal, or a poor boy escaped from some institution. Ah, yes, Eugene, you read too many comic books."

My aunt continued to sing and to shuffle her shoes against the warm pine floor.

"He was," I said, with greater adamance, "a runaway from the juvenile detention center in Indiantown. He broke into my kitchen, didn't he? He was a kleptomaniac—a very imaginative kleptomaniac."

My aunt ceased the meticulous motion of her pen upon her draft paper, set aside her compass, and leaned back in her chair, her eyes glowing with the same passion as my sister's had when she imagined Eugene had flown. "He was," Catherine said, her voice joyous and deep, "a prophet."

"You're mad. He was just a boy, a very lonely boy."

Catherine remained as undaunted by my skepticism as I by her faith. "There've been plenty of boy prophets in this world. No," she said, her face radiant, "he was just who you believe he was. Didn't you see him fly?"

I said that of course I had not seen him fly. Lillian had seen him fly, I said, but Lillian always saw exactly what she wished to see. "He's either dead or gone. I saw him bleed in the woods. He was a child."

"He was childlike, perhaps, but he dreamed very well." My aunt picked up her pen and resumed her work, sighing, as if all the world could not be hers, or at least as if these maps would be a struggle. "Didn't you want to see him fly?"

"Not if he was a boy, I didn't. I didn't want to see him killed." My aunt was again humming that maddeningly cheerful tune. I stared at her and said I would have to visit her more often, for surely this lonely life had made her half-crazed. "What are you doing out here, anyway? Living alone all these years—were you running away from some guy?"

My aunt laughed. "No. I've been living out here with the one you call Eugene." As I listened to Catherine talk a huge horror seemed to collect, compact, and fall leaden on my shoulders. She told me that she had known Eugene, the one my sister called Relga, at least forty years. "Forty years ago he was a little plumper, perhaps, but he looked about the same. I've seen him do things more marvelous than fly. He's lived out here as long as I can remember."

"Then why," I said, "if all this is true, if you did know him, why didn't you show him to my mother? Why did you keep him a secret?"

"I never kept him a secret. He wasn't mine to keep. Your mother saw him more times than I could count. She never paid him any attention."

"And why not?"

My aunt shook her head. "Because he looked human, and not like a very special human at that. He was always small. He tried to save her. Maybe he did save her, who knows?"

"I know," I cried. "She killed herself. I saw her body."

"I didn't," Catherine said, and all the muscles of her face seemed to slacken with sadness. "I didn't see her body, but I've seen your Eugene fly. You didn't see Eugene fly, but you saw her body. I don't know," she said. "I just don't know."

"But you've got a gift," I said, "and you know how to use it. You've got to know something."

"I know that I'm a woman, and that in the morning I plan to get up early and work until I'm tired enough to sleep. I know I have memories. I remember when your mother had a gift. Once it was very strong in Sally. The day she bought her land out here, the gift was very strong."

"Damn all this wishful thinking," I shouted, and my voice seemed to spring infinite miles of wilderness beyond the light cast by my aunt's cabin: into the dark woods the sound of it carried, and it seemed to echo with the desolate wind and diminish the light of the moon.

"I never damn my wishful thinking." Catherine's gray-streaked head was bowed over her maps; with compass and pens she worked quickly now, breathing rapidly, her sunburned cheeks growing redder. "There," she said at last, turning around to face me. "I never damn my wishful thinking at all, when I'm wishing well."

I rushed across the room and rubbed clear a spot on a frosted pane. "He's gone," I said. My body felt crumpled and wasted as I stared onto the porch, down the front path, and into my aunt's gardens. Eugene was not there. "Even if he wasn't who I thought he was, I liked him very much. I loved him—so he shouldn't have left. He's gone forever."

"He isn't gone. I saw him not an hour ago, just before you walked into my house. Put down that analytical finger," my aunt said as she walked toward me. If I had not seen Eugene fly, she asked, and if I had been so confused about my mother's death, how in the world could I know that he was gone? "He might be standing right beside you, for all you know."

A shiver of enormous gladness, quite independent of logic, ran through me. "I don't see him," I said, "but I'd like to. I don't care who he was. I'd like to see him again."

"Then look," said my aunt. "It's all in the practice. Every magician knows that."

I opened the front door and stood for a few moments on the porch. No outer-space alien waited by my aunt's gardens to judge me. "Is it Christmas yet?" I asked.

"I think it is," Catherine said. I hugged her for a long while, until she broke away and said, "Go on home, Ruby, and don't be a stranger. It's lonely and hard even for me, and I do have, as you call it, the gift."

"Should I look into the future with mine?" I cried, stepping backward over the hard, frosty ground, my hands running along the ice-glazed wire fence of Catherine's vegetable gardens.

"I should think so," my aunt said. "I should hope so."

I ran through the woods along the river, already practicing with a magician's concentration productive and pleasurable feats of imagination. The energy I put into reviving my swamp man and calling my husband home made me feel giddy, and as I neared the spot where the path curved toward my house, I stopped and leaned against a tree.

Through the brush I saw some lights and heard some

joyous voices, which might, I thought, belong to fairies, or comforting ghosts, or sublime creatures from another planet. But when I broke through the palmetto fronds and wound my way through the mangroves, I saw only Lillian and her friends, partly obscured by the river's mist, standing at the foot of my dock. Their flashlights pointed up toward the black, starry sky.

"Christmas is coming," Lillian said. "I can hear it." My sister said that on this morning the stars with their diffused light made music not unlike Bach's *Brandenburg Concertos,* just as Mother had promised.

The stars, the women said, recalling Relga's description of the space ships in which the humanlike aliens would travel to earth, were unusually bright and beautiful and seemed to form remarkable geometric patterns. As they repeated the stories Relga had told them by his campsite in the woods, they laughed quietly. Together they fell silent, and then they were staring at each other just as they had stared at Relga when they first pronounced him to be the alien for whom they had searched so long.

"He said the aliens look like humans. Who knows but any of us. . . ?" Lillian said, leaving her thought uncompleted, as aliens did not want to be confronted with the fact of their identity.

"Who knows but *you?*" the other women said.

Lyla Zimmerman, who must have caught hope from the others, for, as Janet Monsterville always said, the light spreads, said in a hoarse, happy voice, "Who knows but me?"

As I stole away they were embracing each other, but carefully, gently, as if they were in awe to touch such good and noble flesh.

Walking alone on the path toward home I began to sing, and then it seemed I could hear another voice, one that anticipated every word and every note, singing along with me.

"Swamp man?" I called.

I heard a sudden familiar laugh and was knocked to the wet ground by a slight figure that seemed more air than flesh that early Christmas morning.

"Eugene?" I called again. "Swamp man?" When the creature groaned, I groaned gladly to his tune.

"I'll catch you again." I wandered in and out of the brush, darting off the path and then onto its hard surface again, my breath making imprints of spirit in the nearly freezing air.

As I neared the pole fence that surrounded my property, I saw the small figure scamper across the lawn.

"I love you," I called. I ran toward the house on feet somehow lighter with my errand and stopped just yards from the front porch.

Artie was standing on the porch in the midst of luggage so ripped and torn the bags might well have been attacked by some wild and vicious beast. His hand was in his mouth, and he was gazing about in wonderment as I came up the steps.

"I was going to leave you, Ruby. I had decided that," Artie said, shivering and staring off into the woods. "But this thing, this animal or ghost—"

"And you don't know which or what," I said.

"That's right. It attacked me and my bags. Some lips brushed my ear"—and my husband grimaced—"and a voice said he loved me. Don't laugh at me now, but I do believe that was my father, reaching out to me from beyond, telling me not to worry so much. You always said this house was haunted. I lost consciousness for a while—I thought, Ruby, that I was a goner." Artie scratched his white curls and cleared his throat. "However, I have the feeling this is not the year for me to depart."

"I'm glad," I said. Looking around the porch at the strewn clothing, at the ties and socks flung over the railings and into the jasmine hedges, I began to laugh.

Artie smiled, although his eyes still looked startled, and repeated, "Not the year for me to depart."

Very early that morning we lay somewhat shyly in bed, sighing and watching the hall and listening to the calls of the Everglades animals outside. Toward four o'clock we turned off the television and the lights; we yawned and said how tired we were.

"I heard a noise in the hall," Artie said.

I said, "There's a howling in the woods."

While a somber wind blew against the frosted windows, while the bobcats screeched and the alligators bellowed, we hit upon the way to ease our shyness and the night, by repeating all the old enduring stories we knew. Toward daybreak, when we imagined we had run out of stories, we became nervous and quiet and sat up in bed and thought and said that we had nothing left to tell. The shrieking of some animal directly below our windows made me believe all was lost, but Artie said, "I have an idea." He held up a proud finger.

"Once upon a time," he said, as we settled beneath the blankets once more, "lived a young-hearted king, in France, I believe this was, Ruby, who wandered as a beggar among his subjects until he forgot who he was."

"I love that story," I said, still troubled. "But be careful with the ending."

Artie smiled, and his face was wonderfully illuminated, as if the last light of the stars had rushed into his eyes and made them glow. "I'll be careful. Once upon a time," he began again, "lived a good, young-hearted king, who wandered, as a beggar, among his people, for many, many years."